THE COLONY

Audrey Magee was born in Ireland and lives in Wicklow. Her first novel, *The Undertaking*, was shortlisted for the Women's Prize for Fiction, for France's Festival du Premier Roman and for the Irish Book Awards. It was also nominated for the Dublin Literary Award and the Walter Scott Prize for Historical Fiction.

The Undertaking has been translated into ten languages and is being adapted for film.

by the same author

THE UNDERTAKING

AUDREY MAGEE

THE COLONY

faber

First published in 2022
by Faber & Faber Ltd
Bloomsbury House
74–77 Great Russell Street
London WC1B 3DA
This export edition published in 2022

Typeset by Typo•glyphix, Burton-on-Trent DE14 3HE
Printed in the UK by CPI Group (UK) Ltd, Croydon CR0 4YY

A CIP record for this book
is available from the British Library

ISBN 978-0-571-36760-3

2 4 6 8 10 9 7 5 3 1

To the memory of John Magee

truths are illusions about which one has forgotten that
this is what they are

FRIEDRICH NIETZSCHE
On Truth and Lie in an Extra-Moral Sense

He handed the easel to the boatman, reaching down the pier wall towards the sea.

Have you got it?

I do, Mr Lloyd.

His brushes and paints were in a mahogany chest wrapped in layers of thick, white plastic. He carried the chest to the edge of the pier.

This one is heavy, he said.

It'll be grand, Mr Lloyd. Pass it down.

He knelt on the concrete and slid the chest down the wall towards the boatman, the white plastic slipping under his fingers.

I can't hold it, he said.

Let it go, Mr Lloyd.

He sat on his heels and watched the boatman tuck the chest and easel under the seat near the prow, binding each to the other with lurid blue string.

Are they secure?

They're grand, Mr Lloyd.

I hope they're secure.

As I said, they're grand.

He stood up and brushed the dust and dirt from his trousers.

The boatman lifted his arm, offering his hand.

Just yourself then, Mr Lloyd, sir.

Lloyd nodded. He handed his canvas pack to the boatman and stepped cautiously onto the ladder set into the crumbling pier.

Turn around, Mr Lloyd. Your back to me.

He looked down, at the small boat, at the sea. He hesitated. Stalled.

You'll be grand, Mr Lloyd.

He turned and dropped his right leg to search for the first step beneath him, his hands gripping the rusting metal as his leg dangled, his eyes shut tight, against the possibilities

of catching skin

cutting fingers

blemishing hands

of slipping

on steps

coated in seaweed and slime

of falling

falling into the sea

The step is under you, Mr Lloyd.

I can't find it.

Relax your knee, Mr Lloyd. Reach.

I can't.

You'll be grand.

He dropped his knee and found the step. He paused, gripping still to the ladder.

Only two steps left, Mr Lloyd.

He moved his hands down the ladder, then his legs. He stopped on the third step. He looked down, at the gap between his feet and the low-lying boat.

It's too far.

Just reach with your leg, Mr Lloyd.

Lloyd shook his head, his body. He looked down again, at his backpack, his easel, his chest of paints bound already to the journey across the sea in a handmade boat. He dropped his right leg, then his left, but clung still to the ladder.

self-portrait I: falling
self-portrait II: drowning
self-portrait III: disappearing
self-portrait IV: under the water
self-portrait V: the disappeared

Let go, Mr Lloyd.

I can't.

You'll be grand.

He crashed into the boat, tipping it to one side, soaking his trousers, his boots and socks, water seeping between his toes as the boatman pumped his right leg against the swirl of sea splashing over the top of the boat, his leg feverish until the currach was again balanced. The boatman bent forward, to rest on his knees. He was panting.

My feet are wet.

You're lucky it's only your feet, Mr Lloyd.

The boatman pointed at the stern.

Go and sit down, Mr Lloyd.

But my feet are wet.

The boatman stilled his breath.

That's boats for you, Mr Lloyd.

Lloyd shuffled towards the back of the boat, hanging from the boatman's callused hands as he turned to sit on a narrow, splintered plank.

I hate wet feet, he said.

He reached his hands towards the boatman.

I'll take my backpack now. Thank you.

The boatman handed him his pack and Lloyd placed it on his knees, away from the water sloshing still about the bottom of the boat.

I won't object if you change your mind, Mr Lloyd. And I'll not charge you. Not all of it, anyway.

I'll carry on as planned, thank you.

It's not common any more. To cross like this.

I'm aware of that.

And it can be a hard crossing.

I've read that.

Harder than anywhere else.

Thank you. I'll be fine.

He closed the buttons of his waxed coat and pulled on his new tweed cap, its green and brown tones blending with the rest of his clothing.

self-portrait: preparing for the sea crossing

He reached down his legs and flicked the beaded water from his trousers, from his socks, from the laces of his boots.

Will you be staying long, Mr Lloyd?

For the summer.

That'll do you.

Lloyd straightened the pack on his lap.

I'm ready, he said.

Grand.

Shouldn't we go?

Soon enough.

How long?

Not long.

But we're missing all the daylight.

The boatman laughed.

It's June, Mr Lloyd.

And?

Plenty of light left in that sky.

What's the forecast?

The boatman looked at the sky.

Calm day, thank God.

But that could change.

It could, Mr Lloyd.

Will it?

Oh, it will, Mr Lloyd.

So we should go now. Before it changes.

Not yet, Mr Lloyd.

Lloyd sighed. He closed his eyes and lifted his face to the sun, surprised by its warmth when he had expected only northern cold, northern rain. He absorbed the heat for some minutes, and opened his eyes again. The boatman was standing as he had been, looking towards land, his body shifting with the rhythm of the water that lapped gently against the pier wall. Lloyd sighed again.

I really think we should go, he said.

Not yet, Mr Lloyd.

I am very keen to get there. To settle in.

It's early yet, Mr Lloyd.

The boatman reached into the inside of his jacket and took out a cigarette. He detached the filter and flicked it into the sea.

A fish might eat that, said Lloyd.

It might.

That's not good for the fish.

The boatman shrugged.

It'll be more careful next time.

Lloyd closed his eyes, but opened them again.

I want to leave, he said.

Not yet, Mr Lloyd.

I have paid you a lot of money, he said.

Indeed you have, Mr Lloyd, and I appreciate it.

And I'd like to go now.

I understand that.

So let's go.

As I said, not yet, Mr Lloyd.

Why ever not? I'm ready.

The boatman drew deeply on the cigarette. Lloyd sighed, blowing through his lips, and poked at the boat, sticking his heels and fingers into the wooden frame coated with canvas and tar.

Did you build it? said Lloyd.

I did.

Did it take long?

It did.

How long?

Long enough.

self-portrait: conversation with the boatman

He pulled a small sketchpad and pencil from a side pocket on his pack. He turned to a blank sheet and began to draw the pier, stubby and inelegant but encrusted with barnacles and seaweed that glistened in the sunshine, the shells and fronds still wet from the morning tide. He drew the rope leading from the pier to the boat and was starting on the frame of the currach when the boatman spoke.

Here he is. The man himself.

Lloyd looked up.

Who?

Francis Gillan.

Who's he?

The boatman tossed the last of his cigarette into the sea. He cupped his hands and blew into his palms, rubbing each into the other.

It's a long way, Mr Lloyd.

And?

I can't row it on my own.

You should have said.

I just did, Mr Lloyd.

Francis dropped from the ladder into the currach, landing lightly on the floor of the boat, his movements barely rippling the water.

Lloyd sighed

7

balletic

poised

movements unlike mine

He nodded at Francis.

Hello, he said.

Francis tugged the rope from the ring in the wall.

Dia is Muire dhuit, he said.

The first boatman laughed.

No English from him, he said. Not this morning, anyway.

The boatmen lifted long, skinny sticks, one in each hand.

We'll go now, said the boatman.

Lloyd returned his sketchpad and pencil to their pocket.

At last, he said.

The boatmen dropped the sticks into the water.

Are they oars?

They are indeed, Mr Lloyd.

They have no blades. No paddles.

Some do. Some don't.

Don't you need them?

If we get there, we don't.

The men pushed against the wall and Lloyd gripped the sides of the boat, digging his fingers into the canvas and tar, into the coarse fragility of a homemade boat as it headed out into the Atlantic Ocean, into the strangeness, the unfamiliar

the not

willowed rivers

coxswains' callings

muscled shoulders, tanned skin

sunglasses, caps and counting
not that
the familiar
no
They moved towards the harbour mouth, past small trawlers and
rowing boats with outboard engines. The boatman pointed at
a vessel that was smaller than the trawlers but larger than the
currach.

That's the one that'll bring your bags, he said.

Lloyd nodded.

It's how the other visitors come across.

Are there many visitors?

No.

That's good.

You'd be better off on that boat, Mr Lloyd.

Lloyd closed his eyes, shutting out the boatman. He opened
them again.

I'm happy in this one.

The big one is safer, Mr Lloyd. It has an engine and sails.

I'll be fine.

Right so, Mr Lloyd, sir.

They left the harbour, passing rocks blackened and washed
smooth by waves, gulls resting on the stagnant surface, staring
as they rowed past.

self-portrait: with gulls and rocks

self-portrait: with boatmen, gulls and rocks

How long will it take?

Three, four hours. It depends.

9

It's ten miles, isn't it?

Nine. That other boat of mine takes a bit more than an hour.

I like this boat. It's closer to the sea.

The boatman pulled on the oars.

It's that all right.

Lloyd leaned to one side and dropped his hand into the sea, spreading his fingers to harrow the water.

self-portrait: becoming an island man

self-portrait: going native

He wiped his chilled hand over his trousers. He lifted his pack and laid it behind him.

That's risky, said the boatman.

It'll be fine, said Lloyd.

He leaned against the pack and moved his fingers as though drawing the boatmen while they rowed

small men

slight men

hips, shoulders, backs

flowing

over anchored legs

Your boat is a different shape to the pictures in my book.

Different boats for different parts, Mr Lloyd.

This one looks deeper.

Deeper boats for deeper waters. The shallow boats are grand for islands that are close in.

Not this one?

No, too far.

Is it safe?

This boat?

Yes.

The boatman shrugged.

It's a bit late to be asking.

Lloyd laughed.

I suppose it is.

self-portrait: going native with the island men

And do they leak?

They do, Mr Lloyd.

The tar on my garage roof always leaks, he said.

That happens with tar.

Does it happen with this boat?

I patched it recently.

And do they sink?

Oh, they do.

Has this one?

The boatman shook his head, slowly.

Well, we are in it, Mr Lloyd.

Yes, he said. I suppose we are.

He reached behind him and again retrieved his sketchbook and pencil from his pack. He looked at the sky and began to draw

gulls

swirling and twisting

hovering, banking

across

cloudless blue

island series: view from the boat I

He looked then at the sea

rolling to shore
to rocks, to land
rolling from
white-fringed blue
to
green-fringed grey
island series: view from the boat II
A bird rose from the water beside him
black feathers
splashed white
red legs
bright
one still dangling
island series: view from the boat III
He closed the sketchpad.

Was that a puffin?

A guillemot, Mr Lloyd. A black one.

It looks like a puffin.

Do you think so?

I really want to see a puffin.

You might, Mr Lloyd. If you stay long enough.

How long?

A month anyway.

He had packed a book about birds in his luggage, a guide with photographs, measurements, names, calls, winter and summer colourings, information about breeding and feeding, details about diving birds, skimming birds, plunging birds, details to differentiate terns from gulls, cormorants from shags, details

that would allow him to draw and paint them, to blend them
into a seascape, a landscape
create them
as they already are
    And do you have seals?
    The odd one over this side, but there's a colony on the island.
    Wonderful creatures.
    Terrible snorers.
    Are they?
    Terrible racket out of them.
The boat lurched forward, pitching him at the boatman's
knees, slamming his pack against his back. He straightened
himself, brought his pack back onto his lap and shoved his
sketchbook and pencil into their pocket. A surge of water
rushed at his head and face. The boatman shouted at him.
    Hold on.
Lloyd dug his feet into the boat's ribs, his hands into its sides.
He shouted back.
    I told you that we should have left earlier.
The boatman yelled at him.
    It's the Atlantic Ocean, Mr Lloyd. In a currach.
Waves knocked the boat left, then right, shoving him from
one side to the other, bouncing him, knocking him, rolling
him, jerking his neck, his back.
    You'll get used to it, Mr Lloyd.
He dug his hands and feet deeper into the boat.
    I don't want to get used to it.
    We can go back, Mr Lloyd.

No. No. We'll go on.

You'd be better in the bigger boat.

I want to do it this way.

Right so, Mr Lloyd. Your choice.

Lloyd watched the two men as they rowed from one wave to
the next.

island series: the boatmen I

sinewy

agile strength

in a flat-bottomed boat

island series: the boatmen II

sun-stained hands

skinny sticks

slapping the ocean

island series: the boatmen III

leaning towards land

then away

towards and away

island series: the boatmen IV

gaze

on sea to come

on endlessness

He closed his eyes.

It's better with your eyes open, Mr Lloyd.

He shook his head.

No, it's not.

As you like, Mr Lloyd.

He snatched his new hat from his head, leaned over the side

and vomited. He wiped his mouth and chin with the sleeve of his new coat. The gulls arrived and devoured what had been his, battling intermittently with their beaks.

Disgusting creatures, he said.

They're not fussy, anyway, said the boatman.

Lloyd closed his eyes again.

How much longer?

We've just left, Mr Lloyd.

Yes, of course.

As I said before, Mr Lloyd, we can go back if you want.

No. I'll be all right.

He slumped into the stern.

I hate boats, he said. Always have.

You might have considered that before now, Mr Lloyd.

Lloyd vomited a second time. The gulls swooped again.

I didn't expect it to be this rough, he said.

It's a calm day today, Mr Lloyd. Bit of wind on the water, that's all.

It feels worse.

That's the currach for you.

A surge of water splashed over the prow, over his chest of paints.

Are my paints safe?

As safe as we are, Mr Lloyd.

That's comforting.

self-portrait: at sea

I'd like you to sing, he said.

We don't sing, Mr Lloyd.

But I need something to focus on. Counting or singing.

Not in this boat.

I read in a book that you people always sing while rowing.

Not a very good book then, is it, Mr Lloyd?

I came here because of it.

The boatman looked past Lloyd, at the land behind.

You need a better book, Mr Lloyd.

It seems that I do.

Lloyd looked around him, at the expanse of sea.

And how do you know which way to go?

It can be hard all right in a fog.

What if one descends quickly?

That's us then.

And who will know?

The boatman shrugged.

They'll see we're not home for tea.

And that's it.

That's it.

self-portrait: drowning I
white-capped waves
engulfing the boat
self-portrait: drowning II
cold salty water
burrowing into paints
into flesh
self-portrait: drowning III
diluting paint
fragmenting flesh
self-portrait: drowning IV

drifts of
grey brown
red yellow
blue green
   How much longer?
   A while yet, Mr Lloyd.

The policeman's wife waits at the front door for her friend. It is Saturday afternoon, June 2nd. They are going shopping in Armagh, as they do every week. The sun is shining. Her five children are about the house and her husband, David, is on the street in front of her, in his uniform, leaning into his friend's car, chatting.

A dark car drives by. She hears a loud bang and assumes that the car has crashed, but David is buckled over and clinging to the door of his friend's car, blood spilling across the front of his white shirt. He falls to the ground. David Alan Dunne, a thirty-six-year-old Protestant, is dead. His thirty-one-year-old friend, David Stinson, a Protestant man married with three children, is dead too.

The Irish National Liberation Army claims responsibility.

Do you see it, Mr Lloyd?

What?

Straight ahead.

He saw a wave in front of him, larger than usual.

Hold on. We'll get over this.

The men rowed to the crest and he saw a large rock surrounded by ocean.

Is that it?

That's it.

And then it was gone, behind a wall of water.

I had expected more. Something bigger.

That's all there is.

He peered through intermittent gaps in the waves, watching the island grow in size and colour, the grey of the rock fragmenting as he got closer, broken by patches of green grass, strips of yellow sand and flecks of whitewashed houses.

They're on their own out here, he said.

They are, Mr Lloyd.

On the edge of Europe.

That's it, Mr Lloyd.

self-portrait I: *de novo*

self-portrait II: *ab initio*

Do they speak English?

Bits. You'll make yourself understood.

But you do.

I had more schooling than most.

Gets you more work, I suppose. Having English.

Rowing a boat is the same in every language, Mr Lloyd.

He picked out a cove, a slipway and a beach. He could see the remains of houses by the cove and further up the hill, away from the sea, a cluster of newer houses with brightly coloured doors and grey slated roofs. He could see donkeys too, in a field on the edge of the island.

island series: view from the currach

A wave whacked the boat and knocked him sideways. The boatmen shouted at each other.

Hang on, Mr Lloyd.

A wave hit them from the other side. The boatmen rose out of their seats and dug their oars deeper into the water, straining their shoulders, necks and faces. Lloyd tightened his grip on the boat and tucked his head into the frame of his shoulders. He shouted at the boatman.

I want to get off.

The boatman shouted back.

That's the plan, Mr Lloyd. Sir.

The two men battled against the water as it changed from blue to grey, from slate grey to black, the surface and the under-belly of the water churning and mixing to shove and pitch the boat, tossing and bouncing them from one wave to the next, the boatmen unable to row against the force of the water, only to use the oars as balancing poles against the turbulence, to prevent the boat from tipping over.

Lloyd dropped into the belly of the boat, into the stale, dirty water, the pack still on his lap, his fingers clinging still to the sides of the boat. He could see men and women spilling from the houses onto the cliff. Onto the path that led to the cove. A bank of water rushed at the boat and landed on top of him, soaking his head and chest

géricault's raft

lloyd's bloody currach

He vomited a third time, bile and bilious foam slipping down his chest and over his pack, but of no interest to the gulls. He rubbed his mouth across the shoulder of his jacket.

I hate bloody boats.

He shouted at the boatmen.

I hate this fucking boat.

They were focused instead on the rock cutting into the ocean, splitting, splintering, shredding the water, bouncing the boat from side to side, forwards and back, veins and arteries bulging in their necks as they fought to turn the boat towards the old men and women waving at them from the slipway in the cove. Lloyd wanted to wave back, to signal his arrival, but a wave kicked the prow of the boat and flicked it into a spin, a tumult of sea, sky and land swirling around him, faster and faster, round and around, the boatmen shouting, yelling

that language

guttural

until they rowed out of the spin and into the stillness of the cove, towards the slipway scattered with islanders in dark clothes, men, women and children, silent and staring. The boatmen dropped the oars and slumped forward, abandoning the currach to the old island men who waded into the water

shoes

no boots

no wellington here

The old island men lifted the easel, chest and oars from the boat. The boatmen stepped out of the boat, though Lloyd stayed as he was, on the floor of the boat in a puddle of water, his fingernails embedded in the tar. An old island man spoke to him.

Amach leat anois.

The old man beckoned Lloyd with his hand.

Amach leat anois.

Lloyd nodded, but did not move. The old man beckoned again.

Out.

He took the old man's hand, then his arm, clinging to a coarse wool jacket as he stepped onto the slab of pock-marked concrete, his legs trembling, then buckling.

self-portrait: as newborn foal

He leaned against the cliff caked in desiccated barnacles and lichen, and watched as the old island men lifted the boat from the water and turned it upside down to carry it over their heads and shoulders, as it was photographed in his book about the island.

island series: the walking boat

The boatmen and the islanders left the slipway, trailing the old men with the boat, the oars, his easel, his chest of paints and brushes, but he stayed behind to wash his face, his hair, relieved by the salty freshness against his skin. He dunked his sleeve into the water, rubbed at the stains on his coat and bag, and followed them out of the cove, water dripping from his coat and hair as the old island men set down the boat at the top of the slipway.

They walked on then, up the hill towards the village, Lloyd at the end of a silent, straggling line that led to a house. He went inside. A woman nodded at him and directed him to the head of a table of blue painted wood, a melamine surface inserted into its frame, bits of old food trapped and rotting between the resin and the wood.

She placed a cup, saucer and plate in front of him. She poured tea from a large metal pot. A second woman, younger with wavy, auburn hair drifting down her chest, offered him bread.

An mbeidh greim aráin agat?

He shook his head. She moved away

hair

drifting

down

washes and ink

brown tones

simple lines

soft

The boatmen took two slices each, talking as they covered the bread with butter, then jam, the same knife used for both until there was butter in the jam and jam in the butter.

He poured from the jug, bigger and heavier than he had anticipated. Milky tea spilled onto the table. He looked for a napkin but found none. He waved his hand, but the older woman had her back to him. He clicked his fingers. She turned, paused, and walked back to the table with a fresh cup. And a saucer. She mopped his spillage, poured more tea and added the milk. He drank, glad of the astringent warmth.

I have told them that you have come to paint.

Francis Gillan was speaking to him.

That's right.

And that you will stay until the end of the summer.

That's also correct.

They want to know what you're painting.

I have come to paint the cliffs. That's all.

They don't want you to paint them.

Then I won't.

The woman poured more tea and milk. Lloyd drank. Still more men came into the kitchen, sliding caps from their heads to their pockets as they sat down. They looked at Lloyd, drank tea and ate bread.

self-portrait: objectified

He turned away from the men, all of them old, away too from Francis, and towards the first boatman.

How many people live on the island?

Ninety-two, Mr Lloyd. Twelve families.

And who among them speaks English?

The children have a good grasp of it.

Among the adults?

Those with good English have left.

He again declined the bread.

And the size of the island?

Three miles long and half a mile wide.

Where will I stay?

I'll show you.

When?

We'll have our tea first, Mr Lloyd.

The boatmen talked to the old island men, toothless mouths in suit jackets crusted by dirt and sea salt, faces deeply furrowed, etched by wind and sea salt

a fingernail through oils

The sea surged again and coursed through him. He closed his eyes to still his stomach, but the waves continued rushing through him, mixing with the throaty sounds of the language that he did not understand and the cloying, suffocating smells of burning turf and boiling meat.

self-portrait: nausea

He stood up. Abruptly. He beckoned the first boatman.

I need to lie down.

In a minute, Mr Lloyd. I'm just finishing.

No. Now.

The boatman returned his cup to the table and stood up slowly. He pulled on his cap and nodded at the other men, at the women who stood by the fire, a ladle hanging limply from the fingers of the younger woman, Mairéad Ní Ghiolláin. They watched

Lloyd leave, quelling their laughter until he and the boatman had walked outside and past the three windows running the length of the house. Mairéad's laughter was raucous. The older woman, Bean Uí Néill, carried a fresh pot of tea to the table.

Did you ever see the like? she said.

I thought Micheál was going to hit him, said Mairéad.

He's lucky we didn't drown him, said Francis.

They all laughed.

The pure arrogance of the man, said Bean Uí Néill.

And vomit all down his chest, said Mairéad.

They laughed again.

Obnoxious is the only word for him, said Bean Uí Néill.

Unbelievable, said Mairéad.

And did you see the way he clicked his fingers at me? said Bean Uí Néill. Did you all see that?

We did, Mam. As though you were some Indian tea-boy.

In my own house, Mairéad. Who does he think he is?

The old men laughed, mouths open, heads rolling backwards.

You're a tough house to please, said Francis.

He's lucky that I didn't pour the tea over his head, said Bean Uí Néill.

That I didn't throw the bread at him, said Mairéad.

Francis put his hands in the air.

Ah, now stop, he said.

What? said Mairéad. He thinks we're all thick.

The poor man, said Francis. A visitor to this place.

That we're illiterate, said Mairéad. That we have no English at all.

The poor man, said Francis.

Mairéad stared at him.

Is this Francis Gillan feeling sympathy for an Englishman?

Ah, Mairéad, it's his first time here.

That doesn't give him the right to be rude to us.

His first time on a currach, Mairéad.

His choice, Francis.

Ah, you're being awful hard on the poor man.

The room quietened. Stilled.

Francis clicked his fingers.

The islanders collapsed in laughter.

You should have seen him on the boat, he said.

Francis held up his cup. Bean Uí Néill poured for him. She gave him more bread.

He was sick the whole way across, said Francis. And talking to himself. Muttering like an old woman.

Seeing him in the cove was enough for me, said Bean Uí Néill. He was in a desperate state.

Why did he do it, Francis? said Mairéad.

Francis shook his head.

I don't know.

He could have taken the other boat like everybody else, said Mairéad.

This fella doesn't consider himself to be the same as everybody else.

But a currach, said Mairéad. That's very different.

And he paid a lot of money for the pleasure, said Francis.

Bean Uí Néill shivered.

You couldn't pay me to get back into one of those boats, she said.

I was slow to do it myself, said Francis. It had been a while.

We could see that, said Bean Uí Néill. And you out there on the rocks.

He leaned back into the chair.

You get used to the motor very quickly.

Lucky to have got away with it.

Francis shrugged.

We were grand, Bean Uí Néill.

I hope that it was worth it, she said.

It was.

How much?

Not a chance, Bean Uí Néill.

Go on, Francis. How much?

He shook his head. She gathered the plates, saucers and cups into a pile in front of her.

What's his name anyway?

Mr Lloyd, said Francis. Of London.

Anything to do with that bank? she said.

Must be, said Francis, given the amount he paid to come across.

They laughed, then stopped. Micheál was walking past the three windows, towards the door.

Ah, he's chewing a wasp, said Mairéad.

He threw open the door.

His lordship wants the furniture moved, he said.

This fella is a handful, said Bean Uí Néill.

And he wants the bed dismantled, said Micheál.

The bed?

Yes, Mairéad. The bed. We'll need a spanner.

We've never had this before, said Bean Uí Néill.

We have not, said Micheál.

Every other visitor has been happy with the bed.

Not this one, said Micheál. He's in there giving out about everything.

Francis and two of the old men followed Micheál into the cottage, into a roughly plastered room that smelt of mould, the whitewashed wall blistering and crumbling in patches close to the floor. Lloyd was beside a small window overlooking the sea, the mildewed net curtain brushing against his cheek.

I told you that I needed a house with light.

You have the lanterns, Mr Lloyd.

For my work.

I'll get you more lanterns.

Lloyd shook his head and led them into the next room furnished with a double bed covered in a faded green bedspread, a wardrobe and a dressing table that no longer had its mirror. The walls were drier though the window was as small as the first.

We're not carrying that wardrobe upstairs, Mr Lloyd.

Get it out of this room.

Do your painting upstairs, Mr Lloyd. There's an empty room up there.

There's no light up there.

You said there's no light down here, so what's the difference? Lloyd dragged the mattress from the bed.

Let's get on. Please.

The four men took apart the bed and carried it upstairs. They followed with the dressing table but dragged the wardrobe into the main room that had a large hearth for cooking, a table and six chairs.

Will that do you now, Mr Lloyd?

It's a bit better.

Right, that'll do, so.

The men left and Lloyd opened the doors and windows. He removed all the curtains and dropped them into a corner of the main room, behind the door. He erected his easel in the bedroom that no longer had a bed, and turned it almost perpendicular to the window, angling it to catch the light without casting shadow. He took the narrowest drawer from the dressing table and balanced it across two kitchen chairs to the left of the easel. He carried the mahogany chest, still wet with sea, from the front door to the studio and unwrapped the plastic, holding his breath as he unlocked the chest and raised the lid

paints intact

untainted by sea

untouched

He sighed and transferred the contents of the chest to the drawer: palettes, palette knives, eight bristle brushes, eight sable brushes, three bottles of turpentine, three of linseed oil, one of size, cloths, tape, jars, bottles, primers, pencils, pens,

inks and charcoal, as well as a penknife, scissors, string, and an
apron, black to absorb the sun. And then the paints, orange,
yellow, red, ochre
sunflowers
red roofs
market stalls
heat rising
of no use here
cold, wet land of grey
of green, brown, blue
    Are those paints?
He startled. A boy was at his side
more man
than boy
though still boy
    Are those paints?
    Don't you knock?
    No.
    Well, you should. This is my studio now.
    Tea is ready.
    I'm not hungry.
    Are those paints?
    Yes. What's your name?
    James Gillan.
The artist reached out his hand.
    The son of Francis Gillan?
James shook his head.
    No. That's my uncle.

James pointed then at the drawer.

Can I have a go?

No. They're for my work.

Well, the tea is ready.

Thank you, but I'll get something later.

There is no later.

Lloyd sighed.

In that case, I should come now, as you suggest.

Lloyd followed him back to the house. James carried the white plastic discarded by Lloyd.

Do you live here?

I do. It's my granny's house.

And who owns the one I am using?

Micheál's brother.

Where does he live?

In America.

That's not on the island.

It's not, said James. He owns two houses here. Rents them out. Gets loads of money from people like you.

An absentee landlord, said Lloyd.

An Irish one, said James.

Does that make a difference?

Nothing for me in it either way.

He sat in the same place as before. Micheál and Francis were already at the table. Bean Uí Néill set down plates of fried fish, mashed potato and boiled cabbage. He poked at the food with his fork but did not eat.

You should eat, Mr Lloyd, said Micheál.

32

I'm not hungry.

It's dinner at one o'clock every day, Mr Lloyd, and tea at half past six.

So this is tea?

It is.

It looks like dinner. What does dinner look like?

Tea.

Lloyd laughed.

I'm not sure I'll get the hang of this.

It's easy enough, Mr Lloyd. You eat the same food most times.

Mairéad poured tea and Bean Uí Néill cut into an apple tart. He ate and drank.

You'll be better for that, said Micheál.

I will, he said.

The artist stood up and nodded at the two women by the fire.

Thank you.

They nodded back.

Tá fáilte romhat.

I'll go for a walk now, he said. To get my bearings.

It's a good evening for it, said Micheál.

What's the best way to go?

Whatever way you want.

I want to see the cliffs.

You'll not get lost, Mr Lloyd.

That's good to know.

Though you might fall off.

Thank you. I'll bear that in mind.

He retrieved his coat, his hat, his sketchpad, his pencil and

climbed the hill through the village, past the old men leaning against a low wall, cigarettes in hands, in mouths, dogs at
their feet. They waved at him, smiled at him, and watched as
he negotiated the path, uncertain of his route, knowing only
that he should leave, get away from the eyes staring at him,
the mouths talking of him, his breath and step faster than was
comfortable, slowing only when he was away from the village,
walking past piles of turf covered in blue, orange and white
plastic, tied down with rope but flapping nonetheless in the
evening wind. He walked by the vegetable patch, alongside
rows of potatoes, cabbages and onions coated in layers of
rotting seaweed, hens pecking at the soil beneath. He passed
three cows, two pigs, several more stray hens, four donkeys
and a flock of sheep grazing freely on grass that grew more
thickly across his path, a path that became a trail as he travelled further from the village into the open wilderness of the
island, the earth moist underfoot but the grass yellowed and
dried, stripped and burnt by the wind. He spotted rabbits
hopping, bouncing, and birds rising from the grass, calling as
they flew upwards into the evening sun. He whistled then and
walked on, pausing when the trail faded, disappeared into the
grass. He looked around for a route but failed to find one and
headed instead across untrodden grass towards the steepest
part of the island, halting to sketch a tree beaten by wind into
a tight ball of twisted branch and trunk, and again to draw
a small lake, the sun sparkling on the water. He hummed,
climbing the hill in search of the cliffs he had come to paint,
noticing that the ground sloped more steeply, that it pressed

into the backs of his legs as he headed to the western edge
of the island, towards the evening sun, still high in the sky,
higher than he was used to. His stomach fluttered
anticipation
excitement
self-portrait: blind date
He walked towards the edge of the cliff, pitched his body
forward and closed his eyes
book truth
walking boat
book untruth
singing boatmen
untruth
truth
one all
cliffs as decider
He opened his eyes and looked down on the cliffs. He kicked
at the wind-burnt grass
pastels
blue
green
tinges of pink
sunday painters
and park railings
unworthy
of oils
of mildew
rain and cold

of cabbage

potato

and fish that's fried

He slumped onto the grass and buried his head into his arms.

self-portrait: blind date, the aftermath

He calculated his losses, the money spent on boats, trains and buses, the deposit on the house, and the fresh expense of travelling south

to sunflowers

red roofs

parched earth

glistening sea

to painting already done

He stood up and looked again at the cliffs, hoping to see them differently, as they were in the book. He shook his head and turned back towards the village, walking along the edge of the island, pushing against a strengthening wind. He tucked his hat into his pocket, disgruntled by the ferocity as he climbed upwards in search of a path, scanning for a route back to his cottage to pack his bags and leave with the boatmen, to return back again

to the sated

the smug

the dealers

their darlings

auerbach

bacon

and freud

the dealers' darlings
the darling dealer
The wind became too strong and he dropped to his knees, uncertain of the way back. He crawled to the top of a slope, to the edge of the island in the hope of seeing lights from the village. He looked down. On cliffs. As they were in the book, raw, rugged, violent beauty, the ocean thunderous as it crashed into the rock two hundred feet beneath his knees and hands. He flopped onto his stomach and reached further over the edge, the force of the ocean against the rock reverberating through his flesh, into his bones

beauty

unearthed

unseen

unpainted

worthy

of oils

He laughed

of mildew

rain and cold

of cabbage

potato

and fish that's fried

He stayed on his belly, watching as the setting sun lit the west-facing cliff, a light show to unearth the pinks, reds, oranges, yellows embedded in the rock, colours he had not expected to find so far to the north. He drew them in his sketchbook and scrambled on hands and knees along the cliff's edge to peer at caves and archways cut by the ocean, to draw the herring gulls, cormorants and terns, squawking and caking the rock in a rich white fertiliser it could not absorb, to sketch how the light fell this far to the north, knowing that at dawn it would be different, as it would be at midday, at four in the afternoon, in rain, in fog, in winter, in autumn, in summer, in spring, the interactions between sun and rock boundless, infinite.

He rolled onto his back and stared into the darkening sky, humming

one truth

two truths

three truths

the men do sing while rowing

though

not

for

me

In the morning, after breakfast of porridge, tea and bread, he asked Bean Uí Néill a question. He spoke slowly, enunciating each syllable.

Do you know what time the mailboat arrives?

She turned off the radio and shouted. James came running.

Bí ag caint leis, she said.

What is it you want? he said.

The mailboat. What time does it arrive?

Tomorrow, Mr Lloyd.

I thought that it would be today.

It's Sunday today.

But I want my luggage.

No boat on a Sunday, Mr Lloyd.

What am I supposed to do until tomorrow?

James shrugged.

Wait.

Lloyd carried a chair outside, standing it on the slate slab set into the earth by the front door of his cottage. He opened his sketchpad and began to draw the village, the cottages, the houses, the men and women moving from one door to another, dogs, cats and hens roaming the single street. He drew the sea, the path leading down to the sea. He drew James, walking towards him with a cup and a plate, tea and bread, the milk already added, the jam and butter thinly spread.

This will keep you going, Mr Lloyd.

Thank you, James.

He received the cup and plate.

What are you up to this morning?

Mass.

I didn't see a church.

The schoolhouse.

And a priest?

James shrugged.

Bean Uí Néill knows enough.

James left and Lloyd drew the islanders again, better dressed this time, the men in suit jackets with hair combed back, the women in dresses, cardigans and lipstick.

island scene: mass on sunday

Micheál waved his arm and shouted at him.

Are you coming in, Mr Lloyd?

Lloyd shook his head.

Not for me.

He gathered his coat, his hat, tucked his sketchpad and pencil into his pocket and walked along the island's edge, staying with the sun in the south and east, with slopes more gentle on his legs. He sat on grass and looked out on the expanse of sea around the island, the sunlight glittering across its surface, the birds diving and banking, soaking in his distance from London, from others, from them, their exhibitions, reviews, plaudits, their scene

her

there

in their midst

the darling dealer

their midst

her midst

not mine

He lay down. To wait. Though the wind chilled him. He sat up and looked again at the vastness of the sea, greyer than before.

self-portrait: on the edge

He returned to the village and sat again in the same place for his evening meal. The boatmen were still there. Francis leaned into him.

You've been drawing the islanders.

I have. Going to Mass.

You said you wouldn't.

Did I? I forgot.
It didn't take you long, Mr Lloyd.
What didn't?
To forget.

The colonel with the Queen's Own Highlanders shouts at two policemen in South Armagh, telling them not to go any further. Superintendent Stanley Hanna is forty-eight years of age and his colleague, Constable Kevin Thompson, is twenty-two years old and engaged to be married. Both men are Protestant.

The policemen signal that they have heard the colonel but carry on regardless, down a country lane in Clonalig just after nine o'clock on Sunday evening, June 3rd. They stop at a wall to investigate a milk churn. The churn is packed with 200 lbs of explosives. The IRA is watching.

The IRA detonates the bomb, exploding it in the faces of the two police officers, killing them instantly.

After breakfast, he asked James again about the arrival time of the mailboat.

In the next hour, he said. Two hours. Three. It depends.

On what?

Many things. Mostly the sea.

How can I tell?

Look at the sea, said James. Then you'll know.

That's it?

James shrugged.

That's it.

Lloyd walked down to the cove, the air still cool. He scanned the sea for movement, for sails, for an engine, but found nothing. He drifted then through the ruins that had once been homes and scrambled down to the beach where dozens of seals were resting, indifferent to his arrival. He drew the cove, the cliff path, the houses, the ruins and then the seals, a fresh page as one, larger than the others, left the herd and shuffled towards the sea, muscles undulating to drag his bulk across the beach

fish skin

sand burn

amphibious joy

Lloyd drew the seal at the water's edge, sketching as it flicked its flippers against the wet sand, as it threw itself at the waves until the sea was deep enough for it to dive. It bent its head, bound its neck to its spine and cut gracefully into the water.

island series: metamorphosis

He closed his sketchbook and walked back up the cliff path to his cottage. He returned the kitchen chair to the slate slab and sat down, uncertain of what to do next, of how to wait in a place where nothing happens

a place

without need

of

happenings

He began to draw the islanders again, the women moving from one house to another trading tools, laundry baskets, irons, saucepans, the old men gathered at the wall, smoking cigarettes and pipes. Micheál and Francis joined them. Francis lit a cigarette and looked across at the artist's cottage. Lloyd closed his sketchpad and stood up. He returned inside, to the studio, and fingered the paints in the drawer by the easel, stroking the metal tubes

presence

future

potential

He took the pencils and charcoals from their packets and laid them on the easel, ready to start, first with pencil, then charcoal, using their softness and fluidity to learn the contours of the cliffs and the fall of light across the rock, moving, when ready, to paint, to paper, to canvas.

He looked again through the window at the sea, searching once more for his suitcases packed with that paper and canvas. He could see nothing. He returned to his chair at the front of the house and watched from there, gulls cutting across the sky, gulls milling at the island's edge.

At eleven, James arrived with tea and a slice of bread, again with butter and jam.

Thank you, James. Any news on the boat?

The boy looked across the sea.

No.

Any idea how much longer?

No.

Lloyd took the cup and plate.

How old are you, James?

Fifteen.

You're still at school?

He shrugged.

I don't know. Maybe.

What does that mean?

I want to leave.

You don't like it?

They don't like islanders.

Why don't they like islanders?

They think we're poor and stupid.

That's not very nice.

James shrugged.

No different to your lot. You all think the same way.

Lloyd drank from the cup.

It's good tea.

Granny makes the tea. Nobody else is let.

Why not?

No reason. Just a rule.

She's a busy woman, James. Doing Mass and tea.

She is.

Well, it's good tea, James.

James nodded.

Godly tea, Mr Lloyd.

They laughed. Lloyd stretched the plate towards James.

Would you like some, James?

I would.

James sat on the ground, a distance from Lloyd, his eyes still on the sea as he chewed.

What made you come here, Mr Lloyd?

The cliffs.

Do you not have cliffs in England?

Not like these ones.

What's the difference?

They're rugged here, wild.

Lloyd set the cup and plate on the ground, the ceramic scratching against the grit and small stones.

I like being on the edge, James. Away from London.

island series: metamorphosis II

James stood up and walked towards the cove.

Where are you going?

46

The boat, Mr Lloyd.

He scanned the horizon. He saw nothing. James shook his head.

Do you not see it?

No.

You need to sharpen that artist's eye, Mr Lloyd.

Doors opened and people moved towards the cove. Lloyd stared still at the sea, unable to see the boat. He followed the islanders to the slipway. Micheál and Francis were at the water's edge, the currach beside them, watching the boat motor into the cove.

I didn't see it at all, he said.

What?

The boat. Out at sea.

Can you see it now? said Micheál.

Lloyd frowned, peering still at the sea.

I can. I just need more practice.

That's all it is, Mr Lloyd.

Lloyd pointed at the currach, a box with books and emptied medicine bottles beneath the prow, but not tied in place.

You're going back? said Lloyd.

We are, said Micheál.

More hard rowing.

Micheál shook his head.

That boat has an engine, Mr Lloyd.

The boatmen and the old island men rowed two currachs to the bigger boat and returned with three suitcases of matching leather and the weekly shopping packed into plastic crates and cardboard boxes, flour, sugar and tea, pouches of tobacco, packets of cigarettes, bottles of beer, medicines, chocolate, cake, toothpaste, shampoo, batteries, pens, pencils, notebooks, letters, postcards, newspapers and books. The islanders took what they had ordered, handed money to Micheál who left, his currach tied to the rear of the bigger boat.

The old men carried the suitcases up the hill to the village. Lloyd followed, walking beside James who was carrying a box of groceries, two books perched on top of the shopping. Lloyd picked the books from the box, a novel, *The Dark Side of the Sun*, and a history of the Native Americans.

Are these for you, James?

They are.

Are they any good?

Don't know yet. Just got them.

Lloyd opened both books.

She sends me two every week.

Who is she?

The librarian.

That's impressive.

James shifted the box in his arms.

Always a novel and then a history or geography book. Sometimes science. Or nature.

And do you like her choices?

Usually. If I don't, I write a note.

Lloyd returned the books to the box.

I might ask her for a book about painting, said James.

Does your mother get books?

She's not a great reader. Finished school at twelve.

And your grandmother?

She can't read. Radio for her.

I hear that. It's always on.

Always, Mr Lloyd. It'd drive you mad.

The old men dropped the suitcases, just inside the door to the cottage. He lifted them into the studio, opened them and sighed, relieved that they were as he had left them

all is

as was

unblemished

untouched

He unpacked his tripod, sketchpads, canvases, paper, painting board, small easel, and the rectangular teak box that he would fill with paints and take to the cliffs. He unpacked too his boots, raincoats, rain trousers, books, binoculars, flask and camera, and his gatherings of other people's work

as gauguin travelled

west

north

south

books, postcards, pictures from newspapers, from magazines, catalogues, as well as photographs and drawings. He stuck them to walls, to doors, upstairs, downstairs, and mounted his large sketchpad on the easel. He stood by the door and looked at the studio.

self-portrait: artist in residence

James landed into the cottage with the chair Lloyd had left outside.

I told you to knock, James.

I did. With the chair.

A proper knock.

It's about to rain.

You should knock with your hand.

I will when it's not raining.

James tucked the chair under the table.

I like the decorating, Mr Lloyd.

Thank you, James.

But it smells awful in here.

It does.

And it's cold.

It is.

You need to keep a fire on the go, Mr Lloyd. All the time.

Do I?

Even when the sun is scalding.

I doubt that troubles you too much, James.

What?

A scalding sun.

Do you know how to build a fire, Mr Lloyd?

With turf?

There's nothing else.

I don't, James.

I'll show you.

Thank you.

He followed James through the rear door to a pile of turf and kindling.

This is yours. You take from here for your fire, but not from anywhere else.

What would happen if I did?

James stared at him.

It's never happened, Mr Lloyd. Nobody does that here.

James built a tepee of turf over kindling and crumpled newspaper. He lit it.

Just keep it going, said James. It'll get rid of the smell and the cold.

Thank you, James.

And cover it with ash in the evening. It'll start easy then in the morning.

James looked around the room, at the three suitcases stacked beside the wardrobe.

You brought a lot of stuff.

I did.

Why do you need so much?

For my work. Do you want to see my studio?

James followed into the room that had once been a bedroom.

I like it better this way, Mr Lloyd.

He moved around the room, touching the easel, the paints, the brushes, stroking them.

Can I have a go, Mr Lloyd?

Maybe. Not today.

James left and Lloyd, the doors and windows closed, the fire burning, began his work. He attached paper to the easel and lifted a pencil to sketch long lines up and down the page, a low hum slipping through his lips as his fingers and hand moved across the sheet, hunting to recreate that first encounter, his first sighting of that ferocious beauty, page after page of light and dark, of unshaded and shaded, working late into the night and again in the early morning, relishing the stillness of the village, of the island, his doors and windows open to flood the cottage with light, with the sounds of the sea and the songs of the birds.

James came to him with a bowl of porridge, a pot of tea, buttered bread, a cup, cutlery, and milk in a second cup.

You missed breakfast.

Thank you, James.

You went to bed very late. And you were up very early.

Are you spying on me?

You've no curtains. You took them down.

Of course.

We'd know anyway. Even with curtains.

There's no hiding place then?

None.

Lloyd poured tea.

What's that like, James?

What?

Living in a place where everybody knows everything about you.

He shrugged.

They only think they know you.

Lloyd lifted the pot towards James.

Would you like some tea, James?

I might as well.

Lloyd fetched a glass jar from his studio and transferred the milk into it. He handed the cup to James. They sat side by side at the table, looking through the window at the sky.

Not a bad day, said James.

What will you do today?

I'm supposed to be fishing later.

You don't sound enthusiastic.

I'm not.

Do you not like fishing?

I don't like boats.

That's disadvantageous in a fisherman.

It is, Mr Lloyd.

James shuddered.

I hate being on the sea.

So do I, said Lloyd.

James laughed.

We know that.

Lloyd poured more tea.

Is your dad a fisherman?

Used to be.

Have I met him? Where is he?

At the bottom of the sea. With my granddad and uncle. Three of them. One fishing trip.

That's dreadful.

It is.

How old were you?

A baby.

I can see why you don't like fishing.

I don't like it anyway.

James emptied his cup.

That must have been a terrible shock to your mother.

It was. Her husband. Her father. Her brother.

That's really dreadful.

That it is, Mr Lloyd.

Any other uncles, James? Apart from Francis.

James shook his head.

Not here. He's the only one on the island.

But Francis doesn't live here, said Lloyd.

James shrugged.

He acts as though he does.

James stood up. He lifted the dishes.

What's your mother's name, by the way?

Mairéad.

She has beautiful hair.

I'll tell her.

Lloyd laughed.

No. Don't. And your granny's name?

Bean Uí Néill. Mrs O'Neill in English. Do you like rabbit?

Very much.

I might catch a rabbit instead.

How do you catch a rabbit?

I have a few different ways. I catch birds too. And get eggs from nests.

You won't go hungry, James.

I keep the house well fed, Mr Lloyd.

So I should be nice to you.

Very nice, Mr Lloyd.

James left, taking the dishes, and Lloyd packed paper, pencils and charcoal to take to the cliffs, to work beyond first impressions and remembrance. He packed his book about birds too, and walked across the island, the wind blowing at his face, through his hair, into his clothes, puffing up his jacket and reddening his cheeks.

self-portrait: on the edge of europe

He looked down on rock that had been in shade on that first evening, picking out deep blues, pale blues, pinks and silvers, the colours shimmering in the sun. He lay on his stomach, on the still dewy grass, and stared at how the sun lit the cliff, illuminating tiny particles of rock and sand pressed into each other millions of years before, highlighting too the ancient structure of the cliff face, planed in some parts, roughly cut in others, the rock hacked, serrated and puckered during that violent separation from the mainland

agony

swirling still

through water and wind

He began to draw, working quickly before the clouds returned with coats of grey and brown, sketching first the cliff, the sea foaming at its base, and then the birds, landing, taking off, the rock as refuge, though he was confused by the gulls and terns, and by the array of black birds, for not all were cormorants. He looked up the guidebook and found images of shags but little else, as it was a guide to birds in English gardens and on English cliffs. He threw the book onto the grass

no guide at all

    Though James might know

    Know what?

James stood over him, a dead rabbit hanging from each hand.

    Sorry?

    You said that James might know something.

    Did I? Can I draw you, James? Just like that.

    Francis said you weren't to draw us.

    Did he? I'll be very fast.

Lloyd flipped to a new page, his pencil scrambling to capture the freshness of youth and death, the boy's dark hair, his blue eyes, his wrongly buttoned shirt and his too short trousers, his scuffed shoes and socks that no longer had elastic, his fingers clasping the rabbits' hind feet, their eyes wide with shock, their bodies still to stiffen, the dribble of blood from each mouth yet to congeal, his pencil feverish, his throat humming until his breath shifted and a bestial groan rose from his chest, a signal that he had achieved. His hand relaxed and he filled out the boy's face, shading his eyes, his mouth

no triumph

everyday

hunt for food

He drew the boy's skin, creamy white with flecks of pink on his cheeks.

    Like your mother, James.

    What?

You look like your mother.

James bent to the ground.

Are you done? Can I drop these lads?

Lloyd stopped drawing.

Yes. Thank you. I have finished.

He stretched the rabbits across the grass, one on top of the other.

You did well there, James.

Not bad.

No gun. No knife. How did you do it?

I have my ways.

I imagine that you do.

He turned the sketch to show it to James.

What do you think?

James stared at it for several moments.

Is that what I look like?

Lloyd turned the drawing to look at it again.

It's what I see.

I look very scruffy, said James.

Lloyd shrugged.

You could probably do with a new pair of trousers.

You'd better give my granny more money, so.

He looked again at the drawing of himself.

But it's good, Mr Lloyd.

I'll paint it and call it *James with Two Rabbits*.

Can I have it then?

I don't know. It depends.

On what?

On many things.

Lloyd closed the sketchpad.

So, tell me what you know about birds, James. My book is useless.

I know a bit. Bean Uí Fhloinn taught me.

What?

Bean Uí Fhloinn. My great-granny. She knows a lot about birds.

I'll talk to her then.

James shook his head.

She has no English.

None?

Not a word.

What about everybody else?

Some understand but don't talk, some talk a bit.

What about your mother?

She knows a bit, but doesn't speak.

Why not?

James shrugged.

I don't know. Prefers not to.

So how can I talk to your great-granny about the birds?

You can't.

You'll have to teach me.

Lloyd dropped the sketchpad beside the rabbits, the grass dried by the morning's wind. James picked it up and turned the pages until he found the drawings of himself.

What does it depend on?

I'm sorry?

The picture of me. Why can't I have it?

It's my drawing.

But of me.

It's my work, James.

We should at least share it, Mr Lloyd.

It doesn't work like that.

How does it work?

Lloyd pointed at the rabbits.

Don't you have to skin those?

I do.

You'd better get going. The hide might stick to the skin.

I've plenty of time yet, Mr Lloyd.

Well, I have work to do out here, James.

I'll be quiet. I'll just watch.

I'd prefer you to leave.

Lloyd stayed until late afternoon when the rocks and cliff were again in shadow. He walked back to the village, washed and went to the kitchen for his evening meal. Bean Uí Néill slapped a plate of rabbit stew and mashed potatoes onto the table in front of him.

Thank you, he said.

James whispered.

You're in trouble, Mr Lloyd.

What have I done?

You drew me. You said you wouldn't.

Did I?

He lifted his knife and fork.

Is this my last supper, James?

59

It could be.

He ate.

It's a very good last supper, James.

Lloyd raised his voice.

That's wonderful rabbit, Mrs O'Neill.

James translated. Bean Uí Néill jutted her chin at the artist.

I'm in big trouble, James.

You are, Mr Lloyd.

They laughed.

So, how do you catch the rabbits?

I'll show you sometime.

I'd like that.

But only if you stop talking to yourself. No rabbit is going to come out of a hole with you muttering outside.

I suppose not.

And humming too. Do you know you hum?

Do I?

You do. You make a lot of noise for a quiet man.

I like to keep myself company.

There was no dessert, and the tea was cold and syrupy.

My punishment goes on, James.

I agree, said Lloyd. It is good with the tea.

Lloyd stood up.

Thank you, Mrs O'Neill.

Lloyd left and returned to his cottage to close the door and resume his work, drawing James with the rabbits, working through the evening at the kitchen table, using pencil, then charcoal, twisting and turning his wrist to prevent smudges, filling sheet after sheet of paper with images of the boy.

James arrived with breakfast.

That's a lot of me, he said.

Take a look, James. Tell me what you think.

James picked through the drawings of his eyes, of his hands, his lips, of the rabbits' eyes and mouths, of blood congealing, the island boy as hunter, gatherer, me as hunter, gatherer, as island boy.

It's all very good, Mr Lloyd. But strange.

To see yourself?

Maybe.

I'm sure it is.

Lloyd ate and poured two cups of tea.

Take some tea, said Lloyd.

The artist gathered the drawings into a pile and slid them down the table, away from the tea. James sat down.

How is your grandmother today, James?

Still giving out about you.

Ah.

She thinks that I'll get a big head from looking at myself.

Lloyd stirred the milk into his tea.

And what do you think?

I don't know. It's different, anyway. Seeing yourself like that.

They looked through the window at the sea, sitting side by side, drinking tea.

What's today's plan, Mr Lloyd?

I'll prepare my canvases.

Will you draw me again?

Lloyd shook his head.

Not today.

Lloyd refilled the cups.

What will you do, James?

Not much.

You can help me if you want.

Doing what?

Coating my canvases. Priming them.

James shrugged.

Grand. There's nothing else going on.

Wonderful. Get the fire going, James.

James rekindled the ashes and established a flame. Lloyd set the size on the edge of the heat and bent over the fire, a stick in his hand, stirring the gelatinous mixture in a blackened

pot

old masters

rooms

like this

cold

dark

but dutch

Most artists don't do this, said Lloyd.

What do the others do?

Buy them ready to use.

Lloyd divided the content of the pot and handed a brush to James.

What should I do? said James.

Copy me.

Lloyd laid two small canvases on the table, dipped his brush into the pot and began to coat one canvas, starting in the left-hand corner and working towards the right. James copied him on the second canvas.

There's no colour, said James. Nothing.

That'll come later. When this has dried.

What's the point of painting if there's no colour?

That's what my wife says.

You should listen to her.

James brushed as Lloyd had shown him, the boy's strokes even and rhythmical, his breath softening to near silence, the door open to the sounds of sea and birds, the breeze light enough to freshen the cottage without ruffling the ash in the grate.

self-portrait: preparing canvas with the island boy

They coated twelve canvases. James washed the brushes with white spirits, as Lloyd showed him.

So why do you do it, Mr Lloyd, when you can buy them coated?

I like the ritual. Doing it as has been done for hundreds of years.

Why?

So that it's all my work, I suppose.

You didn't make the canvas, Mr Lloyd.

True, but all the painting is mine.

Not true any more. This painting is mine.

Lloyd nodded, slowly.

That is true, James.

Are you going to the cliffs today, Mr Lloyd?

I am.

Can I go with you?

No.

James picked up the emptied porridge bowl.

Are you finished with the tea?

Yes, I have.

He gathered the cups and pot.

Thank you, James.

You're grand, Mr Lloyd.

We'll do the second coat tomorrow.

Then can I paint?

Maybe.

Alexander Gore is a full-time member of the Ulster Defence Regiment standing outside his barracks on Belfast's Malone Road just after eleven on Wednesday morning, June 6th. He is twenty-three years of age, Protestant and has been married for four months. His nineteen-year-old wife is pregnant with their first child.

A truck drives down the Malone Road towards the barracks. Two IRA men in the truck open fire and kill Alexander Gore.

On his way to the cliffs – his tweed cap on his head, his hands deep in the pockets of his dark waxed coat – an old woman dressed in black waved at him.

Dia dhuit, Mr Lloyd.

He waved back, the air cool on his hand.

Hello.

He laughed, loudly

brittany, 1889

bonjour monsieur gauguin II

self-portrait

He walked on, whistling

ireland, 1979

dia dhuit mr lloyd

self-portrait

Joseph McKee is walking on Saturday, June 9th to a butcher shop in Belfast, close to the amusement arcade on Castle Street where he works as a doorman. He is thirty-four years old, a Catholic and a member of the Official IRA. Two men from the Ulster Defence Association pull up beside him on a motorbike and shoot him four times in the back of the head, revving the engine to mask the sound of the gun.

He used charcoal, picking off and blowing away pieces that broke from the stem, his fingers working to capture the dance of shade and light that, when perfected, would allow him to begin with oils, blue, grey, green, black and beige for the cliffs isolated beauty

continent's outpost

empire's edge

and black, grey, dark blue, light blue, white and silver for the foaming, glittering sea, and blue for the endlessness of sky, azure blue, sky blue, turquoise blue, gentian blue, cobalt blue, Prussian blue, Persian blue, France blue, layered and thickened, indigo, Payne's grey, Mars black, ivory black, reaching into infinity.

Sitting closer to the edge, he drew the contours of the cliff and a line close to the top of his page. Above the line, outside the frame of his picture, he drew the sun as it was in the sky, almost straight above him. He tracked the fall of light onto the cliff face, and traced it onto his page, copying how the sun shaded and lit the outcrops, the caves, the folds and creases in the rock. He trailed the light as it fell directly onto the cliff, as it was filtered and fragmented through passing cloud, each moment of sun and shade different to the one that went before.

He turned to a fresh page and drew again the outline of the cliff. He switched back to pencil and worked around the base of the rock, digging, hunting to recreate the moment when the island splits open the sea, when grey granite dissects the ocean on its path across the earth, a thunderous roar that catapults water into the air, turning it to foam, to froth, to bead and sparkle in the mid-morning sun.

A shadow fell over his work. He looked up. At the sky. Hunting for the clouds. But the shadow was from behind. He turned. It was James, again, this time holding a flask and a bundle wrapped in a tea towel. Lloyd threw down his pencil. The lead snapped against a small stone.

What do you want?

You forgot something to eat.

Did I?

Yes.

James set down the food.

And you went without breakfast.

Did I?

Are you not starving? I'd be starving without my breakfast. Lloyd dropped his sketchpad onto the grass. He turned from the cliff.

Is that tea?

It is, Mr Lloyd.

Some tea would be nice.

James poured.

I brought a second cup, Mr Lloyd. Just in case.

That was clever of you.

James poured tea for himself.

So, are you not starving, Mr Lloyd?

Some days I can go without. I must be part camel.

James stretched along the grass.

There's brack in there, too, Mr Lloyd. With the sandwich.

What's brack?

Fruit cake.

Does that mean your granny has forgiven me?

My mam made that for you.

She was allowed to make the tea?

My granny refused to.

Lloyd smiled.

I must be in big trouble.

You are.

James pointed at the tea towel.

I love brack with my tea, he said.

Is that so?

It is.

Would you like some, James?

I wouldn't mind. If you're offering.

They ate and drank.

I agree, said Lloyd. It is good with tea.

James picked up the sketchpad.

That's powerful work, Mr Lloyd.

Thank you, James.

Bean Uí Fhloinn says the sea is rising.

Is that the old woman in black? Your great-granny?

Yes.

I saw her. A very old woman.

That'd be her.

How does she know that? About the sea.

She'll tell you the fairies told her. That they're worried about drowning.

Do you believe her?

James laughed. He shook his head.

It's from looking at the rocks. At the differences since she was a child.

Has it changed by much?

Small amounts. But she sees it.

Lloyd poured more tea and looked down on the sea.

We should be safe enough up here, James.

We're grand for today, anyway, Mr Lloyd.

James turned the pages and looked at the other drawings.

You've scribbled over some of them.

Yes. I do that.

Why?

They're not good enough.

How do you know when they're good enough?

You just know.

How though?

You feel happy. Content.

Looking at this, you must be a miserable fella.

Lloyd laughed.

Will you paint me today, Mr Lloyd?

No, not you today, James.

Why not?

I'm working on the cliffs.

When will you finish me?

When I have painted the cliffs.

James lay down on the grass.

I'll be an old man, so.

He closed his eyes.

It's nice out here, he said. Away from everybody.

It is, James.

The British Army and the Royal Ulster Constabulary intercept the IRA in a cattle truck near Keady, South Armagh, on Saturday evening, June 9th.

Police believe the IRA is positioning the truck for a rocket attack. A gun battle ensues between the British soldiers and the IRA men in the back of the cattle truck. The truck speeds away, the British soldiers claiming that they hit the IRA men, that they hear screaming from the lorry.

A prison officer also shoots at the cattle truck, firing his shotgun three times at the IRA men.

The IRA men escape across the border into the Irish Republic. The cattle truck is set on fire in a quarry and, when darkness falls, three IRA men are dropped at the door of Monaghan hospital. Two are injured, but Peadar McElvanna, a twenty-four-year-old Catholic man from Convent Lodge, Armagh, is dead.

He saw the boat on the horizon and headed down towards the cove, although he had nothing to collect, no reason to join the islanders already gathered on the slipway, the women in summer dresses and cardigans, hair tidied, lips coloured, shoulders straightened, standing upright among the old men sucking on pipes, lips smacking against each other, the small sound audible to him in the cove raucous with sea and birds.

self-portrait: acclimatising

self-portrait: becoming an islander

James stood by the water's edge. He nodded at the artist.

Busy day, Mr Lloyd.

So it seems.

Lloyd leaned against the cove wall, against the lichen and barnacles, and watched the scene unfold.

island series: arrival of the mailboat

He drew the islanders, the cove, the mailboat, the sea, then Mairéad, a shimmering green scarf in her hair, the fabric tumbling into her auburn curls, then himself, sketching himself sketching them.

self-portrait: with the islanders and the mailboat in the cove

self-portrait: company without obligations

self-portrait: contentment

The islanders began to wave, harder as the boat drew nearer, as they saw that a man at the prow, tall and tanned, was waving at them.

island series: the islanders' welcome

The man, his hair bleached by sun, jumped off the boat and into the water, still in the sea as he shook men's hands and kissed women's cheeks, first left, then right. He tousled the boys' hair and swung the girls into the air, laughter reverberating around the cove. Lloyd pressed his back against the lichen and barnacles and sidled along the cliff, away from the gathering, from the excitement.

self-portrait I: not for me
self-portrait II: not for me, the englishman

The man, still in the water, walked towards Lloyd. He stepped onto the slipway, spilling seawater over the concrete. He reached out his hand.

So you're the Sasanach?

I'm sorry?

The Englishman. That's what they call you.

Is that a compliment?

Depends on the politics, I suppose.

They shook hands.

I am Jean-Pierre Masson.

You're French?

Yes. Paris.

This is a bit of a change then.

Masson shrugged.

I come every summer.

An unusual place to holiday, said Lloyd.

I could say the same of you.

I'm not on holiday.

Nor am I, Mr Lloyd.

Masson led the islanders back up the path, singing in French as he went, the girls spinning and skipping behind him, the women giggling and leaning into each other, Mairéad among them. Lloyd followed, walking behind with the old men, trailing them into the kitchen where the table was covered with apple tarts, rhubarb tarts, fruit cake and scones, the jam and cream set out in decorated bowls and the milk poured into small jugs. Bean Uí Néill seated Masson at the head of the table, but left Lloyd to find a place of his own. He sat halfway down the table, close to Micheál. Bean Uí Néill poured tea while Mairéad offered scones. Lloyd took one.

Thank you, he said.

He cut it open and ate it without jam, without cream.

How long will you be here, Mr Masson?

Call me JP.

I'm happy with Mr Masson.

Suit yourself.

So, how long will you be here?

Three months. And you?

About the same.

I love it here, said Masson. It's my fourth summer, you know.

Lloyd turned away, towards Micheál.

Quite a party here today, said Lloyd.

There always is when JP arrives, said Micheál.

So I see.

And how are you getting on, Mr Lloyd?

Well enough, thank you. James is looking after me.

I hear that Bean Uí Néill is in a rage with you.

I'm sure that it will pass, he said.

Micheál smiled.

Don't count on it.

Lloyd nodded at the old woman in the corner, to the side of the fire. She lifted her hand towards him.

Dia dhuit, Mr Lloyd.

Hello.

She was older than the old men, though the skin on her face was softer, the fissures less pronounced, the pale creaminess of her cheeks fragmented by tiny capillaries burst open by wind

pin tip

red paint

across

rich cream

after rembrandt

The Frenchman was taking gifts from his bag, boxes of chocolates wrapped in silver paper and blue ribbon. Lloyd looked down at his hands and rubbed charcoal from his fingers

not here

to ingratiate

to please

here

to paint

77

He rubbed at his knuckles, his head down but his eyes turned to watch as Masson moved around the room distributing chocolates and kisses to the women, lingering with Mairéad, auburn hair and shimmering green drifting down her back, laughing as she thanked him. Masson sat down again.

Such wonderful people, he said.

You speak the language, Mr Masson?

Yes, I study Irish. Gaelic, as you prefer to call it.

I have no preference.

Then we'll go with Irish.

Masson drank from his cup.

I'm a linguist, Mr Lloyd, and I specialise in languages threatened with extinction.

And you're here to save Gaelic?

Masson returned the cup slowly to its saucer.

I want to help, yes.

How can you help a language that is almost dead?

I'm writing a book.

Lloyd stretched his arms into the air, right, then left.

I suggest that you and your book are fifty years too late, Mr Masson.

Yes, that is what the speakers of English like to believe.

And what do the French think, Mr Masson?

That Irish is an ancient and beautiful language worthy of our support.

Lloyd lifted his cup for more tea.

The young people want English, Mr Masson.

Young people want many things, Mr Lloyd.

Bean Uí Néill poured tea.

Languages die, said Lloyd, because the speakers give up on them.

That can be a contributing factor, yes.

Isn't that then the speakers' choice? The freedom of their will.

That choice, that freedom, is often more curtailed and complicated than you might think.

Is it? I abandon Irish because English is more advantageous to me. I can get a better job, travel further.

As I said, it is more complicated than you suggest.

Masson sat back into his chair.

And what type of art do you do, Mr Lloyd?

Landscape. I am here to paint the cliffs.

Ah, another painter who wants to be Monet.

That's rather rude.

Isn't every cliff painter trying to emulate Monet?

I am not trying to emulate anybody. Least of all Monet.

Masson took the scone offered by Mairéad.

I imagine Monet is too genteel for you, Mr Lloyd. Too subtle.

Too boring. Too nice. Too bourgeois. Too bloody French.

Masson sighed.

How do you do that? said Masson.

Do what?

Paint what another artist has done so definitively?

How can you write yet another book about the demise of Gaelic?

79

My book is different.

My art is different.

Micheál stood up.

We should sort you out, JP. Get you settled.

Where are you staying? said Lloyd.

Micheál pulled on his cap.

He'll be beside you, Mr Lloyd.

Lloyd ran his hands along his thighs, flattening the green corduroy of his trousers.

I paid to be on my own.

You're on your own, Mr Lloyd. You have a whole house to yourself.

I paid you to be alone here.

You rented the cottage, Mr Lloyd. Not the island.

Masson stood up. He picked up his bag and pointed at Lloyd.

And I should have been told about him.

What about him, JP?

An English speaker on the island, Micheál.

English speakers come to the island all the time, JP.

Not for three months.

Everyone is welcome, JP. Whatever language you speak.

Masson shook his head.

That's the problem, Micheál, that's why the language is dying.

He left. Micheál followed, and the room emptied, the tea party at an end. Lloyd stayed on, sipping at his already cold tea, but then left. The women flopped onto the emptied chairs, into their own language.

That went well, said Mairéad.

They laughed, cursorily.

They'll be best friends by the end of the summer, said Francis.

Bean Uí Néill tugged at the ribbon and opened the chocolates decorated with pink and blue sugars, chocolate flakes and tiny fragments of nut.

They are very beautiful, she said. It's almost a shame to eat them.

She popped a round white truffle into her mouth.

I'm saving mine, said Mairéad.

For what? said Francis.

Until I'm ready.

Ready for what? You either want a chocolate or you don't.

There's the moment, Francis.

Here she goes. What moment, Mairéad?

The moment when they're all gone. If I don't eat them, I save myself from that moment.

Nothing is straightforward with you, is it? Not even a bloody chocolate.

She shrugged.

Some things are, Francis.

Bean Uí Néill sent the chocolates down the table towards her mother, Bean Uí Fhloinn. The old woman shook her head.

Too sweet for me.

Bean Uí Néill took a second chocolate and closed the box.

So, are we ready for a summer of these two men?

It'll be pure entertainment, said Mairéad.

Will it? said Bean Uí Néill.

A spectacle, Mam.

I don't like it. Two foreigners at the same time.

Just sit back and watch, Mam. Enjoy it.

They'll be at each other all summer, said Bean Uí Néill.

Battle of the ego, said Francis. France versus England.

They think they own the place, said Bean Uí Néill.

Nothing new there, said Francis.

Bean Uí Néill sighed, loudly.

I don't like having two of them.

It's not that bad, Mam.

It is. I've enough English to know.

Ah, they're just being stupid, said Mairéad.

Well, I don't like it.

It'll be grand, Mam.

No, Mairéad. One is grand. Two is more than we can manage.

It's only a bit more cooking and cleaning, said Mairéad.

Bean Uí Néill shook her head.

I don't like it. Don't want it.

It's just after the quiet of the winter, Mam. You'll get used to it.

No. I won't. And I don't like that Englishman drawing James.

Ah, Mam. Not that again. They're having a bit of fun together, that's all.

Francis lifted his cup. Bean Uí Néill poured tea for him.

Your mother is right, Mairéad. He shouldn't be drawing James.

Leave it, Francis. Nothing to do with you.

I'm his uncle.

Mairéad opened her chocolates, ate one, then a second. And a third.

We'll get used to them, Mam, said Mairéad. They'll get used to each other.

I don't like it.

And we need the money, Mam.

We do, Mairéad. Especially when that son of yours refuses to fish.

Mairéad stood up. She scraped the jam back into the jar and gathered the remaining cream in a bowl.

I'll use that for butter, she said.

Bean Uí Néill cut another slice of rhubarb tart for Francis. She added cream from the bowl.

I wonder how Micheál's getting on, she said.

I'd say they're giving him hell, said Francis.

Well, he deserves it, said Bean Uí Néill. Taking their money and lying to them.

Ah, now, said Francis. He didn't lie.

He did, Francis.

More just that he didn't fully inform.

They laughed.

He should have told JP that the Englishman was coming, said Mairéad.

And risk three months' money? said Francis. He's not going to do that.

No, I suppose he's not.

But he'll skip away again tomorrow, said Bean Uí Néill,

leaving us with his mess.

Ah, you'll do well out of it too, said Francis.

Not as well as Micheál.

Nobody does as well as Micheál, Mam.

Mairéad gathered the plates and cups, wiped the table with a damp cloth and carried the dishes into the back kitchen. She made fresh tea and sat again at the table. She poured tea for Bean Uí Fhloinn.

What do you make of it all, Bean Uí Fhloinn?

The old woman rapped her fingers against the wooden arm of her chair.

Truth is elusive when money is in the room.

Mairéad laughed and patted the old woman's shoulder.

It is that, Bean Uí Fhloinn.

It'll be a strange summer right enough, Mairéad.

The old woman sipped from her cup.

Ah, you love JP, Bean Uí Fhloinn.

I do. And we know him well enough at this stage. Know the routine of what happens when he's here.

We do, said Bean Uí Néill. And we enjoy it.

Mairéad passed tea to her mother, to Francis.

But we don't know about him and this Englishman, said Bean Uí Fhloinn. That's new for us. Something we don't know.

So what do we do, Mam? said Bean Uí Néill.

Let Micheál do the running for the minute, said Bean Uí Fhloinn, and then we'll see.

They drank tea and waited in near silence until Micheál returned.

Well? said Mairéad. What happened?

The Sasanach wants to move. Says that he wants a more isolated house with better light.

And what did you say?

I told him that short of uprooting the house and taking off the roof, there was nothing I could do for him.

They laughed.

And JP? said Mairéad.

Fine, until he discovered that he was sharing a turf pile with Lloyd.

What's wrong with that?

That was the end of him, ranting that he doesn't want to be anywhere near an English speaker. 'I am here for the Irish language,' he said, 'I need full immersion.'

What did you do?

I threw him into the sea, Mairéad. Full immersion.

They laughed again. Mairéad poured tea for him.

Seriously, what did you do?

I had to split the pile in half. One side for JP, the other for the Sasanach.

Imagine that, said Mairéad. A Frenchman and an Englishman squabbling over our turf.

They've been squabbling over our turf for centuries, said Francis.

I suppose they have.

He leaned into her, whispered to her.

You'd like that, Mairéad, wouldn't you?

Like what?

Being squabbled over.

She pushed him away.

No, I wouldn't, Francis.

Bean Uí Néill stood up.

Right, we have a meal to make. Out, the lot of you.

Mairéad took the scarf from her head, tied her hair into a bun and went into the small backyard to gather turf, hurrying her task as Lloyd and Masson were already outside, on the other side of the wall, throwing clumps of turf into fraying baskets, backs and buttocks against each other, Lloyd working quickly but clumsily, Masson slower and more meticulous in his movements, still bent at the task when Lloyd declared himself finished and picked up his half-filled basket to return to his cottage. He slammed the door, bolted it and shouted through it at the Frenchman.

Go to hell, he said.

Masson clicked his tongue.

Quel mec, he said.

He continued to fill his basket, gathering for himself the clods scattered about the dividing line drawn into the dust by the heel of Micheál's boot.

Quel idiot.

His basket full, he dropped it at the back door of his cottage and walked across the concrete to the lean-to, propped against the toilet house, where he found the sweeping brush that he used every year to clean the yard, the bristles worn, the wood weathered, the top of the handle broken and splintering. As it was, he said. As it always has been. He began to sweep, tidying the yard as he did at the start of every summer, gathering turf scraps, dust and dirt. A dog settling into its basket, he said. He brushed along Micheál's line but not over it, each stroke further dividing the concrete yard, light grey on one side, dark grey on the other. Swept. Unswept. Clean. Dirty. He picked up the turf straddling the dividing line and threw it into his basket. Mine, Lloyd, for I was here first. The whole yard is mine. Always has been. And damn you, anyway. For being here. For intruding. Damn you too, Micheál. For not letting me know. For taking my money, more money than last year, without telling me that he would be here. An Englishman. In this, my final summer. He shouldn't be here, not on this island, not in this yard, for this is my place, my retreat, where I sit, alone, at the end of the day, hidden by the whitewashed walls from the rest of the island, from the islanders, the evening sun on my closed eyes as I dissect the day's language and analyse the phrases and inflections, the intonations and borrowings, hunting for influences of English, for traces of that foreign language creeping onto the island, into the houses, into the mouths and onto the tongues of the islanders, tracking those tiny utterances that signal change, marking the beginning of the end of Irish on the island, these thoughts, this knowledge, encased and protected by the smallness and stillness of this yard, with only the birds to hear my mutterings, as it was in the wood-panelled courtyard of my grandmother's house on the edge of the village far from the town, further still from the city, sitting on my own at the circular table cast of iron, under the willow tree, the birds above me, around me, witness to my childhood mumblings on those early summer mornings, my parents, my aunts, my cousins still sleeping, my grandmother in the kitchen, humming as she prepared my hot chocolate, a freshness and softness to her movements that would later, as the day aged, become irritated and hardened, but then, in the early morning, as I sat outside, alone in the courtyard, as she stirred the chocolate powder into the warm milk, she was gentle, smiling as she set the blue and white bowl in front of me, smiling still when she returned from the kitchen with a basket of bread, with butter and jam, with a teaspoon, a knife, a napkin and a glass of water, setting them all in front of me, ruffling my hair, telling me how happy she was to see me again, to have me to stay, and I, aware even then of the transience of our intimacy, kissed her hand, her skin not yet old but beginning to grow old, holding her until she pulled away and returned to the kitchen, her slippers slapping the tiled floor still to be warmed by the day's sun, leaving me alone again with the birds. As it had been here. As I had been here. Alone, in this yard, until now, until the arrival of this Englishman with his English talk. Masson lifted the brush and slammed it against the concrete. Damn you, Lloyd. This yard is mine. It will be impossible for me to sit out here, to consider the day in silence because you'll be there, next door, making noise, and, worse than that, speaking English, an arrogance that I now have to incorporate into my work because your presence influences the outcome, the findings, undermining everything I have done, and I resent that, Lloyd, resent your arrogance, your intrusion, your dominance, your upending of the years that I have spent chronicling the demise of this language, years of cold summers in a damp, mildewed cottage that I scrub and bleach only to watch the blackness return as I sit at the kitchen table picking over slight linguistic shifts in this ancient, dying language, tracking tiny but significant movements from one summer to the next to prove a generational incorporation of English into Irish, a gradual but noticeable shift towards bilingualism, eventually, I imagine, to monolingualism, but gradual, Lloyd, do you hear me? A linguistic evolution that was occurring slowly until you turned up to destroy my work because the shift now to English will be sudden and violent, more in keeping with the linguistic history of Irish towns and their hinterlands than with a remote island. The Irish here was almost pure, Lloyd, tainted only by the schoolchildren learning English, by the intermittent visits of emigrants returning from Boston and London with their sophisticated otherness, and by mercenaries in linguistic mediation, men like Micheál who want only to communicate, indifferent to the medium or its need for protection until it one day dawns that the loss of Irish and the rise in English reduces his capacity to earn, to be the man in the middle, the broker, he who can shrug his shoulders and claim misunderstanding when the yard that has always been mine is taken from me without notice or discussion, when an Englishman moves in beside me, without notice or discussion, Micheál the Middleman indifferent as he destroys five years of my work, no, more than five, as it took me so long to find this island and to learn their version of Irish, but he is indifferent because he is earning from it, fattening his wallet, improving his lot at my expense, at the expense of my work.

Masson reached under the overhang of turf with the brush to gather more dust and debris, and collected his sweepings into a pile. He returned to the lean-to to collect a shovel encrusted with cement and heavier than it should be. He tilted the shovel and brushed up the sweepings, though dust slipped underneath as the lip was too high and too uneven, leaving him again to wonder, as he did every year, whether he should have brought dustpans and brushes for the island women, for Bean Uí Néill and Mairéad who scoop their sweepings onto scraps of cardboard or onto the small black shovel that they use at the grate, cursing as they scatter fire dust over the already swept floor, but decided again this year against it, opting for the chocolates, even though they were more expensive, as he was on the island to observe rather than influence, to take note rather than change. Masson lifted the shovel and threw the dust and dirt over the Englishman's pile of turf.

He heard James then, shouting, in English.

Tea is ready, he said.

James knocked on his door and went into the studio.

It's on the table, Mr Lloyd.

Lloyd continued painting.

You can bring it here, thank you.

James fiddled with the handle of the door.

I can't do that, Mr Lloyd.

You do it with my breakfast.

That's different.

There's no reason why it should be. I pay you all enough.

The boy turned to leave.

Just bring my dinner here, James.

I can't, Mr Lloyd. Not allowed.

Who says?

My grandmother. You'll have to talk to her.

Lloyd sighed, slowly.

I'm already in her bad books.

You are, Mr Lloyd.

He wiped the wet paint from his hands.

So it's go with you or starve.

That's it, Mr Lloyd.

Will that dreadful Frenchman be there?

There's nowhere else to eat.

Is Micheál still here?

He is.

That helps.

Francis is too, said James.

That is of less assistance.

Lloyd picked up his hat and coat.

I'll go to the cliffs after dinner.

It looks like rain.

Then I'll get wet.

Don't forget to fix your fire, Mr Lloyd.

I'm past caring, James.

The men were already eating when Lloyd sat down. Bean Uí Néill placed a plate of food in front of him, fried mackerel, mashed potato and cabbage.

The ubiquitous cabbage, said Lloyd. Just like Paris.

Masson shrugged.

We're not in Paris, Mr Lloyd.

That I had noticed.

He began to eat.

And you don't mind?

I mind many things, Mr Lloyd.

You don't mind eating this food.

I didn't come for the food, Mr Lloyd.

That was wise.

Lloyd pushed his fork at the food, at the mackerel swimming in oil that was not its own, at the potato that was still lumpy, at the insipid cabbage too long boiled in water. He sighed and mashed the fish into the potato, and added the cabbage, pressing his fork onto the food until the three ingredients blended and glistened with fat. He lifted the mixture to his mouth

body of fish

into body of man

cold flesh

cold fat

congealing

tongue and teeth

congealed

He swallowed and retched

discreet

well-mannered

good man lloyd

He returned his fork and knife to the plate, uncertain of

how to continue, even though he was hungry and the food looked and tasted as it did on other evenings. He pummelled the mixture again and added salt and dusty white pepper. He shovelled the food into his mouth and swallowed

no tasting

no thinking

good man lloyd

He cleared his plate and looked up and down the table, the islanders mesmerised by Masson's narrative, the Frenchman speaking in their language but using the facial gestures and hand movements of his own language.

self-portrait: outsider

He picked at the paint on his hands, peeling off strips of blue and grey, picking at splashes of white, his head bent, focused on the task, on the growing pile of paint scrapings on the table. Micheál was speaking, calling to him. He looked up.

Mr Lloyd, do you want us to speak English for you?

That would be nice.

Masson shook his head. He continued to speak in Irish.

This is an Irish-speaking island, he said.

With an English-speaking visitor, said Micheál.

It's his choice to come here.

And we're delighted to have him.

He chose to come to an Irish-speaking island.

We speak English too, JP.

Is that what you told him, Micheál? To persuade him to come here.

Micheál switched again to English.

93

JP is very passionate about the Irish language, Mr Lloyd.

Masson turned too to English.

Micheál is not, he said.

It's my language, JP. I can use it as I please.

What about Mairéad and Bean Uí Néill? said Masson.

What about them?

They don't speak English.

They understand more than you think, said Micheál.

It's their house, said Masson. And they speak Irish.

As I said, they'll be grand.

Bean Uí Néill set an apple tart on the table.

You are killing your own language, said Masson.

She cut into the tart, hitting the knife against the plate.

Irish is stronger than you think, said Micheál.

It is weaker than you believe, Micheál.

Micheál shrugged.

Than you like to believe, JP.

Bean Uí Néill served Lloyd first, and poured tea for him

grace

and

favour

mine today

It's theirs to kill, said Lloyd. Not yours.

Masson shook his head.

You can't speak on this. You have spent centuries trying to
annihilate this language, this culture.

Lloyd stuck his fork into his tart. He ate two pieces and drank
some tea.

94

France is no better, said Lloyd. Look at Algeria. At Cameroon. At the Pacific Islands.

You're deflecting.

Lloyd shrugged.

This is about Ireland, said Masson. About the Irish language.

And do the Irish have a say, said Lloyd, in your great plan for saving the language?

The English don't, said Masson.

Lloyd finished his tea, his tart, and walked out into the rain that James had predicted. It was windy too. He abandoned plans for the cliffs and returned instead to his cottage. It was cold. The fire had gone out

island's

simmering fires

beyond me

He once more built a frame of newspaper, sticks and turf and squatted to see the fire move through his structure, watching the flames lick the timber and dried earth, releasing the cloying smoke that seeped into the room and coated his clothes, his books, smothering the smell of damp and mildew taking root on the surface of his shoes and boots

of my skin

smearing me

in smells

of them

their past

present still

in this turf that burns

ancient grievances
buried in this burning earth
cow dung
pigs' excrement
rotten potatoes
famished bones
the fetid blood of war
of poverty
of blame
smothering me
suffocating
english lavender
dry-cleaned tweed
though he smells still
of paris
of coffee
of chocolate
his turf untainted

He heard Masson shouting. He was calling for James. The boy shouted back.

Jesus fucking Christ.

He hit the poker against the grate.

Masson shouted louder.

Lloyd hit the grate again and again, the clangorous protest reverberating around the village, ceasing only when Masson arrived at the artist's door.

Stop that noise, he said.

I am trying to work, said Lloyd.

Nobody is stopping you, said Masson.

You are. With your talking.

I am entitled to talk.

I need silence for my work.

Masson laughed.

So it seems.

Lloyd dropped the poker.

You're just too loud, he said. You have to be quiet.

Masson shook his head.

Incredible man, he said.

I need silence, said Lloyd. It is why I am here.

And I need conversation.

Have that conversation elsewhere.

Right here, Mr Lloyd, is my workplace.

I am asking only that you respect my work.

I make the same request of you, mon arriviste.

Fuck you.

Lloyd went to his studio, the room further from Masson's cottage, and opened a fresh sheet of paper. He drew circles, small, grey, slow circles that grew bigger, darker, faster, frenzied turning of hand and wrist until his anger dissipated and his hand slowed. He switched then to charcoal and began on James, his hand calm over the page, his mind settling into the solitude of work as he outlined the shape of the boy's head, his hair, his ears, his nose, his lips, his eyes

fresh-skinned

dewy-eyed

rabbit killer

egg thief

He filled sheets with the boy's eyes and lips, working to find the balance between the softness of his age and the harshness of island life. He aged him by drawing lines under his eyes

rembrandt

ageing titus

not my son

but

irish boy

by english artist

He scribbled over the eyes and started again, reverted to pencil but still drew eyes that were too old or too young, too dark, too lined, not lined enough. He turned to a fresh page and sketched James in his entirety. He replaced the rabbits with two rifles

hard little man

delight in london

fame

He softened the boy's features

baby-faced rebel

delight in new york

fortune

He started again on still more fresh paper but reverted to the rabbits, the boy's fingers lightly but firmly gripping the dead feet

island series: james with two rabbits

indifference

london

obscurity

new york

poverty

Masson was outside his window, shouting. He dropped the pencil and sketchpad to the floor.

This is impossible. Utterly impossible.

He went outside, but Masson was gone and the rain had stopped. He fetched his hat and coat and used the last of the evening light to walk to the cliffs, hunkering on the edge and staring down on the waves rushing at the rocks. He drew the sea, the rocks, the weakening sun, working until the light faded and he walked back to the village lit by the flickering of kerosene lamps and turf fires. He went to Bean Uí Néill's house and knocked on the door. They called him in, to join them at the table, a bottle of whiskey in the centre of the circle that included Masson.

Will you have a glass? said Micheál.

Thank you.

Bean Uí Néill pointed at a chair. He sat down. Micheál poured whiskey into a cup.

I've just been out on the cliffs.

A nice evening for it.

It was. The light was wonderful.

Micheál smiled.

That's good to hear, Mr Lloyd.

The artist lifted his cup.

Cheers, everybody.

He drank, flinched, unused to the rawness. His eyes watered.

Micheál laughed.

Not your usual London whiskey, Mr Lloyd.

No, Micheál, it's a bit stronger.

He swallowed what remained in his cup.

I want a studio on the cliffs, he said.

Micheál snorted.

A studio?

A shed. A tent. Anything at all – just a place to work in silence.

There's nothing out there, Mr Lloyd, said Micheál.

I know, but I'll pay you twice – once for the rental of the house, a second time for my studio on the cliff.

You can't rent something that doesn't exist, Mr Lloyd.

Not even from Micheál, said Masson.

They laughed. Micheál refilled his cup.

It would be better if I was away from the village, said Lloyd.

It would, said Masson.

I need to be on my own, said Lloyd.

James came out of the shadows by the fireplace and stood at the end of the table.

There's the old signalling hut, he said. You could stay in that.

That's in a heap, James, said Micheál.

It's not that bad, he said. I sit there sometimes. When it rains.

Is it dry? said Lloyd.

It is.

Could I sleep in it?

People used to. But there's no bed in it.

I can make you a bed, said Micheál.

Lloyd nodded.

Thank you, he said. I don't need much.

There won't be much, Mr Lloyd.

Lloyd finished his whiskey.

Can you show it to me tomorrow, James?

I can, Mr Lloyd.

Thank you.

It rained overnight and he followed James through the still wet grass along a path that was barely visible.

I haven't been this way, said Lloyd.

Nobody comes out here.

That's what I want.

The trail disappeared, the tufted grass difficult to walk through, his legs tired when they reached a narrow, elongated cliff surrounded by water.

The island's finger, said James.

I never knew it was here.

Why would you?

They walked up a hill, its steepness reverberating in the back of Lloyd's legs. At the top was a concrete hut, perched and close to the edge and surrounded by sea.

Quite a view, he said.

It is that, said James.

What's it like in winter?

Don't know.

James shoved at the battered red door no longer on its bottom hinge and Lloyd followed him into dull, dingy light. The hut was tiny and divided in two – a gas stove, a table, a fireplace, two buckets and three shelves in the front section; four shelves and a bedside locker in the back section.

It's perfect, James.

James laughed.

Oh, it is, Mr Lloyd. Perfect.

Lloyd laughed.

It is perfect, James.

It's hard out here, Mr Lloyd.

I imagine it is.

Especially when the weather is against you.

I'll be all right, James.

They went outside, into the light, and walked around the concrete hut, stepping over glass fragments from window panes.

No toilet?

No, Mr Lloyd.

Running water?

No.

This will be interesting.

It will, Mr Lloyd.

Have you ever stayed out here?

No. I come out here a bit. To get away from them all.

But not to stay?

There's no bed.

I'll get one, said Lloyd, and you can use it when I'm gone.

How long will you stay out here?

Until the end of summer.

Will you stay out here the whole time?

We'll see.

They moved to the edge of the promontory and looked down on the sea, their bodies bent against the rising wind.

It's perfect, James. Absolutely perfect.

Lloyd sat on the edge.

This can be your winter hideaway, James.

James shook his head.

Only if I come on my hands and knees, Mr Lloyd. You can't walk here in winter.

So who warns the ships?

They're on their own in winter. Always have been.

Not much of a signalling station.

Not in winter, anyway.

Who built it?

Your lot, said James. They wanted the highest point.

Nothing like using local knowledge, is there, James?

We should go, Mr Lloyd. Before it rains.

The rain fell as they reached the village, needle-sharp on their faces. Bean Uí Néill handed them towels that were hard but warm.

Thank you, Mrs O'Neill.

She nodded at him.

I'd like to move into the hut as soon as I can, he said.

James translated, and his grandmother sent him to fetch Micheál.

It'll take about a week to organise, Mr Lloyd.

That's fine, Micheál.

You pay me for the repairs.

All right.

And the rent. Half of what you pay for the cottage.

Who owns the hut?

Don't worry, I'll pass it on.

When the rain stopped, he took the yard brush, shovel and cloths and returned to the hut. James followed with two buckets, a bottle of washing-up liquid and a flask of tea.

I'm going to have to work out a toilet, James. A hole in the ground isn't very pleasant.

At least you can sit on a bucket, said James.

There is that.

But the metal is cold. Especially at night.

That is also a consideration, James.

They swept and tidied, and in the early afternoon walked about half a mile to a small cove of stones to draw salted water from the sea.

I could wash here, said Lloyd.

Not in that, Mr Lloyd.

Why not?

Look at the currents.

I'm a good swimmer.

Send us so a postcard from America.

Lloyd sat down beside James to look at the waves crashing onto the shore.

I have aunties and uncles in America, said James.

Would you go there?

Too long in a boat.

You could fly.

Too long in a plane.

Lloyd laughed.

You'll be staying here in that case.

I'll live in the hut after you.

Micheál will want rent from you.

He will, said James. But I won't pay him.

James laughed.

You're the only one doing that, Mr Lloyd.

They watched the swirl of the sea.

I like the sound of London though, said James.

It's a good city.

The waves rolled onto the shore, clawing at the sand.

What will you do for food? said James.

Beans, eggs, that sort of thing.

I'll show you where to get fresh water.

Thank you.

James leaned back onto his elbows.

My granny thinks you'll be back with us every day for dinner and tea.

I'll turn up sometimes.

She won't like it.

She'll be happy to be rid of me.

That may be, but she won't want you skinny. Your people thinking she wouldn't feed you.

What, James? 'Irish Starve English Artist.'

The boy laughed.

It'll be all over the BBC, James. *The Times* will send a reporter to track down your grandmother. The evil Irish granny who starved the great British artist.

That's it, Mr Lloyd.

Tell her not to worry, James. I'm tougher than you think.

Than you look?

Lloyd sighed.

I hope so.

James stretched out on the grass.

So are you that, Mr Lloyd?

What?

A great British artist.

Not yet. But I hope to be. Want to be.

How do you become one?

By moving into a concrete hut on the edge of a cliff.

James laughed.

That should work.

Lloyd too lay on the grass.

Will you really stay out there until the end of the summer, Mr Lloyd?

I'll stay until Masson leaves.

That's the rest of the summer, so.

The old island men worked with Micheál and Francis to repair the windows and door, to fix the roof and clean the chimney. They built a bed that was rudimentary but usable, erected shelves, and hammered wood into the base of the door to stop rain seeping into the hut. When the work was complete, the other islanders and Masson walked out to see the hut.

self-portrait: exhibited

You'll go mad out here, said Masson.

I was going mad back there.

The islanders walked around the hut, inside and out. Mairéad, the green scarf through her hair, left a parcel of food on the table and sat with the others on the grass, using shared cups to drink tea made by Lloyd with water from the spring and shared plates for the fruit cake carried across by Bean Uí Néill. She whispered to James.

She's worried you'll be lonely, Mr Lloyd.

Tell her that that's very kind, James. But I'll be fine. I'm used to my own company.

James translated.

Now she wants to know if you're married, Mr Lloyd.

I am.

What is your wife's name?

Judith.

Where is she? Can she come here to keep you company?

Lloyd shook his head.

This would not be her sort of thing. She's in London. She's an art dealer. She buys and sells paintings.

Does she buy yours? said Masson.

Not any more. Our tastes have diverged.

But you're still married?

For the moment, yes. And you?

No.

Lloyd turned to the islanders.

And you, Micheál?

I am, he said. To a woman across the way. From over beyond.

What does that mean?

She's not an island woman, Mr Lloyd.

What's the difference?

An island woman is happy without shops – isn't that right, Mairéad?

Mairéad said nothing.

And Francis? said Lloyd. Are you married?

Micheál laughed.

Francis is waiting on Mairéad.

Francis whistled and looked at the sky. Mairéad leaned forward to wrap the remainder of the fruit cake in a tea towel, to gather the cups.

Ah, she'll come round to it, said Micheál. Eventually.

She stood up and went into the hut, setting the cups and fruit cake on the table, muttering, mumbling, swearing, at them, at their plans, at her mother out there on the grass issuing instructions, telling Lloyd to cover the ham with a bowl, ordering James to translate what she had said, instructing Francis and Micheál to carry the cleaning tools back to the village. Do this. Do that. Morning. Noon. And night. She rinsed the cups, returned them to the shelf and dried her hands, but lingered in the hut, moving slowly, quietly, touching the easel, his brushes, his paints, opening his sketchbooks, his art books, lingering over the women painted in oils, drawn in charcoal, painted in ink. Dead women who are still alive, talking to me through the artist's hand. She walked out of the hut and down the promontory, ahead of the others, leaving Lloyd behind on the edge of the cliff. He picked up his sketchpad and began to draw, in pencil, and to hum.

The Artist's Hut I

A single shelf between the fireplace and window, holding four cups, four plates, two bowls, two saucepans, two knives, two forks and four spoons, light falling on the corner of the small table and chair underneath.

The Artist's Hut II

Two shelves over the counter on the wall dividing the kitchen from the bedroom bearing food – a tin of tea, tins of beans and soup, two bottles of milk, porridge oats, bread loosely wrapped in a blue and white tea towel, potatoes, turnip, cabbage, sugar in a jar, fruit cake in a green and white tea towel, and a hunk of honeyed ham on a plate, fat glistening in the evening light.

The Artist's Hut III

Candles, matches, wellington boots and a bucket beside the door; hat and coat hanging from two hooks attached to the back of the door. Heavily shaded.

The Artist's Hut IV

Paints, pencils, charcoal, paper, paintboxes, backpack and easel lined against the wall running from the door to the end of the bed. A mixture of light and shade.

The Artist's Hut V

A bed and two shelves on either side of the window, clothes neatly folded, books neatly stacked. All in shadow.

He signed them, Lloyd, and went outside to draw the exterior, the decaying front door, the weathered windows and puckered concrete, the roof of corrugated iron, and the birds overhead as they drifted and curled with the Atlantic winds.

John Hannigan is a Protestant man with three children. He is thirty-three years of age and in charge of the cemetery in Omagh, Co. Tyrone. He is also a part-time member of the Ulster Defence Regiment.

He is walking to work on Tuesday morning, June 19th. It is 7.30 a.m. He stops off at his local sweet shop. As he leaves the shop, an IRA man steps out of an orange Volkswagen and shoots John Hannigan twice in the head and five times in the body, killing him.

Masson tapped on the door and nudged it open, smiling as he approached, as he bent down to kiss her, to take her hand and stroke the blue-veined skin, softer and thinner than the summer before, her smile more flaccid, wrinkles in lips once held taut by teeth. She waved him away, chastising his kisses.

Foolish Frenchman, she said.

He smiled, relieved that she was still here, in this house, in this chair, still as he first met her four years before, drinking her dark, syrupy tea and smoking from her blackened clay pipe, her knitting in the basket by her chair. He patted her again, and smoothed the black shawl stretched across her shoulders.

Are you well, Bean Uí Fhloinn?

As well as can be expected.

You look well, anyway.

As you do yourself, JP.

He opened his recorder, took notebooks and pens from his bag. He poured tea into two cups. She drew on her pipe.

I see that you have sent the Englishman to the cliffs.

Masson nodded.

It seems that the village isn't big enough for the two of us, Bean Uí Fhloinn.

Two bulls in a field.

They leaned into each other and laughed.

Are you happy to start?

She set down her pipe and cleared her throat. He turned on the recorder. She began to speak, her Irish more guttural than his.

I'm an old woman now, my body weak but my memory strong. I was born here, on this island, eighty-nine years ago. It's a long time now since my birth, and the world is a different place. Better in some ways, worse in others. My father was a fisherman, out at sea every day but Sunday, while my mother was home on the shore with the other women, skirts hitched to gather food provided by the good Lord, picking whelks and weed from the rocks and sea, sending me as a young child to scramble and reach places she could not.

He patted her hand, encouraging her onwards, coaxing her to again tell her story, as she had told it to him over the previous three summers.

The men still fish on the island, but the women and children no longer go down to the shore, no longer forage, and it's a great pity, causing me great sadness, for there is a lot of nutrition down there, a lot of goodness in the weed and shells to keep illness off the island. But nobody listens to me. An old woman like me. Blathering on. They prefer instead to run down to Micheál's boat for chocolate and cake, handing over money for food already made, food filled with salt and sugar, so far from the health offered up by the island. You should work for your food, JP. Working for your food keeps you strong. That's my way of thinking, anyway.

She drew on her pipe and drank tea, and he again patted her hand, smiling, encouraging her onwards, though her words came more slowly than before and her breath was shallower than it had been, a crispy rattle as she inhaled. Fragility. Previously unheard. Not on any other recordings. He stroked her hand. You're worrying me, Bean Uí Fhloinn. Unsettling me. More than if it was my own grandmother breathing like this. My own mother. For I spent months searching for you, Bean Uí Fhloinn, hunting up and down the western coastline, in and out of houses, on and off islands, told repeatedly that I was too late, that all those women, all those men, were dead, buried, the language with them, but here you are, Bean Uí Fhloinn, defiant in your presence, in your speech, refusing to modernise, to adapt to this English invasion, refusing to pepper your language with this other language, to make yourself seem more relevant, for you understand your relevance, to the language, to the island, to me, old woman as totem, reminding us of what is being lost, of how life used to be.

Are you listening to me at all, JP?

I am, Bean Uí Fhloinn. Go on.

There was no boat to bring us things or take things away, leaving us on our own for most of the time, dependent on what God, the sea and the land gave us, which suited me well enough for I was happy that way and I had none of this looking over the shoulder to see what was coming in from beyond, wondering what life was like over there, because my view was limited. I knew nothing else and I had no yearning for something I knew nothing of, though later on others were

113

desperate to go. My own children, all they could do was talk about America, morning and evening, frantic for it, though I didn't bother with it, JP. For as long as there is food and a place to rest I see no point in searching the earth for a place to do the same thing, though I know that in times gone by people in these parts had no choice, it was to leave or to starve, but I was born in a more fortunate time, when that was all over and we could eat well enough, though we wouldn't get fat, mind you, but I'm not sure there's much good in that, anyhow. Masson lifted her hand and kissed it, listening for shifts in her language, in her syntax, hunting for markers of change in intonation, inflection, articulation, but found none as she told her story in the same way as last year, and the years before, nothing to undermine my study of the island's linguistic patterns, this longitudinal analysis of four generations of one family, work that will be upended by this Englishman if you drop your barrier against him, Bean Uí Fhloinn. Against his English. You need only to resist his influence, resist his incursions for two and a half months more. Then I will be done, Bean Uí Fhloinn. A book, a doctorate and a faculty place.

Are you all right, JP?

I am. Fine. Please, carry on, Bean Uí Fhloinn.

She dragged on her pipe.

You look a bit pale, JP.

Bit tired, that's all. Keep going.

I go down to the shore sometimes with the boy, James, and I hitch up my skirts as my mother did and I walk along picking whelks from the rocks, rinsing them in fresh water and eating them. It does me good, not only the freshness but knowing that I am doing what my mother did, what her mother did before her, all the way back for hundreds of years. I enjoy that. That connection with the past. Being part of something older than myself. It makes me feel less alone, JP, less frantic about what time I have left, because I am not leading, only following.

He poured more tea.

I have only been across the way three times, once to bury my mother, the second time to bury my father and the third time to bury my husband. It'll be time soon to cross again. I didn't have to go across for Áine's husband as he was drowned. But you know all that, JP. Three good men lost on an autumn day. My son-in-law, my grandson and my granddaughter's husband. Gone. Never to come home. Not even for their own funerals. That was a hard time, JP. But as I say, you get hard times wherever you are. They have a great way of following people. Though it took a long time for the island to recover. You can imagine. The worst of it was watching Mairéad, and she with the baby. He was only months old at the time. Her husband gone. Her father gone. Her brother gone too. That Holy Trinity of men. And nothing to replace them. Only for the baby, JP, she wouldn't be with us. And that's the truth of it. But that James is a good lad. Very good to his mother. And to his grandmother. He's good to me too. And God is good to him. He is good to us all.

She blessed herself. He drank his tea.

There aren't many of us, I know, willing to live like this any more. Áine, Bean Uí Néill, is the only one of my children still on the island. And she now without a husband or a son. My other children are under the sea, little Séamus who slipped off the rocks, God rest him and have mercy on him, or above the ground and living in Boston. American now. Too soft for this life. You see, there's a harshness to life here, JP, that not everyone can manage. There's a harshness everywhere, I know, city or country, but here it is more exposed, stripped bare by the weather and our isolation. That simplicity doesn't suit a lot of people. They say it bores them, but I have watched. It's not boredom, JP. It's fear. The barrenness and rawness frightens them. Sends them away to cloak themselves in timetables, bills, holidays and houses, in sofas, kitchen counters and curtains, a life of buying and owning to mask the bareness of existence. Hide its harshness. Make it more palatable. Tolerable. But I wonder if it does? Maybe, as James is the only young man still with us. The rest have gone, fled, leaving us the wrinkly old men with no teeth.

He smiled at her. She continued.

In other places, places with trees and shelter, the baseness of life is easier to disguise, to dress up as something more elaborate than it really is. I see them, you know, even now on this island, running back and forth across the sea, thinking it will be better over there only to find that they miss here. But they can only return triumphant, coming back with something nobody else has – a new hat, better shoes, a bigger belly, a pair of wellington boots. My own children have returned from America in that way. Trying to prove that they were right to leave. That we were fools to stay. Suitcases stuffed with fancy clothes and tales of where they've been, of who they have met, adamant that their toehold on this earth is higher than ours, of greater value. And for what? If it is to secure food and warmth, yes, I understand that. But much of it is this hunt for affirmation in a world that affirms little, if anything at all. As though some title could confirm who you are. Some house or car could prove your worth. I suppose that it works for some. Men think it attracts women, I suppose, but what type of man is that? And what type of woman is that, JP? Be thankful to God for what you've got, I say, and stop all the time chasing after the next new shiny thing. Sure, that makes us no better than the magpie.

He checked the recorder, the amount of tape still left on the reel to capture her sounds, but also her thinking, her commitment to the language. For how shall I place her? Explain her to them? Will I tell my professor that she is a Stoic? For the Stoics would be proud of you, Bean Uí Fhloinn. Socrates would enjoy her, too, an old toothless woman huddled in front of a turf fire, though he would bore quickly on the limits she puts on her thinking. Diogenes? He'd admire the simplicity of your life, Bean Uí Fhloinn, but despise your adherence to convention while the two Christians, Augustine and Aquinas, would ironically tire quickly of your unquestioning acceptance of God. Nietzsche would obviously abhor your slavish acceptance of the way you live, a life inherited from your mother, from your grandmother, but Schopenhauer would admire you, Bean Uí Fhloinn. He'd like your rejection of society's superficiality, your refusal to be the magpie.

He turned off the recorder.

Maybe I will tell them in Paris that she is a true existentialist, a west of Ireland Heidegger fighting against technology, against change. Bean Uí Fhloinn and her Dasein. Bean Uí Fhloinn, philosophy unvarnished. Before it gets painted over in obscuring terms and conditions by each generational attempt to answer the unanswerable. The as yet unanswered.

He laughed.

Really now, what's so funny?

I enjoy being with you, Bean Uí Fhloinn.

You have a funny way of showing it. Laughing at your own jokes.

I do, I suppose.

He poured more tea into their cups. She added milk and they drank.

So what about the Englishman, Bean Uí Fhloinn?

What about him, JP?

Should he stay here? Speaking English the way he does.

He's away on the cliff now. Out of harm's way.

The first rain and he'll be back.

We'll see what happens, JP.

Masson stood and packed away his recorder.

My professor has been listening to you, Bean Uí Fhloinn.

Is that right, JP?

He didn't understand anything of course, but he was mesmerised by the melody, by the ancientness.

It is a good age, JP.

And very beautiful.

That too.

We agreed a title for my thesis. For my work.

And what's that?

'Evolution or Demise? The linguistic patterns in the Irish language over four generations. A five-year comparative study of one island family.'

That's a mouthful, JP.

It is.

She sucked on her pipe, but it had gone out. She packed it with tobacco.

The Englishman will show you the demise quickly enough.

He will, Bean Uí Fhloinn.

She lit the fresh tobacco and cradled the flame with her hand, drawing air through the pipe, smacking her lips against each other until the fire took hold in the bowl.

Only you can stop him, Bean Uí Fhloinn.

She sat back into her chair and smoked.

There's not much hope if you're relying on an old woman like me, JP.

He kissed her hand and draped the strap of his recorder over his shoulder.

I'll let you rest, he said.

You have enough then, JP?

Plenty to be getting on with, Bean Uí Fhloinn.

He poured more tea into her cup, kissed her on each cheek and closed the door quietly behind him. He met James on the path back to his cottage.

What are you up to, Séamus?

My name is James. And you know that.

Your Irish name is Séamus.

I use my English name.

I prefer the Irish.

It's not your choice, JP.

Francis Barney Sullivan is at home in his terraced house on Bombay Street in Belfast, close to the wall dividing Catholics from Protestants. It is teatime on Wednesday, June 20th. He is with his wife and two children, a six-year-old boy and a four-year-old girl.

Two youths knock on the front door and ask for him. Francis Barney Sullivan starts to run. The two young men chase him through the hall and into the kitchen. They shoot the thirty-four-year-old Catholic man in the back as his wife looks on. He is dead on arrival at hospital, killed by the Ulster Defence Association.

Masson sat on a chair in the yard, the evening sun on his closed eyes, the sounds of Bean Uí Fhloinn swirling inside his head, her inflections, intonations, phrasings, her rasping breath, her syntax, her throaty laugh, smoke-lined. His mind sought to hold them there, inside his head, to pin them down, to analyse them, process them, categorise them, but they would not still, would not settle in the yard tainted by Englishness, the inside of his head agitated by the molecules of foreign tongue lingering in the air, clinging still to the surface of the wall, to the chair, to the sods of turf, diluting her presence until bit by bit the sounds of her slipped from him and left him with the sounds of the island, the sea against the rocks, the birds calling, the men talking at the village wall, the women working still in the houses, Bean Uí Néill and Mairéad in the back kitchen talking of the work to do before the day's end, the floors to clean, the pots to scrub, the grate to empty, the fire to build, the radio on as they worked, the broadcasting men discursive in softer, southern accents, talking of the regularity of the killings, the seeming intractability of violence up there, over there, across the border, Mairéad joining in their conversation, talking at them, over them, talking to wonder whether the woman who saw her husband shot would ever recover, whether the children heard the shooting and saw their daddy on the kitchen floor covered in his own blood, dying, Mam, they saw their own father dying and how could they ever get over that and wouldn't they always be traumatised by the night their daddy died, question after question until Bean Uí Néill turned off the radio because it's wrong, Mairéad, to be immersed in this talk of death on a summer's evening, a lovely summer's evening like this one, and she turned the conversation instead to the life of the Englishman, out there on the cliffs, do you think he gets lonely, Mairéad? Bored? Hungry? I don't know, Mam. Why do you think he went to live out there? Do you think it's a form of madness, that type of isolation? I don't know, Mam, but he was happy enough to go, to be there, alone, on his own, away from JP and his talking, and he craned then to listen more closely, but their voices moved to the front of the house, out of his hearing, leaving him with the sounds of water rushing at the rocks, of seals barking on the beach, of birds calling to those still at sea, cormorants, gannets and gulls shouting that night was coming, that it was time to return to the cliffs, the guttural, grating, squawking of their evening song so different to the birds at his grandmother's house, in the willow tree above the circular table cast of iron, goldfinches, blue tits, swallows and doves, my mother pointing upwards to match the different evening songs to the birds, demanding my focus on the trilling and chirping, pinning down my attention to distract from the sounds of the kitchen, from the laughter that did not include us, although my father, her husband, was there, laughing with them, my grandmother, my cousins, my aunts, while we waited outside, in the dusk that was almost dark, guests waiting for coffee and dessert, my mother insisting that it was wonderful to be outside listening to birds as she used to during her childhood in the city by the sea with birds more exotic than these, breathing air that was hotter and drier than at my grandmother's house, much hotter and drier than at our home, an apartment in the northern rain and dark, on the fifth floor, the ocean visible but distant and laced with winds and storms that caused her sometimes to weep, so that we should enjoy it here, my love, in the evening warmth under the tree, listening to the birds, not at all worrying about the noise from the kitchen, about their laughter, though she sees that now I am weeping because they are allowed to help, Maman, my cousins are helping and I am not, they are allowed to carry cake and whip cream and I am not because Grand-maman told me to stay with you, told me not to move, to stay out here with you in the near dark while they are in there in the brightness, laughing, Maman, having fun, playing games that I cannot play because I am to stay here with you, and she takes my hand to hers, kisses it and whispers to me, you are the family prince, Jean-Pierre, the one who will be king, the one too precious to waste on the drudgery of work, but I like work, Maman, I like whipping cream and carrying cake, and I don't understand because Grand-maman is kind to me in the morning, before everyone is awake, she likes me then, when I am on my own, without you, without Papa, without my cousins, she likes me that way, but not this way, when everybody is here, she is mean to me then, hard, and my mother ruffles my hair, telling me that it is not my fault, that my grandmother is being strange and behaving oddly, a thing of old age, she says, running her hand through my hair, drawing me to her, holding me until they again sit at the table, my father, my grandmother, my aunts, my cousins, all of them talking in rapid rural tones that I struggle to grasp and my mother has no chance of understanding so that she sits in silence as they talk of funerals and presidential candidates, her dark eyes slightly elevated, as though watching the birds close their eyes under darkened leaves, her soldier husband, my father, touching her intermittently on the arm to ask her to join in, irritated as she again explains that she cannot understand what it is that they are saying so that he once more asks his mother and sisters to speak the French that they learnt at school, the same French that his wife, my mother, has studied at school, at university, the same French that she speaks at home, with him, in the north, but they ignore him, ignore her, and continue in their patois until my soldier father, her husband, has drunk enough to go into battle on her behalf, warring against his mother and sisters with the vehemence and passion he once displayed as a soldier fighting in the desert against his wife's people on behalf of his country, his anger rising until he is raging against his family, against his country's treatment of people like his wife, my mother, until my grandmother grows weary, expresses surprise at the speed of time and declares the gathering at an end, sending us all to bed, my father's rage still burning, spilling into the room that we share with him and landing on us, his wife and son, who, he says, have made no effort to include ourselves in his family, sitting out there under the tree waiting to be waited on, refusing to help, like some little prince and his queen, too regal to whip cream or carry cake, and he had not brought her to France for this, had not rescued her from that pit of a country so that she could sit around expecting to be waited on, acting as though she was superior to his family with her college education, paid for by French taxes, as though she was superior to him even though she was nothing without him because he had saved her from that hovel by the sea, its innards bombed, saved her from those men instructing her on how to dress, how to live, but with him she was free to live as she pleased and she chose to be ungrateful, condescending, to him, to his family, and he, as the Frenchman who had rescued her, found that intolerable, and insisted that she should apologise, beg for his forgiveness, and kneeling in front of me, unbuttoning my shirt, preparing me for bed, tears rolling down her cheeks, she apologises for not understanding his family, and pledges to try harder next time, and he, satisfied by her tears and kneeling, goes back downstairs to drink some more, leaving us to crawl into bed together, to close our eyes against him until morning when we would pack and supply excuses as to why we would not return for Christmas, but would return the following July, waving as we drove away, the traces of their lips on my cheeks, of their hands on my arms fading as we returned, just the three of us, to the north.

John Henry Scott drives a milk tanker and is known as Jack. He drives from farm to farm in Co. Tyrone to collect milk and follows the same route every day. He is forty-nine years of age, a Protestant, and is married with nine children. He is also a reserve member of the Royal Ulster Constabulary, and is about to celebrate his silver wedding anniversary.

He is driving along the shores of Lough Neagh on Friday afternoon, June 22nd. The IRA opens fire and shoots him several times in the head and body. The tanker crashes into the hedge.

He was woken by dawn rain tapping on the corrugated roof, the hut shrouded in mist that seeped into the concrete walls, into the room, chilling the interior. Lloyd buried deeper under the blankets

lifeless light

worthless day

He tried to sleep again, but the rain fell more heavily, drumming at the metal. He dragged the blankets over his head. The noise penetrated, the cold too. He sat up and dressed in the clothes that he had worn the previous day, adding a second pair of socks, his hat, his gloves and his oilskin coat. He rekindled the fire and watched the flames fragment the grey of the hut

inner sanctum

though

grey

still

He urinated in the bucket by the door, made tea and porridge, using the last of the fresh milk, and ate his breakfast on a chair in front of the fire, his shoulders slumped, his head sinking to his chest.

self-portrait: alone

He dumped the dishes in the second bucket, threw more turf on the fire and began to draw birds, long curving strokes for wings, but shorter movement for heads, beaks and eyes, his hand, eye and mind closing in on the sound of the pencil scratching across paper, shutting out the rain hammering against the metal, filling sheet after sheet of birds rising, hovering, climbing, circling, gliding, wheeling, banking, diving, birds breaking the surface of the sea, yellow lashless eyes wide with delight, working until suddenly ravenous, his body shaking with cold, his teeth chattering. He lifted a bowl, slippery with animal fat, but the ham was gone, the beef too. He rubbed his fingers over the bowl to lift the residual fat and licked them. He scanned the shelves, but the beans were gone, the bread too. He unwrapped a tea towel set into a tin and found two eggs. He picked the frying pan from the bucket, scrubbed at it momentarily and dried it with a dirty tea towel. He fried the eggs and ate them from the pan, looking through the window at the thick ribbons of rain.

self-portrait: kicked from the nest

He threw some more turf on the fire and stuffed the dirty tea towel into the gap under the door where rain had gathered

tea, bread, butter and jam

the garrulous one

islanders' darling

embraced

the quiet one

half starved

near arthritic

banished

He took off his boots and climbed back into bed, his coat and hat still on. He closed his eyes, shutting out the hut, the mist, the rain on the roof

famine's revenge

The body of James Joseph Porter is spotted on the side of the road by a man driving to church in Mountnorris, Co. Armagh on Sunday morning, June 24th.

James Joseph Porter, a sixty-four-year-old Protestant farmer and part-time member of the Ulster Defence Regiment, is clothed, though his feet are bare. His head is shattered, destroyed by three or four bullets from a high-velocity weapon fired by the IRA.

The Irish language is dying, but is not yet dead.

Masson looked at his handwriting across the blue-lined page. Spindly. Typically French, he said. He resumed writing.

The death has been a slow one, taking place over centuries as speakers abandon the Irish language for English. In this study, I trace that demise, tracking four members of one family over four generations, the oldest of whom, Bean Uí Fhloinn, speaks only Irish while her great-grandson, Séamus Ó Giolláin, is comfortably bilingual.

Irish is a Celtic language, a branch of the Indo-European language group, and its closest linguistic relations are Scottish Gaelic, Manx Gaelic, Welsh, Breton and Cornish. Manx and Cornish are extinct, while the others struggle for survival, aided, or hindered, to varying degrees, by government policies and public initiatives.

It is difficult to be certain when the Irish language first arrived in Ireland, but the oldest physical remains date back to monuments from the 5th and 6th centuries known as Ogham stones, boulders marked with lines and notches representing the Latin alphabet. Most of these stones carry inscriptions of people's names and scholastic writings, and it is believed that the language remained mainly unchanged until the Viking invasion of Ireland between 900 and 1200. The language survived that conquest, but adapted and acclimatised, as language does, by absorbing Norse words, such as 'ancaire' (anchor), 'bád' (boat), 'stiúir' (rudder), 'bróg' (shoe), 'pingin' (penny) and 'margadh' (market).

He looked through the window, at the rain, at the islanders rushing into the schoolhouse for Bean Uí Néill's Mass. He twisted his pen. Bean Uí Néill. Rome's guardian of the island. The Pope's lieutenant. He returned to his dissertation.

A second invasion, this time by the Anglo-Normans between 1200 and 1500, had a similar, if more intense, impact. Norman words were absorbed into Irish, resulting in words such as 'cóta' (coat), 'hata' (hat), 'gairdín' (garden), 'garsún' (boy), 'giúistís' (justice), 'bardas' (corporation) and 'cúirt' (court), though the English language exerted only a moderate influence over Irish and the two languages existed side by side. Only Dublin, Waterford, Cork and Dundalk were core English-speaking parts of the country. Galway city and the areas around Dublin, Waterford, Cork and Limerick were multilingual while the remainder of the country spoke only Irish. The Anglo-Normans themselves began to learn and use Irish, becoming, as the Catholic priest and historian John Lynch wrote in his 17th-century *Cambrensis Eversus*, 'Hibernicis ipsis Hiberniores', more Irish than the Irish themselves, or 'Níos Gaelaí ná na Gaeil iad fhéin'.

The succession of King Henry VIII to the English throne in 1509 had enduring and devastating consequences for the Irish language. Henry VIII became not only King of Ireland but also head of the Church of Ireland, a newly formed Anglican

Protestant church. He dissolved Catholic monasteries and subdued Irish chieftains and Anglo-Norman lords, and imposed a new societal hierarchy, one no longer based on clan, region and language but on religion. He divided the people into Protestant and Catholic, a division that endures to this day.

Masson looked up. Through the window, at the islanders leaving the schoolhouse after Mass, rushing home through the rain.

Elizabeth I, who inherited the throne in 1558, continued her father's work and expanded Protestantism across Ireland, again routing the Irish-speaking chieftains and their bilingual Anglo-Norman allies. She replaced them with English-speaking Protestant planters and insisted that English be used for all administrative and legal affairs. The Irish language, without administrative status, was useless when buying or selling land, when paying taxes or dealing with the growing number of English landlords. Irish became a second-class language, stirring a quiet linguistic civil war that, like the religious divide, lives on in modern Ireland.

James pushed open the door. He set a cup of tea and a scone with butter and jam on the table.

Thank you, Séamus.

James left without closing the door.

It's James, he said.

Masson stood up, closed the door and returned to his writing.

Conditions for Catholic Irish speakers improved during the reign of Charles I, a Stuart and moderate Anglican who took the throne in 1625, though that improvement was short-lived.

With Charles I beheaded at the end of England's civil war, Oliver Cromwell's parliamentarians wreaked revenge in Ireland on the Gaelic chiefs and Anglo-Norman lords who had supported the deposed king. Cromwell's army killed thousands, deported thousands more and confiscated land to give as reward to his soldiers and financiers. It was a devastating time for the already weakened Irish language, though worse was to come.

James returned.

I forgot to collect your washing.

It's in the bedroom, Séamus. In a pile on the floor.

I'm James.

You should be happy to be called Séamus.

My name is James.

The draconian and devastating Penal Laws were introduced in the wake of the 1691 Treaty of Limerick, the accord underpinning the defeat of the Catholic forces of England's James II and France's Louis XIV on battlefields at the River Boyne and in Aughrim to the Protestant army of England's King William III, known as William of Orange. Irish supporters of James II left Ireland, ceding control of the country and the language to Protestant England. Most of the remaining Catholic lands were handed over to Protestants and, under the new laws, Catholics could not gain equal access to education or political representation, their rights to inheritance were blocked and they were banned from bearing arms or entering the army and professional classes.

James returned with a ham sandwich, buttered brack and a cup of tea.

Thank you.

What are you writing anyway?

A history of the Irish language.

That's mad exciting, JP.

Masson smiled.

To me it is.

I prefer Mr Lloyd's art.

You'd better go and find him then.

Ah, he doesn't want anybody near him.

He wants to go mad on his own.

It must be that.

Off you go. I'm working.

The Penal Laws had devastating implications for the language as all schools, courts, leases, rent books, writs and summons were only available in English – this in a country where 80 per cent of the population spoke Irish. Only about one-fifth of the people were bilingual and those speakers tended to work as middlemen, shopkeepers, innkeepers, midwives, servants, pedlars and artisans, all of them providing services to the English-speaking Protestants who were landlords, judges, barristers, attorneys, officers, officials and agents. Those who spoke only Irish were the most impoverished group in society, living in dreadful conditions as tenant farmers dependent on the goodwill of their landlords and the success of the potato crop, their only source of nourishment. In addition, Catholics were obliged to pay tithes to their local Protestant Church of Ireland minister.

Masson glanced upwards, through the window. Lloyd was walking into the village, unshaven, saturated, his shoulders slumped. Masson watched as the Englishman moved across his window, eyes to the ground. He listened as Lloyd opened the door of his cottage and stepped inside. He returned to his writing.

Excluded from the centres of power and education, and from the rapid developments in print across continental Europe, the Irish language became marginalised and increasingly an oral language of the poor, relying on poetry and political verse to disperse ideas and ideals. Irish poetry, previously laments on the relationship with nature and landscape, became politicised with many poets yearning for the moment when Ireland would rise again as a Catholic country that cherished its Gaelic culture.

Monolingual Irish poems gradually became bilingual with poets using Irish and English in the one sentence, or switching language for different verses, creating macaronic works by poets with some fluency in both languages who were writing for an audience in the mid-1700s that had at least some capacity to understand English, a receptive bilingualism such as we see today on this remote island, for example, in Bean Uí Néill, who understands what is being said in English but speaks only Irish.

He watched Lloyd passing his window again, in dry clothes, though unwashed, unshaven, moving towards Bean Uí Néill's kitchen. Lloyd knocked on the door and went in, startling Mairéad, still in her Sunday clothes, by the fire, listening to the radio and knitting, a charcoal grey wool across her lap. She smiled at him.

An bhfuil ocras ort?

He nodded.

She put away the knitting, turned off the radio and stood up. She pointed at the table. He sat down. She prepared a plate of scrambled eggs, bread and scones. She poured tea.

Thank you, he said.

Tá fáilte romhat, she said. You're welcome.

You speak English, he said.

Giota beag, she said. A little.

Bean Uí Néill came into the kitchen. She greeted Lloyd but talked to Mairéad. The women left the kitchen and returned, no longer in Sunday clothes, to prepare food, to build up the fire. He ate and drank, glad of the warmth rushing through him.

Thank you, he said.

He went out again into the rain, to his cottage

mould

mildew marching

unabated

He built his own fire and put water on to boil for a bath and shave. He remounted the curtains and wandered around as the water heated, examining his work on the easel, other people's work on his walls. He picked up his book of Rembrandt drawings

washes and ink

brown tones

simple lines

soft

138

sleeping woman

reading woman

bathing woman

He hummed as he filled the bath, as he scrubbed his skin, shaved his face, the islanders passing his window, moving through the rain, carrying boxes, Micheál and Francis in their wake, dripping water onto the floor of Bean Uí Néill's kitchen.

You should change before you sit down, said Bean Uí Néill. She pointed to the bedroom off the kitchen.

The men's clothes are in there.

Francis set a box on the end of the table and followed Micheál into the other room. Mairéad added buttermilk to the flour, lifting her head as Micheál returned in the clothes of her father, Francis in the clothes of her husband.

How's the weather for tomorrow? said Bean Uí Néill.

Due to clear overnight, said Micheál. We should be grand.

What time will you leave?

The heifer in the cove at seven. That'll give us time.

Bean Uí Néill poured water into the teapot.

I need a good sale, Micheál, she said.

I'll get you that.

To get through the winter.

I'll get you enough for the spring as well, Áine.

Bean Uí Néill stared at him, the man in her husband's clothing.

Not if you keep taking our money, she said.

You get more than I do, Áine.

You must get nothing, so.

Mairéad shaped the bread, patted it.

Terrible goings on up north, she said. One of those men had nine children.

Micheál shook his head.

It's an awful mess.

He was Protestant, said Mairéad. With nine children.

That's unusual, said Bean Uí Néill.

Mairéad slid the bread onto the tray.

Imagine being that wife, she said. All nine looking up at you expecting you to know what to do next.

He should have thought of that before joining the RUC, said Francis.

He was in the reserve, Francis.

Still the RUC.

Maybe he did it for the children. For the money.

The price of the Queen's shilling.

She cut a cross into the surface of the bread.

You seem happy enough to take it from Mr Lloyd, Francis.

What?

The Queen's shilling.

That's different.

Is it?

Aren't we in the Free State, Mairéad?

She stabbed the bread four times.

Is this the same Francis Gillan who says that Ireland will never be free until it is united?

Taking money from an Englishman here is not the same as working for the British against the Irish people.

English money is English money, Francis.

She dropped the bread into the pot over the fire, washed her hands and sat with them.

So what about the Englishman, said Micheál. How's he getting on?

He's just back, said Mairéad. He spent about a week out there.

In this rain? said Micheál.

Day after day of it.

That's rough living.

She laughed.

It smelt rough.

Micheál pointed at the window.

Speak of the devil.

Lloyd came into the kitchen, clean, shaven.

I was hoping for some tea, he said. Maybe something else to eat.

Mairéad poured tea and gave him two scones. He laced both with butter and jam.

So, how is it going out there?

Good, Micheál. The work is going well.

You had a bit of rain.

Lloyd frowned.

A lot of rain, Micheál.

Hard enough out there.

It is. Very.

But you survived it.

Did I?

Well, you are here.

Lloyd shrugged.

Then, yes, I suppose I did.

He ate his first scone.

And what brings you back, Micheál? On a Sunday.

Market day on Wednesday. We're taking a heifer over tomorrow.

On your boat?

It's too far for her to swim.

Lloyd smiled at him.

May I go with you?

Micheál shook his head.

It's not a trip for you, Mr Lloyd.

I'd be better this time, Micheál.

Not for you, Mr Lloyd. Best to watch from the shore.

Lloyd ate his second scone.

When are you leaving?

Early.

What time?

Six in the cove.

Fine. I'll be there.

Grand so, Mr Lloyd.

Lloyd returned to his cottage and slept until James knocked and called him to his evening meal. The rain had stopped. He ate fried fish, potato and cabbage.

Thank you, Mrs O'Neill. That was very good.

She refilled his plate. Masson leaned forward and spoke loudly.

Caithfidh muid Gaeilge a labhairt.

He turned to the Englishman.

I'm sorry, Lloyd, but we have to speak Irish.

Leave it, JP, said Micheál.

No, Micheál. This is an Irish-speaking house.

Is my week away not enough? said Lloyd.

No, it is not. This is an Irish-speaking island.

How much longer should I stay away?

Don't let him rile you, Mr Lloyd.

I'd rather hear him say it, Micheál. How long I should stay on the edge of a cliff without proper food and heat. Without running water.

Until you leave, said Masson.

That's daft, JP, said Micheál.

He shouldn't be here at all, Micheál. This island should be protected from English speakers.

Micheál laughed.

Like a museum, JP?

More a conservation project.

A zoo then?

An Irish-speaking island is a precious thing, Micheál.

You can't lock people onto the island because they speak Irish, JP.

You can if it saves the language.

Nor can you keep other people off because they don't speak Irish.

It's your island. You can do what you want.

Ah, you really are being daft, JP.

Am I? You have this last chance to save the language.

Lloyd leaned forward, towards Masson.

Are you a linguist?

I am.

I thought the job of linguist was to observe, said Lloyd.

I am observing.

You're not. You're influencing. Campaigning.

The language is dying in front of us. Of course I am campaigning to save it.

But that's not your job, said Lloyd. That's not the job of a linguist.

It is now.

Lloyd sighed.

Do I have to go now? Or may I have dessert first? A cup of tea?

Bean Uí Néill set a slice of tart in front of him and poured tea.

Thank you, Mrs O'Neill.

He ate and drank.

So, how long does it have left? said Lloyd. This language.

If James stays on the island his children will speak Irish and English, as might his grandchildren.

If he doesn't?

If he leaves, his children will probably speak English with a working knowledge of Irish. His grandchildren though will speak only English.

So it's hopeless, said Lloyd.

No, it's not, but it needs a national commitment to reverse the pattern.

Micheál sighed.

That's been tried, JP, he said.

We need to protect Irish-speaking areas, said Masson, invest in jobs and keep the Irish speakers in the west.

Nobody stays, JP. Nobody wants to.

Make them stay, said Masson.

How?

Pay people like James to stay on the island, speaking Irish.

What if I don't want to stay? said James.

You're not going anywhere, James, said Francis.

I can if I want.

Francis shook his head.

You're the only man in this house.

You can't make me stay, Francis.

You can't leave these women out here on their own.

I can do what I want, Francis. Go where I want.

Francis leaned back into his chair.

No, James. You can't.

Mairéad stood to gather plates and cups, knives and forks.

Why does it matter if the language disappears? said Lloyd. If everybody speaks English?

It's their language, said Masson. Unique to them.

And?

It carries their history, their thinking, their being.

Micheál pushed his plate and cup towards Mairéad. He pulled a cigarette from inside his jacket.

By God, JP, you're a fierce romantic.

Am I?

He lit the cigarette.

It's a language, JP. A way to talk to each other. To buy bread in a shop. Nothing more.

James slipped out of the kitchen and waited outside until Lloyd returned to his cottage and went upstairs to bed. He ran then, to the cliffs, to the hut, arriving in near darkness. And why shouldn't I? I was the one who told him about it, the remains of light still with him as he stepped into a scattering of tins across the floor, of dishes unwashed and a terrible stench of soured milk and stale urine. The bed was unmade, as though the artist had just got out of it, and his clothes were dumped on the floor or rolled into balls and thrown on the shelf. James bent down to pick up a pair of trousers, but stopped, it's not your mess, James Gillan. No, but it is my hut. The easel had the beginning of an oil painting of the cliffs on its stand and a stack of drawings, all in charcoal or pencil, at its feet. James lit the kerosene lamps and opened the door further to freshen the air. He sat on the floor and sifted through the drawings, of the sea and cliffs, shaking his head as he moved from one to the next, they're too flat, Mr Lloyd, you're not understanding the light at all, you have it sitting on the top of the sea, but it doesn't do that, does it? No, it buries underneath, diving between the waves as a bird might, lighting the water from below as well as above. I'll show you how to do it, Mr Lloyd. If you let me. If you let me use your paints. He rekindled the fire and put water in the kettle to make tea, comfortable that Lloyd was deep in sleep and that nobody else would follow him out to the cliffs at this late hour, most of them never leave the village anyway, too old and dull to come out this way. He

sat on the bed, chewing at the desiccated brack, drinking black
tea, examining the drawings of birds taped to the wall, gulls,
it seems, though their heads are too small for their bodies, a
tern's head on a gull's body, so more practice needed there too,
Mr Lloyd. He finished the tea, the cake and lay down, curling
his knees into his chest, careful not to kick at the drawings
piled at the end of the bed, watching through the window as
the light faded, as night came, a boy Goldilocks, though this
is really my hut, and the bed will in time be my bed with its
smell that is different to my own, to my mother's, to my grandmother's, to my great-grandmother's. All those mothers that I
have to mind. Is this how a man smells? Is this how my father
smelt? What my mother smelt when she lay down beside
him at night, what I smelt when I lay between them? Francis
doesn't smell like this, no, not this, for this is the smell of oil
and paint mixed with sweat and must, of paper, of pencil, of
linseed. Not of Francis. He smells of smoke, of sweat, of salt
and sea. And of fish. He has a smell of fish that never goes,
no matter how newly washed he is, and I hate that smell, that
smell of fish, but I like this smell, your smell, Mr Lloyd, the
smell of an artist, of an Englishman. Imagine that, Francis Gillan, liking the smell of an Englishman, of Englishness. After all
they did to us, James Gillan, you like the smell of an Englishman. Traitor. Turncoat. Off with his head. His legs. His arms.
His knees. Bullet to the brain because I like this smell. Because
I prefer this smell to the smell of you, Francis Gillan and those
bloody fish, and the smell of you panting after my mother,
chasing her with your stinking eyes, your always leering eyes,

why should I like your smell, Francis Gillan, your fishy pant-ing-for-my-mother smell? Can you draw a smell, Mr Lloyd? Paint one? Have you ever tried? Will you paint the smell of me into the painting? And what would that be? The smell of me? The smell of rabbit? Of hen? Maybe I smell of fish already. Maybe I was born smelling of fish. The son and grandson of fishermen who drowned, under the sea to smell eternally of fish. He buried under the covers and rolled from side to side, basting his clothes and skin in the artist's oils and sweat, in pencil, charcoal and paint, rolling until he was certain that he smelt of something other than fish, because if I smell of some-thing other than fish, of paints and oils, they might all see that I should leave, that I am not a fisherman, not a proper island boy, but something that has to be elsewhere, somewhere other than here looking after my mother, my grandmother, my great-grandmother, and now they're giving me the mother tongue to look after as well, to save that mother too, to save it all and the other mothers. I don't want so many mothers.

He stayed until it was fully night and returned to the village, passing the pen with the heifer that was leaving in the morning.

Goodbye now.

He patted her, a gentle hand on her rump.

Good luck, he said.

In the morning, before six, Lloyd dressed quickly and gathered fresh pencils and a new sketchpad to take into the cool morn-ing, the sun already risen but shrouded in cloud and lacking the warmth needed to dry the grass that soaked into his trou-sers as he walked along the path towards the cove, realising as he drew closer that it was empty, with only waves lapping over the rocks and seals sleeping, snoring, on the beach.

He walked back up the path looking for Micheál, but the village was still asleep. He went back down to the cove and began to draw, diffusing the sun even further and turning Micheál's boat into a man-of-war on the cusp of invasion.

island series: seals as first casualties, after turner

He again walked up the cliff path, but stopped at the old village, wandering from one derelict house to the next, the roofs gone, the walls crumbled into boulders of stone and fragments of earth. Gables, though, were still standing. He sat down and drew.

self-portrait: early morning in the ruins
self-portrait: in a soup of grey light

He heard the heifer then, bleating, lowing, and saw her, the animal uncertain of the narrow path, of the seven old men carrying sticks, James in their wake, a stick in his right hand. It was just before seven and the heifer was dark russet, a white stripe down her face, and a rope around her head to serve as a halter. She had rope too reaching under her belly, gathered into a large knot on her spine.

Lloyd fell in behind James, avoiding the cowpats that became looser and more frequent as they approached the sea. The heifer stopped at the top of the slipway, refusing to go any further. Francis and Micheál slipped past, lifted a currach and rowed out to the bigger boat. They climbed on board. Three old men and James stayed with the heifer at the top of the slipway. The four other old men carried two currachs to the water and climbed in, settling the boats just out from the slipway.

Micheál shouted. Lloyd began to draw.

The men and James slapped the sticks onto the heifer's rump and she went forward, stepping onto the concrete, liquid manure pouring from beneath her raised tail. They pushed her further down the slipway, towards the water. A plaintive moan rose from her chest. She turned to go back up the slipway, spinning, swivelling, tripping over herself, but they beat her back down the concrete path, the sticks hard against her rump, her flank, her legs. She bellowed and stumbled towards the sea.

island series: bringing the heifer to market I

They shoved her closer to the water's edge. She flipped around, trying to escape, moving left, moving right, seeking a route between the men.

island series: bringing the heifer to market II

But they blocked her and drove her forward, to the waves rolling onto the concrete. She swivelled again, rushing at James and the old men, but the sticks fell on her, a cascade of long, dense wood over her back and sides, pummelling her flesh, the beating relentless until she entered the sea

fear of water

fear of men

and sticks

heifer's choice

Faeces coloured the sea, and the men in the boats reached to take the heifer's halter, to twist her neck, to keep her nose and mouth out the water. Two men held her, one from each currach, while the two others rowed, dragging the animal through the sea to the bigger boat.

island series: bringing the heifer to market III
Micheál and Francis attached ropes to the loop on the heifer's spine and the six men dragged and heaved the animal up the side of the boat and onto the deck where they quickly bound her legs, head and neck into each other. One old man slipped off Micheál's boat and took the three currachs back to shore. The others left with the heifer, her lowing rising intermittently over the noise of the boat's engine as they left the cove.

island series: bringing the heifer to market IV
The islanders returned to the village, but Lloyd stayed, still drawing, watching as the sea rinsed the slipway, sluicing the concrete, washing her manure into the ocean, dispatching it on its journey across the earth.

island series: bringing the heifer to market V
He closed his sketchpad and walked back up the path. James was sitting at the top of the cliff, looking down on the sea.

Can cows vomit, James?

I don't know.

Horses don't. They can't. But I don't know about cows.

Nor do I, said James.

Do they get seasick?

I don't know.

He had breakfast then and went back to bed, sleeping until he was woken by a knock on the door. It was James with a sand-wich, a cup of tea and a slice of brack.

I have food for you.

Thank you, James.

Were you asleep?

I was.

It's a grand life you have, Mr Lloyd.

I suppose it is.

My mother wants to see your drawings of me, he said.

Lloyd shook his head, chasing away the sleep.

Why?

I don't know. She didn't say.

James shrugged.

She just wants to see them, Mr Lloyd.

They're not finished.

She won't mind.

All right then. Tell her to come.

When?

Now, if she wants.

Lloyd led them into the studio, a cup of tea in his hands.

It's messy. I'm working.

Ná bac, she said.

Don't worry, said James.

He gathered the drawings from different parts of the room and set them, one after another, on the easel, pausing between each one so that she could absorb his interpretation of her son.

Tá siad go hálainn, she said. They're beautiful.

Thank you.

He looked at her, quizzically.

Does Masson know you speak English?

James lifted a finger in front of his lips.

Don't tell him, said James. He'd be very disappointed.

How does he not know?

Mairéad shrugged.

Creideann muid an rud a oireanns dúinn.

We believe what we want to believe, said James.

Lloyd laughed.

Not much of a study then, is it?

He watched as she picked up each drawing and turned it to catch the light

washes and ink

brown tones

simple lines

soft

sleeping woman

reading woman

bathing woman

She ran her fingers over the pencil, touching her son, touching his work, lifting the charcoal off the page.

Wait, he said.

He fetched his book of Rembrandt drawings and opened the drawing of the young woman sleeping, resting her head on her arm, a sheet loosely wrapped around her. He showed it to her.

Can I draw you? he said. Like this?

She touched the woman.

But with your hair long, he said. Not tied up as he has it here. James translated. She took the book from him and walked to the window to look at the drawing in the day's grey light.

It is beautiful, she said. Cén uair a rinneadh é? How old is it?

Over three hundred years.

Seanbhean óg, she said.

A young old woman, said James.

She shook her head.

An old young woman, she said.

Lloyd smiled at her.

She ran her fingers across the drawing, across the woman's face and down the fabric of the sheet, eternal life granted unto her, unto me, if I let him, this Englishman who looks nothing like Jesus. She smiled. A permanence, I suppose. Of sorts.

Tá go maith, she said. I'll do it.

He stared at her.

Are you sure? he said.

She shrugged.

I said yes.

You did, I know. I hadn't expected it.

He laughed.

I had assumed that you would say no.

She closed the book and returned it to him.

Cén uair? she said. When?

This afternoon.

She shook her head.

No. The hut. Anocht. Tonight.

Too dark.

Amárach. Tomorrow?

Yes, he said. Dawn. The light is good.

She smiled at her son.

Mé féin is tú féin i bpictiúirí.

Lloyd looked at James.

What did she say?

She said herself and myself in pictures.

Lloyd smiled.

Indeed.

Lloyd returned to tidy the hut, to prepare it for her. He organised first his drawings, stacking those that he would keep neatly under his bed, and bundling the rest to wait by the fire for burning. He tidied his clothes, cleaned the table, emptied the grate, swept the floor, and set out for the sea, a metal bucket in each hand, one from the kitchen, filled with dirty crockery, the second his toilet bucket, emptied but scattered with traces of faeces and urine. He carried the two along the rocky path and through tufty grass to the cove that he had found with James. He removed his shoes and socks, and walked with the two buckets into the water that swirled furiously around his feet, its iciness rushing at his spine and teeth, reddening his feet and legs. He bent down to rinse the buckets, but stopped.

self-portrait: washing in my own shit, after dalí

He laughed

too puerile

too funny

too much money

He returned the toilet bucket to the sand and immersed the bucket of crockery, using the salted water as an abrasive over old stains on bowls, plates and cups. He then dunked the toilet bucket, watching as the waves snatched and diluted his remains.

self-portrait: around the world I go
He snorted.
self-portrait: international artist
He sat on the sand, waiting for the wind and sun to dry his
feet and hands, his feet short and broad with thick, dark hair
curling from the toes, his hands long and elegant, as though
manicured.
self-portrait: as hands and feet
self-portrait: as beauty and beast
He traced the water moving through the cove, arriving on the
left and sweeping in an arc with such force to the right that it
was hopeless to think he would emerge, that he could swim
against it
though
who
to notice
to care
the dealers' darlings
oblivious
the darling dealer
indifferent
The air too cold to dry his feet, he rubbed them with his fingers, his hands, his socks, wearing wet socks and damp boots
on his return to the hut. James was sitting on the ground,
leaning against the door.
    I want to be an artist, he said.
Lloyd set down his buckets.
    And how are you this afternoon, James?

I want you to teach me how to paint, Mr Lloyd.

Sorry, James. Not today. I'm working.

You're not supposed to work on Sundays.

I do.

Tomorrow?

No. No students.

James followed Lloyd into the hut.

So, will you teach me?

No.

But you have to.

Actually, I don't.

Please.

A box of food was sitting on the table.

Granny sent that over for you.

I didn't know that I was staying.

She thinks you are.

Lloyd looked in the box.

There's a lot of food, James. More than usual.

She must like you.

He began to unpack the food. Beef, more ham than usual and a dozen eggs instead of six.

You have to teach me, Mr Lloyd.

That's rather rude, James.

James moved to the wall.

Can I ask you something, Mr Lloyd?

You may.

James pointed at the pictures.

Are those gulls or terns?

Gulls.

Their heads are too small. They're tern heads.

Right.

And you're not understanding the way the light falls on the sea.

Is that right, James?

You're seeing it the wrong way.

Am I now?

Yes, Mr Lloyd.

And how would you know that?

I look at the sea all the time, Mr Lloyd. There's nothing else to do.

Lloyd unpicked one of his drawings of the sea from the wall. He handed it to James.

All right. Tell me how I should be seeing it.

From underneath the sea as well as above.

What do you mean?

The light doesn't just stay on the surface of the water.

I suppose it doesn't.

It gets broken up and some of it ends up underneath.

So?

It should look as though it is being lit from below as well as above.

That's interesting, James.

See. I can be helpful. Useful.

You can, James.

Now teach me how to paint, Mr Lloyd.

I'm working, James.

I'll work beside you.

No, James. I work alone.

Well, can I have some paint and brushes? Some paper.

Not here.

At the cottage?

Lloyd sighed.

I really don't want to take on a student.

I'll tell Granny that you're going to draw my mother.

Lloyd gasped, theatrically, his hand on his chest.

You wouldn't, James.

The boy laughed.

I would. And I'll tell her too that Mam will be wearing only a sheet.

Lloyd shooed James towards the door.

Out of here, James. Start with pencils and charcoal. No paints.

Yes, Mr Lloyd.

I'll be back in a few days to see what you have done.

Can I have a key?

I'm sure you'll find a way in, James.

James laughed.

You're right. I will.

Lloyd returned the dishes to the shelf and emptied the box of food, stacking the remaining shelves with bread, fruit cake, beans, tins of soup, and the vegetables, as they were before, potatoes, cabbage and turnip

english artist

exiled

159

french linguist

embraced

He carried the fresh milk and butter outside to store against the north-facing wall, encasing them in a sunscreen of stone and slate. He went back inside and lit a fire, encouraging the flame with discarded drawings and scraps of stick, then bits of turf, cautious of smothering it with a clod that was too big or too damp. He made tea, ate beef and bread and sat in front of the fire to wait on Mairéad, to draw gulls with larger heads, to draw the sea with light from underneath as well as above, following the instructions of the island boy who understood light better than the artist, who was taking the key from Bean Uí Néill's kitchen and unlocking the Englishman's cottage, walking into the studio air thickened by paint and linseed oil, by tiny particles of carbon and charcoal. James inhaled deeply, soaking his lungs in this otherness that I could breathe all day, never come out. I'll get Granny to leave breakfast, dinner and tea at the door so that I can stay inside, breathing this air, alone, hidden from them and their smell of fish, hidden from them and their plans for the rest of my life, in here instead, fingering brushes, paint, charcoal and pencils, opening tubes of paint, of red, of yellow, squeezing the colours onto my fingers and drawing yellow and red stripes across my cheeks, my forehead, initiated, apprenticed, the building of an artist.

He squeezed paint onto the palette, turquoise blue, France blue, myosotis blue, cadmium orange, lemon yellow, golden yellow, light green madder, deep green madder, scarlet Persian red, deep ruby, cinnabar green, sea green, olive green, deep rich green and white. Lots of white.

He picked up brushes, thin and thick, and painted a big boat out at sea, its net cast and fish jumping, Micheál and Francis on board, smiling. He started a second picture. Another boat. A currach. Closer to shore. Micheál and Francis sitting in it, but scowling this time as they rowed Lloyd to the island, three brushes in the artist's right hand, held up to the sky, an offering to the gods of art. He painted the island as a mountain scattered with cottages, his grandmother and mother at the door of their house, a teapot and plate of scones in their hands, Masson at his cottage door holding his tape recorder, Bean Uí Fhloinn further up the mountain, closer to the top, leaning on her stick, smiling beatifically, a yellow glow around her, around her cottage. In the bottom right-hand corner, under the sea, he painted a small boat upside down, and wrote his initials, JG, on the hull. James Gillan. Artist. Not fisherman.

He made four other paintings, and began to work then with pencils and charcoal, staying until darkness, until he heard his mother outside, talking to JP. He left through the back door and reached the kitchen before she did.

You missed your tea, she said.

She set a basket of dirty linen on the table.

I did.

He touched the basket.

That JP keeps you busy.

He likes clean clothes.

They only get dirty again.

161

Are you hungry, James?

Starving.

She took a plate covered by a second plate from the edge of the fire and laid it on the table, in front of her son, whose face and hands were splashed with different coloured paints.

The plates are hot, James.

Thanks.

What were you up to?

Nothing.

You were a long time at nothing.

I suppose I was. What were you doing in JP's?

Nothing.

I heard you talking.

You must have been nearby then.

He smiled at her.

I suppose I was.

She ruffled his hair.

You should go to bed, James.

I should.

He left. She washed the plates and cutlery, and stoked the fire. She sat down and lifted the charcoal grey knitting from the basket at the side of the chair. The start of a jumper for James. Dark to hide the dirt. She stretched the knitting across her lap and counted. Eight rows done, two to go, one row plain, one row purl. Ready in time for school, James. If you ever go back. Back to those priests and their ways. She started to knit, sliding one needle over the other and looping the wool. Their quietening of you, James. Their stilling of you. And your nails chewed to the quick. She finished the cuff at the base of the jumper and added six extra stitches to each side. She knitted on, rows of plain and purl to build the foundations of the pattern to come, her own pattern, her design, as she knitted it for Liam, now for James, who tells me nothing, insists only that I shouldn't worry, that they don't like me because I'm an island boy, but don't worry, Mam, because I don't like them either. She counted the stitches. One hundred and thirty four. As it was in the beginning, is now and ever shall be. The knitter's prayer. She continued, three more rows, plain, purl, plain. She stretched the knitting across her thighs, counted the stitches one more time and started on her pattern, blackberry stitch, cable, moss, diamond up the middle and out the other side in reverse, moss, cable, blackberry. She knitted the first blackberry, building three stitches from one, gathering them, wrapping them in purl, and pushing through, the birth of a berry to texture the jumper. She smiled and stroked the woollen knot, a thickening of the wool to keep James warm, as it warmed me, knitted by my mother, though not my grandmother who still calls this English knitting, the English scheme, their guilt for the famine, for the land theft. They take our land, she says, starve us and then to alleviate the poverty, to assuage their guilt, they set us up with knitting. Make jumpers this way and sell them, they said. Earn your living that way, they said. Earn your rent that way, they said, though we liked earning our living the other way, from the land that was our land, the sea that was our sea. But they told us to knit, so now we knit. Well, I'm not knitting, says Bean

Uí Fhloinn. Not that knitting. Their knitting. Their Scottish, English, Irish knitting. I'll do my own knitting. Knit as my mother did. As my grandmother knitted. Mairéad laughed. At Bean Uí Fhloinn sitting up there still, by the fire, with her pipe, her tea and her knitting, defiant, making socks that nobody wants to wear any more, socks with patterns more intricate than these jumpers, socks of waves and weaves, twists and turns, socks that sit in a drawer because my father, her daughter's husband, was the last islander to wear them, dozens of socks in that drawer waiting for him to come back from the sea. Mairéad smiled. At least his feet won't be cold when he comes back from the sea and opens that drawer of socks. She knitted on, twenty plain stitches, the foundation of the cable that will run up the sides of James's chest, from his hip bones to his clavicle. Then the moss stitch, plain, purl, plain, purl, the knitting soothing in the stillness of the sleeping house, the sleeping village, her metal needles sliding one over the other to build the base of the diamond pattern that would run up the centre of the jumper, along James's chest, still skinny, though his voice has broken, and he has shaved once or twice, his chin only, surreptitiously, the hairs washed away, the blade hidden, his father's blade without his father's guidance, without the guidance of a man, for the priests are of no use to him, those men in frocks, and he has no time for Micheál, even less for Francis, his own uncle, though he likes the Englishman well enough. Maybe he talks to the Englishman as he would have talked to his father, a man of little use to him now, under the sea, in one of these jumpers, dark like this one, a bed now for fish, a blanket for crabs, the wool more enduring than his skin and flesh, than his black, black hair. But what of your bones, Liam? The marrow of your bones? Of you? What is left of them? Of you, my love, down there, underneath in the sea grave, the grave sea. Is anything left, or are you all gone? Eaten? Atomised? Diluted and dispersed. Carried from one ocean to the next. Tiny particles of you travelling around the earth. My husband in Australia, in Africa, in South America, travelling the world without me, though he promised that we would go together, leave together, the three of us. But you left without me, Liam. Without us.

She sipped at her tea and knitted on.

How long does a bone last, anyway? A skull? Shorter or longer than a jumper? My brother was wearing a jumper, too. Dark as well, like this one, but made by his mother, my mother, with fewer blackberries so that we could tell them apart in the washing. Though they seldom need washing, these jumpers, as they absorb the smells as well as the sheep. Have you ever met a smelly sheep, Liam? Cows, yes. Goats? Terrible smell out of those billies. But the sheep? Left to its own devices, it's a clean animal. Unlike that Frenchman who is clean only because I clean him.

She reached the other side of the diamond and began the pattern in reverse, moss, cable, blackberry.

My father though, he never wore a jumper, not even in the middle of winter. He wore Bean Uí Fhloinn's socks and shirts, and the sleeveless jacket and scratchy trousers made by the tailor man who came to the island twice a year. He wore a proper jacket to Mass, but on that day, that autumn day, that last day, he was in his traditional clothes, adamant that he felt no cold, though he must have as the water seeped into him, soaking his skin, his lungs, soaking into their skin, their lungs, my father, my husband, my brother. That Holy Trinity of men. Amen. No men. On a still autumn day. Weighed down by wool. By the denseness of knitting. By the denseness of my knitting. My beloved man drowning in my knitting, drowning in my English knitting.

She stretched the beginnings of the jumper across her lap, the foundations laid, the pattern established. She stuck the two needles into the wool, returned them to the basket and stood up, almost silent in her movements out the door and into the Frenchman's house, into his bed, staying until the dark grey of the summer night began to lighten, when she dressed again and left for the cliffs, for the Englishman who was dragging the mattress, sheets, blankets and pillow from his bed to the tiny space in front of the fire, setting the pillow where he could achieve most light from the fire and the window, waiting on daylight to creep through the panes, waiting for her to arrive, uncertain if she would, this woman who would be his sleeping woman. She rattled the door. He opened it, and reached out his hand.

Thank you for coming, he said.

She nodded and shook his hand. He stoked the fire, and added more turf. He handed her the book, open on the page of the sleeping woman.

Like that, he said.

Yes, she said.

I'll go outside, he said.

She removed her clothes and draped the sheet over her body, exposing her feet and legs, resting her head on her arm, copying the image from the book.

He came into the hut.

Thank you, he said.

He adjusted her head slightly and sat on the floor, his eyes shifting rapidly from side to side, up and down, scanning, scrutinising, lucid and blue, hooded with overhangs of flesh though he is still a reasonably young man, about forty, older than Francis, younger than Micheál, his skin softer and less blemished than the island men, the sea men, his body softer too, more rounded, unused to work, a pet dog rather than a working one.

She smiled.

I prefer the working dog myself.

She laughed.

He stopped drawing.

Sorry, he said, did you say something?

She laughed and shook her head.

Please, Mairéad, close your eyes. You're supposed to be asleep.

Céard a dúirt tú?

He closed his eyes.

Tuigim. Yes. I understand.

His pencil moved quickly and his eyes dug more deeply, burrowing into me, soaking me in, absorbing me, though not as Liam did, not as JP does, nor Francis, Francis with his panting tongue. No. Differently to them.

Mairéad.

She opened both eyes.

Yes?

He squinted one eye closed. She laughed.

Asleep, he said.

Yes.

Sleeping. Not squinting.

Her eyes no longer of use, she listened to his pencil moving across the page, the strokes slow, rhythmical, the pencil pulsing softly, soothing her, lulling her away from the village, away from James, from Bean Uí Néill, awake by now, simmering at my absence, at my failure to put the kettle on the fire, the dishes on the table, the day in motion, for that is my job, putting the day in motion, holding it there, in that place, in motion, for the whole day, every day, to do just as she does, as she has done all her life, without question, no question that I have heard anyway.

Sit up, please.

He took the sheet and wrapped it over her shoulders, body and feet, so that only her face was exposed.

We're lucky this morning, he said. Filtered light.

She nodded, though uncertain of his words. She looked at the light reaching through the small window, diffused by cloud and glass, broken into beams that lit different parts of the floor.

Move back a little bit, please.

He pushed through the air with his hands. She moved backwards.

And turn your head.

She turned.

This way.

She turned again.

He sat in front of her then, closer than before, his face pitched forward, leaning into hers so that she could feel his breath, smell his smell, lavender, paint and turpentine. She recoiled a little, but he followed, chasing her with his eyes, his pencil, pinning me down, holding me in place as he drew, looking intermittently at the paper, at the lines and curves on the page, then back at me, at my face, my eyes, scraping and scratching, as though trying to enter me through my eyes.

She smiled.

I think I prefer the way the Frenchman comes in.

Be still, Mairéad.

She nodded.

Stop moving.

Beidh, she said. I will.

Thank you.

Alan John McMillan is walking around Market Square in Crossmaglen in South Armagh, close to the Irish border on Sunday, July 8th, the second day of his tour of duty as a soldier in Northern Ireland. He is nineteen years old and a private in the Queen's Own Highlanders.

He doesn't see the wire protruding from the letterbox of a house on the village square. He walks into the wire, detonating the IRA bomb inside the house. He dies in hospital from his injuries, his Scottish parents at his side.

Masson made a pot of coffee and set it on the table with a clean cup and a jug of milk. He sat down and flicked back over his papers, scanning where he had left off in his narrative of the history of the language, the precursor and context for the analytic and comparative work that he would write too over the summer months. He drank some coffee, gazed briefly at the seascape, and picked up his pen.

The severity of the Penal Laws reduced from 1770, allowing the slow but gradual emergence of a Catholic middle class, though unofficial and often relentless discrimination continued in everyday life, and continues to this day, more than 200 years later, in the north-eastern part of the country still occupied by Britain.

Using violent, economic and legal controls, the English insisted that the Irish adapt to them, to their rules and regulations, a policy and attitude that impacted hugely on the Irish language, its use and its structure – a brief example of which now follows, though I will provide more details later in this dissertation.

The Irish language had no neutral form of respect for addressing strangers or more senior people, such as 'vous' in French or 'Sie' in German. A version of 'vous' began to appear in the 16th century, during the reign of the Anglo-Normans, but disappeared again as Irish became increasingly a domestic and private language with little need of a neutral form. However, England's need for societal hierarchy, even in language, compelled the Irish speakers to adapt and introduce 'sir' or 'sor' when addressing English-speaking men in positions of power, adding a layer of linguistic and social inequality that did not previously exist.

By linguistically reinforcing the divisions already created by violence and economics, the English were able to maintain control and reward those who complied with and slotted into the new hierarchical system, a system of colonisation exercised too by other European powers, including the French. The Irish who accepted the changes imposed by the English fared better economically and socially than those who didn't. By speaking English and anglicising their Irish names, the Catholic people were more likely to get work from English employers who had little interest in learning an Irish name. Those who fared better again were the Catholics who spoke English and converted to Protestantism.

Irish in time became the language of the peasants, of the impoverished, of the uneducated. Thus marginalised, it stood little chance of holding its place as the dominant language or even of being an equal to English. Instead of becoming a bilingual society such as Belgium or Luxembourg, Ireland became diglossic, with Irish as a private language, spoken only at home and in small, mainly rural, communities. English was the public language, the language of commerce and education, the language of social and economic advancement. Parents opted to pay for English lessons for their children and grew dismissive of attempts by Irish-language teachers to preserve the native tongue as English was the gateway to employment, prosperity and emigration, a key need in Ireland after the devastating famine that caused the death of one million Irish people between 1846 and 1848 and led to the emigration of one and a half million more. Irish, as a result, became the lesser language, the language of those who were not advancing socially and economically within the new structure.

Scholars and politicians fought back. Thomas Davis, a Protestant writer and Young Irelander, in 1843 declared Irish a 'national language', and in 1893 Conradh na Gaeilge, the Gaelic League, was established to create a mass movement of support for the Irish language.

But the damage to the language was deep. While Irish was still spoken, its status as a major language was lost and people did not flock to support the language as had been hoped, resulting in the gradual but consistent decline in usage.

The language on this island lives on, for the moment. Bean Uí Fhloinn, the oldest family member of this inter-generational linguistic study, is a monolingual Irish speaker with no knowledge of English whereas her daughter, Áine Uí Néill, and granddaughter, Mairéad Ní Ghiolláin, are receptive bilinguals in that both understand English – though to vary-ing degrees – but only speak through the medium of Irish. Bean Uí Fhloinn's great-grandson, Séamus Ó Giolláin, is the first bilingual member of the family. His primary education on the island was through Irish, but his secondary education on the mainland is through English. He is the first to regularly use the English version of his name, James Gillan.

He heard the Englishman in the cottage next door, speaking. James was talking too, the artist and his pupil discussing the oil painting that Lloyd had lifted off the easel.

I told you to draw first.

I like painting.

Lloyd examined the depiction of the village, in blue and grey oils.

It's very good, James. You have a good eye.

James laughed.

What's a bad eye, Mr Lloyd?

Lloyd returned the painting to the easel.

Keep going, James.

I will, Mr Lloyd.

Now, I have to wash.

You do, Mr Lloyd.

That bad?

James laughed.

I can smell everything off you but fish.

Lloyd ran his hand across his bearded face.

It's been a while.

The true price of art, Mr Lloyd.

It is, James.

James built the fire and carried the bath in from the scullery.

How is the work going, Mr Lloyd?

It's going well. It suits me out there.

Don't tell JP.

I won't, James. He'd banish me forever.

They sat on either side of the tub, waiting for the water to boil.

Did you work on me?

A bit. And I practised my birds. And the light on the sea.

Glad to hear it, Mr Lloyd.

Your work is good, James. You have a natural eye.

Is that the same as a good eye?

You don't have to be taught how to see. You just see.

That's handy.

It is.

Because I don't want to be a fisherman.

I wouldn't want to be a fisherman either.

James shook his head.

You'd be a poor fisherman, Mr Lloyd.

I could get better.

James laughed.

I doubt it.

Lloyd looked at the water, still to boil.

Maybe Micheál could train me. Take me on as an apprentice.

James shook his head.

Micheál is not getting into a boat with you again.

Francis then.

Even less likely.

You'll have to teach me then, James.

James shook his head.

I'm going to be an artist.

It's not an easy life, James.

It's a lot easier than being a fisherman.

It's hard in other ways, James. Ways you can't see.

I prefer the ways I can't see to what I can see fishing.

Lloyd looked at the pot, at the quiff of steam rising from the water.

Will you teach me, Mr Lloyd?

I'm not a teacher, James.

So who will teach me? To draw like you?

You'll have to go to art school.

Where's that?

Dublin, I suppose. Or London. Or Glasgow.

How do I go there?

I don't know, James.

James stood up before the water was fully boiled and dumped it into the bath.

That should do you, Mr Lloyd.

I suppose it will, James.

James returned to the studio and closed the door between them. He drew the sea filled with fish and a boat on the surface. A boy was standing in the boat with a paintbrush in one hand and a fishing net in the other. Under the boat, on the sea-bed, he drew an upturned currach with three bodies scattered around it. He signed it, JG.

Lloyd came into the studio, dressed, his beard gone, his hair clean and combed.

Does your mother know how good you are?

She doesn't know I'm here.

Why not?

He shrugged.

We'll put on a show for her, James. A joint exhibition.

I don't want to.

It's good work.

I don't want her to know what I am doing.

Why not?

James returned to his drawing.

Was the bath hot enough, Mr Lloyd?

It was, James. Thank you.

Lloyd leaned against the window ledge.

Show me your other work, James.

The boy walked to the far corner of the studio and retrieved a small pile of paintings. He handed Lloyd a painting of the studio, viewed from the floor by the door.

What made you think of that?

I saw an ant walking in.

Lloyd laughed.

Let's call it *What the Ant Saw*.

He looked through the remaining paintings.

We'll need more paint, young man.

We will.

And brushes.

And charcoal, Mr Lloyd.

We'll have some sent.

Lloyd swept his hand around the room.

To the artists' colony on the edge of Europe.

James laughed.

That should find us all right.

Michael Kearney is a Catholic man and a member of the IRA. He is twenty years of age and from Glenveagh Drive in West Belfast. On Wednesday, July 11th, he is taken from the city by other IRA members, tortured and shot in the head. His body is dumped near Newtownbutler, Co. Fermanagh, about fifty yards from the Irish border.

Mairéad poured whiskey, the white-yellow liquid flowing freely into cups. They toasted and drank.

It's good, Micheál, said Mairéad. Better than your usual.

She poured again.

So, how is it working out for you, Mr Lloyd? said Micheál. Out there on the cliffs.

It's going very well, Micheál. Better than expected.

Is there much to paint?

The cliffs. The light has been good.

Is that all?

Pretty much, yes.

The cliffs over and over?

Lloyd nodded.

He wants to be Monet, said Masson.

Who's that?

The world's most famous painter of cliffs.

I suppose he's French, said Micheál.

Of course, said Masson.

They laughed and drank.

And how is the writing, JP?

Going well, Micheál. I have finished the history of your language.

Does it have a happy ending, JP?

That remains to be seen, Micheál.

Is that you done then?

Masson shook his head.

Now I begin my study, my comparative work.

Lloyd emptied his cup.

So, what happens next, Masson?

Mairéad poured, a third time.

As I said before, unless there is major investment, the language dies, like Manx or Norse.

And what's so bad about that? said Lloyd.

That's one perspective, said Masson.

I'm a utilitarian, Masson. A pragmatist.

And?

Instead of spending money on a dying language, build houses and hospital beds.

This is an ancient language with an ancient history.

So was Manx. So was Norse. The world is getting on fine without them.

Is that enough for you, Lloyd? To be getting on.

Lloyd shrugged.

We have to get on. To progress.

It's more than that, Lloyd.

You're right, Masson. It's about the common good.

And?

If the common good is better served by English, speak English.

What is the common good? Who defines that?

Better houses, better schools, better hospitals.

You can have those and speak Irish.

Can you? It's not happening here, on this Irish-speaking island. The only thing that is happening here is poverty. And a dearth of opportunity.

Masson tipped back his whiskey.

How can an artist be so indifferent to something so ancient, so beautiful?

If I get sick, I want a good hospital.

And that's it? The only value to language? To get you a good hospital.

And to communicate my symptoms.

Masson threw his hands in the air.

This attitude will make you sick.

Mairéad poured a fourth time. They drank.

This country was colonised, said Lloyd.

Is, said Francis.

Lloyd shrugged.

Language is a casualty of colonisation, he said. India. Sri Lanka. The French in Algeria.

There are similarities, said Masson.

French was imposed on Algeria, on Cameroon. English on Ireland, on Nigeria. To progress you learnt the language of the coloniser.

And?

Lloyd shrugged.

It happened. All over the world.

And?

The damage is done, said Lloyd. Move on. Invest in the living.

The language is still alive, said Masson. Here on this island.

Spoken by a gaggle of old women, said Lloyd.

Mairéad is not old, said Masson. Bean Uí Néill is middle-aged. The language is not as dead as the English may want it to be.

I don't want anything, said Lloyd.

You've always hated the language, said Masson. Been threatened by it. Your people treated this language brutally. Savagely.

Lloyd crossed his arms, stretched out his legs.

Yes, of course, I forgot. The French adored the languages of Algeria, nurtured and nourished the languages of the Berber and Arabs.

You're being facetious, Lloyd.

Am I?

Yes, you are.

Why aren't you in Algeria unpicking the damage caused by French? Why come here giving out to the English for all their awfulness when you have done exactly the same.

I'm a linguist trying to help.

Go help there.

Masson lifted the bottle, stilling his hand, his thoughts, for you'd like that, Mother, wouldn't you? Your son in Algeria. Your linguist son working for you, your language, your heritage. You'd adore that.

He poured into Bean Uí Néill's cup, but slowly, the whiskey trickling from the bottle.

Instead I'm here, far from you, Mother, on a remote rock studying a language that is not your language. Not the result you wanted, Mother. After all those years. All those battles. As far from you as I can be, from those days when, your hand over mine, we walked the streets of the town that was almost a city, more my home than yours, although you led me, adamant that in the narrow streets off the main roads would be a teacher to teach me the language of your childhood, of your people, the people that you said were my people though I did not know them, had not met them, knew them only from photographs and saw that their smile was yours, all of you together, happy on chairs under trees by the sea. Avant la guerre, you said. You stroked their faces and returned them to their place in your handbag. We walked, day after day, rejecting teachers you thought too casual, too focused on conversation, we talk at home, you said, hunting until you found what you were looking for, on a street that was narrower still, up the stairs of a dusty house, past windows overlooking a yard that had once been a garden, the plants uprooted and replaced with a pragmatic swathe of concrete, up and up again we climbed, to the third floor and into a room of twenty desks, battered and stained but arranged into four rows, neat degradation. A man sat at the front of the classroom, in a worn suit at a larger but equally tattered desk. He stood only when we reached him. He invited us to sit, each of us at a desk while he talked about my future learning, about the rightness of choosing him as my teacher because he would expose me to the rigours and demands of Arabic. But the joys too, Madame Masson. The

joys. And it's a brave act, Madame, because most parents, especially mothers, are wimps, cowards who let their children skim
the surface of this great language and settle for a colloquial
knowledge without proper learning or understanding, leaving
these children, these young people as half-knowers, only half
immersed in their roots, half immersed in their history, and
this half-knowing, this half-immersion, was, he said, often
more dangerous than ignorance. The half-knowers who think
they know everything, Madame Masson. But they know
almost nothing and understand even less. You don't want your
son to be a half-knower, Madame Masson. And you nodded
vigorously, Mother.

Whiskey dribbled down the side of Bean Uí Néill's cup.

The teacher shook my hand, welcoming me to the twice-
weekly classes that would start on Monday and last for two
hours. I went on that first Monday to sit with nine others,
all boys, all with skin that was darker than mine, more like
my mother's than mine, the teacher roaming amongst us,
demanding answers, sometimes with his voice, other times
with the back of his hand against my head, so hard that tears
welled and sometimes fell while you, Mother, sat outside on a
chair in the hall, plastic glass between us, me inside learning
an Arabic I would never use, you outside reading a novel in
French and drinking tea from the flask you carried, the flask
emptied by the time I emerged from class, my eyes and cheeks
red. You jutted your chin at me, Mother, ordering me to grow
up, to toughen up, to turn into a man, silence between us as
we walked home in the winter dark.

Francis snatched the bottle.

You're making an awful mess, JP.

He filled the cups.

Sláinte, he said.

They drank.

You should get your own house in order first, said Lloyd.

Masson sighed, loudly.

An Englishman is struggling with my attempt to save Irish.

What's the point? said Lloyd. What are you trying to prove? It's almost dead, anyway.

The point is to persuade people in Ireland and Europe that this language is precious and should be protected.

Why protect a language that most people don't want to speak?

For that, Mr Lloyd, I go back to your Elizabethan poet, Edmund Spenser. He wrote that 'The speech being Irish, the heart must needs be Irish.'

Lloyd yawned.

Such sentimental rubbish.

It's more than sentiment, Lloyd.

Is it? said Lloyd. James and Micheál are no less Irish because they speak English.

Micheál turned to the women.

Is there any tea, Mairéad?

She stood up and moved to the fire.

What do you think, Micheál? said Masson. Are you less Irish when you speak English?

I don't talk politics, Masson. You know that.

We're talking about language, Micheál.

Same thing.

Mairéad took a cardigan from the back of a door.

Ná bac leis an tae, she said.

She left the kitchen and went outside.

What did she say? said Lloyd.

She said forget the tea, said Micheál.

Bean Uí Néill took a scarf from the hook.

Tá mé ag gabháil amach ag siúl.

She too left.

What did she say? said Lloyd.

She's gone for a walk, said Micheál.

He stood up.

I'll go too, he said.

Mise chomh maith, said Francis.

The two men followed the women, the four moving quickly, silent until they reached the back of the village where the vegetables grew.

I've been thrown out of my own house, said Bean Uí Néill.

An eviction, said Francis.

From my own kitchen.

The colonisers have taken over your kitchen, said Francis.

Bean Uí Néill buttoned her cardigan and wrapped the scarf around her head.

Ah, we can't really call JP a coloniser, she said.

The French are as bad, Mam, said Mairéad.

They didn't colonise here, said Bean Uí Néill.

They walked towards the cliffs, in the opposite direction to the hens pecking at the ground as they returned to roost, a slow meander in the approaching dusk.

I hope they don't drink all the whiskey, said Mairéad.

I'll bring you another bottle, said Micheál. A better one.

Micheál and his promises, said Bean Uí Néill.

What does that mean?

Always promising something, aren't you, Micheál?

What are you getting at, Áine?

Don't worry about them, you said. They'll settle. They'll be grand. You'll all be grand together. And now look at me, Micheál. Thrown out of my own house.

It'll settle down, he said.

She snorted.

You're at it again, Micheál. Always talking in the future tense.

She hurried her step and broke away, walking faster towards the cliffs.

Each of them is grand on his own, said Mairéad. One at a time.

It'll settle.

I'm not sure it will, Micheál. You can't have two top dogs.

The battle of the colonisers, said Francis.

Stop it, Francis, said Mairéad. It's bad enough without you drumming it up.

The ground sloped upwards, slowing Bean Uí Néill. The others caught up and walked alongside her through the grass, dried and spiked by the day's sun and wind, still to be soaked and softened by the coming dew. They walked towards the cliffs, towards the sea rushing at the rocks, their bodies bent against the wind, though there was little wind, the bend habitual, inherent, even on an evening still enough for the midges to rise from the grass and bite at their hands, their faces, though none of them noticed, the four focused on reaching the cliffs, the elemental air, the pulse of sea against rock.

Bean Uí Néill inhaled, deeply.

It does you good out here, she said.

It does, said Micheál.

They sat and watched the sun sinking into the sea, a blaze of pinks and reds.

This is better than Mass, said Mairéad.

That's a terrible thing to say, said Bean Uí Néill.

Is it?

It is, Mairéad. Terrible.

The monstrance is shaped like the sun, Mam.

And?

Men in dresses hold it up in the air as though it was the sun.

That's terrible, Mairéad.

They worship it. We're supposed to worship it.

I do, Mairéad.

But here it is, in front of us, Mam. The sun. Not a priest in sight.

You talk nonsense sometimes, Mairéad.

Do I?

Maybe you're a sun worshipper, Mairéad, said Francis. An old Indian squaw.

Or a Greek goddess, Francis.

Francis laughed.

The Greeks don't have red hair, Mairéad.

They might, said Mairéad. How would you know?

I've seen those Greek postcards. Not a redhead on them anywhere.

Mairéad nodded.

I'll give you that, Francis.

A momentous moment.

Bean Uí Néill stretched her legs across the grass.

When is the priest coming back anyway, Micheál? said Bean Uí Néill. I could do with communion.

Haven't heard, Áine.

And confession, Mam. For murderous thoughts.

They laughed.

Bless me, Father, said Francis, for I pushed the Englishman off the cliff.

One Hail Mary, said Micheál.

Bless me, Father, for I have pushed the Frenchman off the cliff.

One Our Father. Two Hail Marys.

They laughed and fell again into silence, watching the sea and listening to the birds, to the usual raucousness of the gulls, but also too to the summer visitors, the throaty call of the corncrake, the squawk of the puffin.

Would you move back, Micheál?

Think I've gone too soft, Áine.

And you, Francis?

I would, Bean Uí Néill. In the right circumstances.

We could do with a man, Francis.

I can see that, Bean Uí Néill.

Mairéad closed her eyes, pulled her knees to her chest.

It's hard in winter, said Bean Uí Néill.

A man would help all right, said Francis.

And you'd come back, Francis?

I would, Bean Uí Néill. As I said, in the right circumstances.

Bean Uí Néill nudged her daughter.

That's good to know, isn't it, Mairéad?

We're managing well enough, Mam.

We're not, Mairéad. Not in winter.

Mairéad opened her eyes, stretched her legs along the grass.

We're doing grand as we are, Mam. And James is getting stronger. Older.

Bean Uí Néill snapped at her daughter.

Is this the James who won't get into a boat? Not much use on an island, is he?

He does everything else, Mam.

Except the very thing we need him to do.

That's not fair, Mam.

We need a man who fishes, Mairéad.

He's a good hunter.

Nobody buys rabbit, Mairéad.

Mairéad shrugged.

I like rabbit, she said.

We need a man who catches fish, Mairéad. Who sells fish.

We don't, Mam. We're doing fine as we are.

Bean Uí Néill shook her head, slowly.

We're not, Mairéad. We're not doing fine as we are.

Micheál cleared his throat.

In fairness, he said, you've done well by yourselves out here.

Bean Uí Néill laughed. Harshly.

So you like to believe, Micheál.

What does that mean?

Those women out there on that island are grand with the pittance I give them.

That's not fair, Áine.

It is fair. You always give me less than you should, Micheál. You won't even give me double for those two back at my kitchen table.

They'll be gone soon enough.

I want one of them gone now.

Which one, Áine?

I have no preference.

Choose one and I'll tell him to go.

You choose, Micheál. You brought them both.

You want one of them gone, Áine, you choose which one.

I can help, said Francis.

Be quiet, Francis, said Mairéad.

You know I won't do that.

I do, Áine.

You always get what you want, Micheál.

So we'll muddle through, then.

Only if you give me more money. The same amount for each man.

But the Englishman is barely at your house. Barely eats.

Then I'll send the Frenchman away.

Micheál laughed.

All right, Áine.

They turned from the cliffs and walked back, the sky darkening as they reached the village. Mairéad closed the henhouse, tapping twice against the door of corrugated iron.

Night, night, hens.

Patrick O'Hanlon is having a drink at the bar of his local bowling club in West Belfast on Sunday night, July 15th. He is celebrating his sixty-ninth birthday. He learns that two men have damaged his car. He rushes outside. Two men in a Ford Cortina have crashed into his parked car. He walks towards the men, both republicans. They shoot him, a married father of three, a Catholic, a retired mechanic and garage owner who twice told police that his car had been hijacked. Patrick O'Hanlon is dead on arrival in hospital.

James carried eggs, fresh milk, ham, two cooked fish, scones, bread and fruit cake to the hut. He tapped on the door. Lloyd was working at the easel.

My granny sent you these.

Thank you.

Lloyd opened up the package.

I think your grandmother is keen for me to stay out here.

James laughed.

Looks that way all right.

Send her my thanks.

How long more will you be?

Longer now.

How's it going?

Well.

So is mine.

Lloyd nodded.

Then you should go back to it, James.

Can I stay here today?

No.

I can tell you the news of the village.

No talk, James. No gossip.

I can be silent either. Not tell you anything.

No, James.

Do you want me to show you the puffins?

No. I'm working. No talk. No gossip. No puffins.

But you said that you wanted to see a puffin.

Lloyd threw down his brush.

Bloody hell, James. Right. Let's go and see a puffin.

They walked towards the cliffs, on the path Lloyd used.

There's nothing out here, James. I know this well by now.

You'll see.

They walked on, James scanning the ground. He hunkered
down.

There's a colony beneath your feet, Mr Lloyd. Moving
underneath without your even knowing.

James stuck his hand into a hole and pulled out a puffin, the
bird's head and beak of cadmium orange spinning in protest,
its feet stamping at the air.

It's tiny, said Lloyd. Smaller than I had expected. And those
claws are sharp.

Good for digging.

Lloyd peered into the hole.

Is there a chick in there?

Maybe. Maybe not.

James reached further into the hole and retrieved a ball of soft
grey feather. He held the mother in one hand, the chick in the
other, laughing as the mother lashed at him with her claws
and beak, as she buckled and twisted, fighting to reach her
chick. The chick was motionless, its eyes fixed on its mother.

We should put them back, James.

Do you want to hold them?

No. Thank you.

They'll spend the winter out at sea. Grey-faced, the fishermen say.

They're pretty grey-faced today, said Lloyd.

They're grand.

They've had enough, James.

He slipped the chick back into the hole and released the mother. She rushed after her baby.

She's frantic, said Lloyd.

She'll be fine, said James. No harm done.

I imagine that the puffin sees it differently.

You wanted to see one, Mr Lloyd.

I did.

Now you have.

I have.

You don't look happy about it.

It seems wrong to wrench them out of their home.

James shrugged.

It's what you wanted, Mr Lloyd.

I'm going back to work, James.

James left and Lloyd sank deeper into solitude.

The IRA parks a pig trailer packed with explosives beside a bus stop in Rosslea, a rural area in Co. Fermanagh. They run a wire from the pig trailer to a mobile home overlooking the bus stop. A man, his wife and their children live in the mobile home. They are taken captive as the IRA waits in the caravan, surveying the road, the bus stop and their bomb.

Four people gather at the bus stop on Tuesday morning, July 17th. They are waiting for the shoppers' bus to Enniskillen. The bus is due at 10.05 a.m. They are all from Rosslea. Two of them are brother and sister, siblings of the man being held captive in the mobile home. The other two people at the bus stop are an elderly mother with her thirty-two-year-old daughter, Sylvia Crowe, a Protestant woman who works in the Faith Mission bookshops.

They hear a vehicle. It is not the bus but a Land Rover, the Ulster Defence Regiment on patrol. The Land Rover approaches the bus stop. The IRA detonates its bomb, killing Sylvia Crowe and injuring the three others at the bus stop, as well as four members of the UDR.

She returned to the hut.

Thank you, he said.

He left, she undressed and draped the sheet as it had been before. She called to him.

Tá mé réidh, Mr Lloyd. I'm ready.

He adjusted her, adjusted the sheet, and began to draw.

She closed her eyes.

I must tell him, tell James to tell him, that I want to be in a simple frame, white or cream, not gold, nothing fancy, but plain. A plain frame for the island woman. And on white walls, Mr Lloyd. Only white walls. A plain frame and plain walls for the widow woman, for the young widow woman out here, on the edge. The young widow island woman. My name on the mainland. What they call me when I walk those streets, enter those shops, those eyes, those fingers, those mouths, looking at me, pointing at me, talking of me, see her, over there, going into that shop, coming out of that shop, that's her, the young widow island woman, you know her, know her story, the young widow island woman who lost her husband, her father, her brother in one day, all of them under the sea, one afternoon, that's her, god help her, god save her, god love her, though god is good for he gave her first a son, a son who

looks like his father so that her husband can live on, thanks
be to god, thanks be to the lord god, a father living through
his son, through him, with him, in him, thanks be to god, his
father's eyes, his father's hair, his father's chin, father, son and
holy ghost, holy ghost of a man, of a husband, a lover, a friend,
not a trace of him anywhere, in rocks, in grasses, in waves, in
clouds, in rain, in prayers, in beads, in crosses, nothing, not
a sign. I have looked, day and night, night and day, hunted
as James hunts those rabbits, but found nothing, so that only
snapshots remain, black and white, eyes squinting in the
island sun, a smile across him, but nothing more, for the sea
took everything, beating him into fragments small enough
to send across the earth on a journey of further erosion and
rendering, pounding him into still smaller particles, atomised
eternity granted unto him, oh lord, but nothing more, nothing
for me to hold at night, to look at in the morning, though
she lives on, this sleeping woman, three hundred years, more,
young still, beautiful, not ravaged by sea, by salt, and so alive
still that I am certain I can smell her breath, staled only by
sleep, her skin unblemished, untouched by age, painted eternity granted unto her, oh lord, though not unto Liam, for
there is no smell rising from those photographs, no breath,
nothing but my memory of him, his musky skin, his armpits,
his groin, a sweet maleness I have not found elsewhere, not in
Francis with his dirty, stinking, fishy smell, nor in JP with his
shop-bought masculinity, nor in this Englishman who smells
of must and oil, of stale sweat, maybe too of lavender, but no
smell from him or anywhere on the island of frankincense,

myrrh or sandalwood, those funereal smells never dispersed over my man's body, over his coffin, for there was nothing to bury, nothing to wake, nothing to dress in his wedding suit, to clean, to kiss, to hold. Nothing. No last taste of sea salt and tobacco from his lips, from his tongue. Though she lives on, this sleeping woman, as though the artist had just kissed her, was about to kiss her again, for he knew her well, as well as I knew Liam, as Liam knew me, as we had known each other before and after our wedding, out on the cliffs on summer nights, on the beach, and then in my bed that became our bed, my sleep then as contented as hers over three hundred years before, a sleep that eludes me now as I toss, turn, pace the floor, walk the cliffs, never again to sleep as she sleeps, as I used to sleep, and would like to sleep again, though I never will, though maybe this artist man, this English artist man, will allow me to sleep as she sleeps, draw me as she is so that I too live on, sleep on, eternal life, eternal sleep, granted unto me.

Open your eyes, Mairéad. Please.

She stared at him, at his pencil moving across the page, his eyes flicking from side to side, his tongue running intermittently across his lips, moistening them, as though preparing to kiss, to taste as that other artist had tasted his sleeping woman, as though he, this Englishman, needs the taste of me to draw me, to know me as she was known, though I have no need of him, no need of the taste of him, need only that he takes me from here, away to live elsewhere, the young widow island woman hanging from a wall in some strange place, a foreign land while I stay, still setting the kettle on the fire, the dishes on the table, the day in motion, breathing in the fragments of my dead man, living with the bits of him that the sea never got. Just as she will be, that poor mother, back in the house where her daughter had lived, swallowing the air in the hope of absorbing some of her, something of her, something left behind by the bomb, the bomb that blew her daughter into tiny fragments. Did they not see them at the bus stop? Did they not see them standing there, the old woman with her daughter, the brother and sister of the man they had taken captive? And still they set off the bomb. Pulled the wire. Exploded their bomb hidden beside a bus stop. Who plants a bomb beside a bus stop? You'll be like me now, old woman. When you go to town, when you walk those streets and enter those shops. Those eyes will look at you. Those mouths will talk of you. Those fingers will point at you. The old mother of the bus-stop daughter. That's her, god help her, god save her, god love her. And you'll go home, old woman, as I do, and you'll stay home, soaking up the fragments of the daughter that they took from you.

That's enough for today, he said.

He stood up.

You can dress.

Go maith.

Sorry?

Good, she said. It's good.

Tea? he said.

She nodded.

Yes, please.

He turned on the gas and put on the kettle.

I have no milk, he said.

She shrugged.

Gan bainne, mar sin.

He turned his back to her and she dressed. She folded the sheet and blankets and set the pillow on top. She went outside. He followed, handing her a cup of black tea.

Thank you, Mairéad.

Tá fáilte romhat. You're welcome.

They stood side by side in the freshness of morning, sunlight glistening on the water, waves rolling over the rocks, gulls swooping, strident even at that early hour, the sky tinged still with pink.

Will you come again?

A rabbit bounced in front of them, knocking dew from blades of grass, droplets arcing in the sunlight.

Yes.

Tomorrow?

Yes.

She handed him the cup, retied her hair and left, walking back towards the village, to her mother.

Where were you?

Walking.

Well for you.

It did me good.

We're behind on breakfast. JP is prowling.

He can wait.

You look tired. Did you sleep at all?

I'll be fine.

Did you get the eggs?

No.

Get the eggs.

When she returned with the basket of eggs, Masson was at the table. He winked at her.

Maidin mhaith, a Mhairéad.

Good morning, JP.

That's English, Mairéad. You don't speak English.

She shrugged, and stood beside her mother at the open fire.

How many eggs?

Eleven.

That'll do. We can do eggs at midday.

And for the evening?

I'll ask James to get rabbits. You cut the bread. The porridge is ready.

James joined the three of them at the table.

You look tired, Mam.

Do I?

You do, Mairéad, said Masson. Did you not sleep?

He smiled at her. She looked at her son.

I went for an early walk, James. That must be why.

Where did you go?

Out. Towards the cliffs.

How is Mr Lloyd?

She held his gaze.

I went the other way, James.

And coming back?

It was early. He was probably asleep.

I'll go out there today, said James. Bring him food.

He'll need milk, said Mairéad.

And more eggs, said Bean Uí Néill.

I'd leave him be, Séamus, said Masson. He's gone there to be on his own.

He needs food. And don't call me Séamus.

Bean Uí Néill poured fresh tea.

Maybe JP is right, said Mairéad. We should leave him be.

But he'll be hungry, Mam.

He'll come back if he's hungry, said Mairéad.

James collected pencils, charcoal and a sketchpad from the studio and headed out across the island, the spider webs unbroken, the dew as it had fallen, undisturbed on the grass blades.

You're a poor liar, Mam.

He scanned the surface of the island around him, looking for grass freshly compressed by rabbits' feet, tracking that movement to a hole where the soil at the entrance had been freshly disturbed. He set his net over the hole, sat beside it and waited for a rabbit to emerge, as one did, shortly after he sat down. He tightened the net around the rabbit, grabbed the rabbit by the legs, lifted it in the air and smashed its head against a rock. He took the rabbit from the bloodied net, dropped it on the grass and drew its startled eyes and pink tongue flopping out the side of its mouth, blood trickling between red-coloured teeth. Death of a rabbit that is fresher than yours, Mr Lloyd. He picked up the rabbit and went on, prowling until he caught and killed a second one. He dropped the two on the ground, paws entangled, and sketched, first with pencil, then with charcoal, over and over to capture that moment of death, sudden in this case, over in seconds, a jolt, but slow for my father as the sea soaked into his jumper, his trousers, filled his boots, too tightly laced to kick off, the fisherman's boots so heavy that it is pointless learning how to swim because death, once in the water, is inevitable in those boots. Best not to wear those boots. Not to be a fisherman. Better to be an artist, drawing death instead of being death.

He picked up the rabbits and turned back towards the village. Micheál and Francis were in the kitchen, drinking tea with his mother and grandmother. He laid the rabbits on the table.

We may stay the night, said Francis. Stay for the feast.

You'll stay anyway, said James.

His grandmother poured tea for him. He sat down.

We're going fishing after this, James, said Francis. Are you coming with us?

I've caught the rabbits. That'll do us for today.

We'll give you a cut of the catch.

He shook his head.

You need to start making money, James.

I'm grand, Francis.

Bean Uí Néill handed James a slice of bread, already coated in butter but not jam.

You should go with them, James, she said.

I'm grand today, Granny.

James poured milk into his tea.

We need you to start earning some money, James, said Bean Uí Néill.

He drank the tea. Ate the bread.

I will, Granny. Just not from fishing.

His grandmother tightened her lips and nodded, slowly.

And what had you in mind, James?

He turned to Micheál.

Are you coming back here after the fishing?

We are, James, said Micheál.

And are you staying the night?

We are.

Will you give my grandmother some fish?

I will, said Micheál.

And money for looking after the two men?

That too, yes.

James drank the remainder of his tea.

Thanks, then we're grand for today.

Mairéad stood up to clear the table.

We're not grand, James, she said.

We have food, Mam.

We do. For today. But not the winter.

We'll worry about the winter in the winter.

She shook her head.

You should go with them, James. Learn the fishing.

He stared at her and slowly returned the cup to the table. He stood up and walked out of the kitchen, towards the studio, his breath shallow, panting as he pushed against the door, shoving it closed so that nobody could follow with a set of heavy boots and knitted jumper. I don't want one of your jumpers, Mam. Those drowning jumpers. Not for me, Mam. I won't do it. I won't be that fisherman. That tradition. That drowning tradition. He opened a fresh sheet of paper and drew in pencil, two rabbits, dead on the grass, three fishermen, dead on the seabed.

Not for me, Mam, he said.

The cries of the gulls penetrated the thin glass panes, calling to each other, but less stridently than earlier for their bellies were full, the anxiety of early morning hunger alleviated so that they could rest, frolic, play, their needs sated. As I want it. The rabbits in, the day's food secure, the hours free now to unfold without obligation. As it is with Bean Uí Fhloinn, up there on the hill. Though it is not like that with you, Micheál, is it? For you always want more, to have more, to own more, a bigger fish, a bigger house, a bigger boat, maybe even one day two boats, two houses, like your brother in America, proof to him that you were right to stay, that you too can toss your scraps at men like Francis, at boys like me, and Francis wants them, your scraps, wants them to lure my mother, to woo her with your scraps so that he can build his own scraps inside her, in his brother's bed. But I want none of them. None of you. I don't want a bigger boat. Or any size of boat. He began to paint, oranges, pinks, yellows, colours that Lloyd did not use, would not miss. Use all the greys, greens, browns, blues, and he'll kick me out. He painted the village, drawing on postcards sent by Granny's sister in America who prefers the blue and white of Greek islands to the green and brown of this one. He nodded. She's probably right. Maybe I should go there. Live there. Though that place too is riddled with boats. He copied the box shape of the Greek houses but set them on his island and painted them orange, pink and yellow. He painted the earth a lurid green and the sky a silver grey, a mixture of rain, clouds and sun. He worked until he heard his mother calling people to the evening meal, surprised to find Lloyd already at the table.

I hadn't expected you back, he said.

The rabbits told me of the mayhem.

It's that all right, said James.

Bean Uí Néill set plates in front of the four men. They had most of the meat. James, his mother and grandmother had scraps of meat and sauce.

I should have got three, said James.

Or caught some fish, said Francis.

They began to eat.

What has happened over the last few days? said Lloyd. Have I missed anything?

Life has gone on in its usual way, said Micheál.

A woman was killed standing at a bus stop, said James. She was younger than Mammy.

We don't talk politics, James, said Micheál.

It's not politics, said James. It's fact. A woman was killed standing at a bus stop. Blown up by a bomb.

That's a shocking way to die, said Lloyd.

That's a shocking way to live, said Francis.

Standing at a bus stop? said James.

Lloyd pointed at James's hands.

I see you've been painting, James.

He looked at his hands, paint-spattered.

I have.

Unusual colours to have chosen.

You took all the decent ones.

Lloyd scanned his own hands.

I suppose I did.

Masson tapped on the table.

B'fhearr liom dá labhraíodh sinn Gaeilge, said Masson.

What did you say? said Lloyd.

I'd prefer if we spoke Irish, said Masson.

Lloyd sighed.

I came back to converse, he said. To talk to people. I can't do that through Irish.

Then learn Irish.

Masson switched to Irish. Lloyd looked at Mairéad, her eyes distant

withdrawn

elsewhere

amendment

current works

future works

He finished eating, bowed in thanks and returned to his cottage, the fire lighting, used cups on the table, paper on the floor, James's painting still on the easel

psychedelic greek

irish island

as she wants from me
dealer wife
half-wife
but never gets
never will
James came in after him.

Sorry, Mr Lloyd. I didn't think you'd be back.

I like it, James. It's original.

You do?

My wife would too.

That's kind of her.

She's not kind.

What is she then?

She runs a gallery. Modern art. Doesn't like my art, though.

Why not?

Too old-fashioned.

I like your art.

Thank you. You're very kind. Unfortunately you are not my wife and you are not running a famous London gallery.

James laughed.

Why doesn't she like it?

Thinks that it's all been done before. That photographs do what I do.

She has a point.

Does she?

You copy what already exists.

That's what she says.

But you're very good at it, Mr Lloyd.

He bowed.

Thank you, James. You're very kind.

He picked up James's painting and scrutinised it.

She'd like this though.

So you said, Mr Lloyd.

She'd like the naivety. But the modernity too.

Is that a good thing, Mr Lloyd?

It might be, James. Bring me your other work.

James laid his paintings and drawings across the floor of the studio. Lloyd studied the work, the boldness of blending the Greek island into the Irish one, the novelty of seeing the studio as the ant did, the freshness of the boy's work contrasting sharply with his own. He closed his eyes and opened them again.

So here's what we'll do, James.

James stood motionless, waiting.

We'll host an exhibition together, in my wife's gallery.

James slapped his hands together.

Brilliant, Mr Lloyd.

You do six paintings, James.

I will.

Good lad.

How many will you do, Mr Lloyd?

I don't know yet. Maybe twenty.

But she doesn't like your work.

She can't refuse me if you are with me. You, the modern, young, naive artist alongside me, the fusty, old but experienced traditionalist.

You're not that old, Mr Lloyd. You still have all your teeth.

Lloyd laughed.

In the art world, I am. There's an obsession with youth. With novelty.

That'll be me then, said James.

Exactly. I'll ride on your coat-tails, James.

So I don't have to be a fisherman.

No fishing for you, young man.

James smiled.

That's grand, Mr Lloyd. Though my granny will be a bag of cats about it.

She will, James.

I'll have to get off the island. Leave. Emigrate.

You will.

I'll live in London.

You'll be too famous to live there. Teenage girls will mob you on the streets.

I'll hide in your house, Mr Lloyd.

Lloyd chuckled.

They'll still find you, James.

Lloyd pressed his hands together, tapping his fingers against his forehead.

We'll call our exhibition *The Islanders*.

But you're not an islander, Mr Lloyd.

I am now.

Lloyd gathered up some fresh clothes, and his book of Rembrandt drawings.

I'll go back out to the cliffs. You keep painting, James.

You've only just come back.

Masson has banned me from talking, so I may as well be at the hut.

He collected more paints and paper, as well as pencils. Most of the charcoal was already used.

We'll have to be careful of our supplies, James.

Maybe your wife could send some. From her gallery.

Lloyd shook his head.

She's not that sort of wife, James.

James looked in the drawer.

I'll write out a list of what we need, Mr Lloyd, and give it to Micheál.

You do that, James.

He left the studio, whistling

bilingual

trilingual

nobody's lingual

not yours, masson

not mine

He knocked on the kitchen door and went in. Mairéad was in the back kitchen washing a pot.

May I have some food, for the cliffs?

'Bhfuil tú ag gabháil siar arís? You're going back? Already?

He nodded and she dried her hands.

Cén uair? When?

Now. Will you come again? To the hut.

I will.

213

She gathered food into a box and handed it to him. She gave him too a bottle of fresh milk.

My tea, she said.

He smiled at her.

Come whenever you want, he said. Even if I'm asleep. The door doesn't lock.

I will, she said.

She went to him again, at dawn, through rain, water dripping on him as she shook him awake.

You're saturated, he said.

He handed her a towel. He dressed while she dried herself.

I'm not sure that it was worth your while. The light is terrible.

She pointed at the fire.

Bigger, she said.

He worked at the fire while she undressed and stretched across the mattress, the sheet over her. He knelt beside her and showed her a different Rembrandt drawing, of a woman's naked back and buttocks, her face towards the wall.

Like this? he said.

She looked at the drawing. Silent.

Nobody will know it's you, he said.

She pushed away the sheet and sat up.

Thank you, Mairéad.

He drew and she looked at his kitchen floor, at the dust, the dirt, the debris of his meals, of his skin, his hair, his nails. She closed her eyes. Not my responsibility. No responsibility, no obligation, only to lie here listening to his pencil across the page, his chest rising and falling, his breath in and out, a slight rasp at the end of his exhalation, as though he might not be healthy in old age, an irrelevance to me drifting with the sound of lead across paper, over and back, light movements, heavy ones, lines, curves and circles, one sheet, then another, the dense morning light unaltered by the passing minutes, though I am, altering, being altered, the young widow island woman evolving into something else, though what that is, I don't know, what that will be, I don't know. Maybe he knows. The artist man. The Englishman. Maybe he knows what I will become as he draws my hair, my back, my buttocks, my hips, my thighs, my feet, unblemished still by age, as she is, that sleeping woman in artist's aspic. And that is what I want, Mr Lloyd. To be lifted away, off, to some place else where I will endure and live beyond the transience of the everyday, a permanence that others get through god, the after-life, the promise of heaven, but I have already looked there, at that, and there is nothing, only a void that once seen cannot be unseen. I need a remedy against its harshness, Mr Lloyd. Against its bleakness. An after-life of my own. An after-life greater than atomised particles of dust across the kitchen floor. An after-life from an Englishman with sad eyes and a sad mouth, burdened by a need to draw, to paint, to live in isolation on the edge of a cliff, a hermit monk, his paints and brushes an offering to his art god.

Turn over, please, Mairéad.

She paused and stared at him, this artist man who will lift me off the island. I will endure only if you are good, Mr Lloyd. If

215

you are as able as the artist who painted the sleeping woman so that I live as she does, unblemished by the icy winds and needling rain that tear at my face every winter until one day my skin will collapse under the strain, break and blemish as the faces of my mother and grandmother have broken and blemished.

Towards me, he said.

She turned. To face him. With her eyes, her mouth, breasts, stomach, hips, her pubic hair, her knees and feet.

Thank you, he said.

She bowed her head, slightly, and closed her eyes.

Eyes open, he said.

She looked at him looking at her, absorbing her through his eyes, through his pencil. He worked feverishly, a light hum rising from his lips.

island series: mairéad I, face and hair
island series: mairéad II, shoulders and breasts
island series: mairéad III, stomach, hips and pubic hair
island series: mairéad IV, legs and feet
island series: mairéad V, back and buttocks
island series: mairéad

He dropped the pencil and sketchpad to the floor, and, panting, groaning, stood up and walked out of the hut. She wrapped herself in the sheet and picked up the sketchpad to look at herself broken into different body parts, page after page of her shoulders, back, buttocks, breasts, stomach, thighs, pubic hair, knees, feet, then detailed sketches of her face, her chin, whole and smudged, her nose, abandoned after three attempts, as though it was too hard, or too uninteresting, and then her eyes, dozens of them, page after page of sad, lonely eyes, sadder than his, as though he is drawing himself rather than me because his eyes are sad, lonely eyes, but mine are not, not that sad, anyway, not as sad and lonely as his.

He came back in and she put down the sketchpad.

What do you think?

She shrugged her shoulders.

You can't tell me what you think?

Tá sé go maith, she said. Good.

He smiled.

Thank you.

She shivered.

Sorry, you must be cold.

He threw more turf on the fire. She dressed.

Eyes, she said.

What about them?

Sad eyes.

He shrugged.

You have sad eyes, Mairéad. Beautiful, but sad.

He made tea and they sat outside, side by side on his waxed coat, listening to the birds at morning song.

Jim Wright and his twenty-one-year-old daughter sit into his car on Friday morning, July 27th.

He is forty-eight years of age, married with four children. A Protestant man, he is an active member of the King William's Defenders Orange Lodge and a former police reservist. He is a gospel singer and participates too in the Salvation Army.

He is giving his daughter a lift to work before going to his own job as store manager of a garage in Portadown, Co. Armagh. His wife is away on holiday.

He turns the ignition. The car explodes, killing him and seriously injuring his daughter.

The Irish National Liberation Army claims responsibility.

That poor woman away on her holiday, said Mairéad.

Well for her, said Bean Uí Néill.

Ah, Mam. Stop.

At least she got the holiday before her husband died. More than I got. Than you got.

Ah, Mam, that's terrible.

I know it is.

Are you all right, Mam?

I don't suppose we'll ever get a holiday, Mairéad.

Probably not. But sure what would you do with it anyway, Mam?

I'd have a grand time. Away from here.

Mairéad shook her head.

No, you wouldn't. You wouldn't sit still.

I could try.

You'd spend the whole time worrying about the hens. Whether James was gathering the eggs.

Bean Uí Néill laughed.

I imagine that's the truth.

She sighed.

But do you not want a holiday, Mairéad? To go to Greece like your aunt?

I've enough island here, Mam.

A city then?

The town is too big for me.

Bean Uí Néill nodded.

It's too big for me too.

Anyway, they might come back while I'm away.

Who?

Liam, Daddy and Séamus.

Bean Uí Néill stared at her daughter.

Do you really believe that, Mairéad?

Mairéad smiled.

No, not really. But it stops me wanting a holiday.

Bean Uí Néill nodded, slowly.

I suppose it does that. Did you clean their house?

The hens?

I did.

Any extra eggs?

None. We had them all.

James Joseph McCann is walking down Obins Street in the mainly Catholic section of Portadown, Co. Armagh, on Saturday, July 28th. He is twenty years of age and a Catholic. A red Ford Escort car pulls up beside him. It's the Ulster Volunteer Force. They shoot him. James Joseph McCann staggers into the doorway of a nearby pub, still conscious but bleeding heavily. He dies soon afterwards in Craigavon Hospital.

Over ten thousand people at that Portadown funeral, Mam.

Turn it up, Mairéad.

They stopped cooking to listen to the newsreader.

That's a huge funeral.

It's half the town, Mairéad.

How many of them will turn up for that poor Catholic fella? And he only walking along the road.

Won't be half the town anyway.

Not that town, Mam.

Masson walked past the windows, his recorder over his shoulder. He waved at them.

Off to see Bean Uí Fhloinn, said Mairéad.

Have you heard her, Mairéad? On his tape?

I have, Mam.

She sounds ancient, said Bean Uí Néill.

Mairéad laughed.

That'll be you, Mam.

It will not.

It will. Twenty years from now. Some French college lad bent over you, declaring that he has found the last Irish speaker in Ireland.

They laughed and made tea while Masson climbed the hill to

tap on the door of Bean Uí Fhloinn's house. She smiled as he bent down to kiss her.

Foolish Frenchman, she said.

He kissed her on each cheek.

It is a pleasure to be foolish around you, he said.

You have a way about you, JP.

She smacked her lips against her pipe.

You're lucky I'm not a younger woman, JP.

They laughed. He poured tea for them both and sat down.

Though Mairéad is, she said.

He nodded.

Indeed.

And beautiful too, said Bean Uí Fhloinn.

That she is.

Bean Uí Fhloinn drank tea.

The Englishman thinks so too.

I'm sure he does.

I see her coming back from there, early in the morning, when I'm on my walks.

From his hut?

She nodded.

Nothing much passes you, Bean Uí Fhloinn.

Nothing at all, JP.

He leaned back into his chair.

So what do you think she is doing out there? With the Englishman.

No idea, JP.

Does she go into the hut?

From what I can see, JP.

What's she doing in there?

You'll have to ask her, JP.

Ah, it's none of my business, Bean Uí Fhloinn.

She smiled at him.

Is it not, JP?

He nodded, slowly.

As I said, nothing passes you, does it?

No, JP, it does not.

Does her mother know?

About you or the Englishman?

Both, I suppose.

She knows about you well enough, said Bean Uí Fhloinn.

He sipped at his tea.

Though you can never be sure, JP. Áine was never the brightest. Easy to fool.

Does she know about the Englishman? About the hut?

Bean Uí Fhloinn shook her head.

No. She knows nothing about that.

What about Francis? What does he know?

He's waiting in the long grass, JP. You know that. We all know that.

He sat forward, his elbows on his thighs, his hands cupped.

So what do I do?

Nothing. Go on as normal. See what happens. If anything at all.

I appreciate your advice, Bean Uí Fhloinn.

She drew on her pipe.

That Englishman has turned the head of the young lad as well, JP.

James?

She nodded, blowing smoke into the room.

He was here telling me that he's going to be an artist, that he's having an exhibition in London.

That's ambitious.

That he's going to live with Mr Lloyd.

She shook her head, slowly.

There'll be nobody to catch the rabbits when he's gone, she said.

No, said Masson.

No more rabbit stew, she said.

He poured more tea.

And how is the writing, JP?

Going well, Bean Uí Fhloinn.

I hope they make you a professor.

He exhaled, sharply.

So do I, Bean Uí Fhloinn.

He placed his cup on the hearth, leaned further forward and took her hands, nodding at her, smiling, adamant that his work be worthy of the doctorate, of the professorship, but worthy too of a wider audience, of newspaper articles, of television news, of radio documentaries. He lifted her hands and kissed them, for I will invite French journalists to meet you, Bean Uí Fhloinn, the last of the pure Irish speakers, the last woman to live like this, the shawl over your shoulders, the clay pipe, the knitted socks, and I will persuade them to interview you, to listen as you speak this ancient language untouched by modernity, untainted by the invasion of English, the language as it was spoken by your parents, your grandparents, by your great-grandparents, a linguistic lineage that stretches back hundreds, thousands, of years. He dropped her hands, but held them still on his lap. And after they have spoken to you, recorded you, photographed you, filmed you, they will turn to me, the French linguist who found you and captured the last moments of this ancient language, the great French linguist who lived alongside this woman in primitive conditions on the edge of Europe for five years, no electricity, no water, a diet of fish and potatoes, and he should be honoured, dear readers, dear listeners, dear viewers, by the President with the Légion d'honneur for services to culture, for his commitment to this dying language, this ancient beauty. He patted her hands. But then the questions will come, as they always do, Bean Uí Fhloinn. Why the Irish language? Why not the language of the Basque country? Or the Breton language, Professor Masson? Didn't you grow up in Brittany? What do your parents think? They must be very proud, or would they have preferred if you stayed at home and studied their language. We'll ask them. And a rush at the staircase, a swirl of recorders, cameras and notebooks hurrying to the fifth floor to find her still at the window overlooking the distant Atlantic, telling the journalists that she is unsure why he has been in Ireland saving the Irish language when he should be in Algeria learning hers, learning Classical Arabic, Literary Arabic, the language that she tried to teach him as a child, week after week of classes with a man who was deeply committed to the language, to Algeria, a man who, week after week, became increasingly aware of my indifference to his passion, aware too that my father was French, a French soldier, a French colonising soldier who had taken my mother from Algeria to France, my skin lighter than his, my name more French, and for that he slapped me, harder than he slapped the other boys as he walked between our desks, an open hand against the back of my head, a stinging flick of his finger against my cheek, staring at me when he lectured over and over on the awful deeds carried out by the French against the Algerians, the mosques turned into cathedrals, the land taken and sold to self-serving Europeans for a pittance, the language debased, the religion prohibited and, worse again, compulsorily renounced to become French. And the famine. Never forget the famine, boys. Especially you, Masson. An extra wallop to the back of my head. You must never forget the famine, Masson. You must always remember how our great country suffered under the hands of the French, the French who turned us into a version of France, pretty little villages, vineyards, clock towers, when we were nomads, shepherds, our own country with proud traditions, our own ancient languages, but none of it was to be tolerated, all of it to be dismissed, stripped away, do you understand that, boys? Understand that you are to continue the great struggle of what it is to be the son of an Algerian.

I lifted my hand.

But my father is French, I said.

He smacked me on the back of my head, harder than usual. I looked to my mother on the other side of the plastic partition. She was reading and sipping tea, a scarf pulled over her head.

George Walsh is a fifty-one-year-old Protestant police officer who is married and has a child. He is sitting in an unmarked car outside the courthouse in Armagh on Tuesday, July 31st. Two INLA gunmen drive towards his car and open fire, spraying him with bullets, killing him.

Did you hear the Cardinal, Mam?

No.

Calling on them to stop the killing.

Do you think they'll listen?

No.

Nor do I.

I suppose he has to try, said Mairéad.

I suppose he does.

Bean Uí Néill handed Mairéad a basket of clothing.

Take that to JP, will you. I hear him in there with that recorder.

He'll go mad listening to her, back and forth with the tape, back and forth.

Bean Uí Néill shook her head.

A madman in the village, a madman on the cliff, that's some summer.

Mairéad took the basket. She placed it on the chair beside Masson.

That's ready for you.

Thank you, Mairéad. Would you like some coffee?

She sat down.

I would.

He set water on the fire to boil.

You look tired, Mairéad.

Do I?

She smiled.

It's probably your fault.

Probably.

He sat back down. He turned on the recorder.

She likes you, JP, the attention you pay her.

I enjoy it, Mairéad.

They listened, her voice cracking, fragmenting.

She's more fragile than I thought, said Mairéad. Older.

She is.

Her language is older too.

Irish is changing rapidly, Mairéad.

She patted his hand.

It's good to have, JP.

The water bubbled, boiled. He made coffee and stood the pot and two cups on the table.

Would you like milk, Mairéad?

I would. And sugar.

He stirred in the sugar and the milk. He turned on the recorder again. They drank and listened.

She knows a lot, he said.

Ah, she talks stuff and nonsense. Story after story.

She's a reliable witness, Mairéad.

That's true, JP. She misses nothing.

He reached towards her and curled her hair behind her ear.

She tells me you've been out at the Englishman's hut.

She drank from the cup, glad of the sweetness.

I was there, and beyond, out on the cliffs.

What were you doing?

What's it to you?

I'm interested.

Why?

He poured more coffee. She added her own sugar, her own milk.

I'm looking for Liam, JP.

Masson lifted his cup.

Of course you are.

He drank.

Well? he said.

Well what?

Have you found him?

She shook her head.

No, not yet.

How often do you go out there, Mairéad, looking for him? She shrugged.

It depends. More in summer than in winter. In winter I stay near here. Down at the cove, on the beach.

Always looking.

Always.

When will you stop?

When I find him. Or a trace of him.

Mairéad stood then.

Thank you for the coffee, JP.

Masson emptied the laundry basket and handed it to her.

Will you come tonight?

As you said yourself, I'm tired.

He resumed his work, filling the room again with sounds of Bean Uí Fhloinn, protector of the language, custodian, defiant of, indifferent to, the conventions of linguistic studies, the ones asserting that women change language faster than men to improve the lot of their children, to increase their children's chances of social advancement. Not Bean Uí Fhloinn. Language loyalist. Linguistic warrior. Nor my mother, insisting on obscure classes in Classical Arabic when I wanted French, to speak French, to read French, to be French. Not as she was. As she is. Up there still on the fifth floor, at the window overlooking the distant sea. Woman in no-man's land.

Walking home from those classes, she told me the stories of the other boys and their mothers, their bodies more covered than hers, their French less polished so that they spoke instead in the Arabic of their childhood streets, telling stories of how they had arrived in France, of where they bought their food, of how they managed in the northern cold, northern rain, when they were used to light and heat, but I had no interest in those stories, those boys, those classmates, as I had classmates of my own, French-speaking ones, boys I wanted to play with, know better, spend time with in the park, on the football pitch, speaking French as they did, though she would not let me out to play with them, insisting instead on those classes, those boys, those good boys who are at lessons, not in parks playing foul-mouthed football. I did not want those boys, my mother's boys, though I could not say that to her, my already sad mother, my already lonely mother, could not tell her that I hated Classical Arabic, hated that teacher, those boys, those women in their dark clothes, that I was a child of ten years too weak to bear the weight of her disappointment. I walked on beside her, silent. Acquiescing to the repeated narrative of her childhood, the days before she met my father, she would tell me of when she was in the Catholic college studying French literature, a young, beautiful Algerian francophone, Francophile, ripe for my handsome father when he came with the war, with his seed of me that he planted in her, that growth declaring that she was no longer Algerian, no longer one of them, no longer safe as she was different to them, French, she assumed, as she got into a boat to leave, to cross the Mediterranean, to land in the country of her dreams, ripe for France as my father had been ripe for her, her reading and thinking ready for the cafés teeming with intellectuals, for the street-corner politics, the discussion and debate over dinner tables, lunch tables, breakfast tables, for the talk of books, of films, of theatre, but found only silence, isolation on the fifth-floor apartment that he, the French soldier, had secured for his new family. Although he was no longer a soldier, rather a mechanic who fixed cars, an expert on the deep cleaning of carburettors, rendering her an expert on the removal of oil stains from overalls, fresh overalls every day, his name over the left breast pocket, though her name was nowhere, other than on letters she received intermittently from her family in Algeria, though they were rare, a woman on the periphery waiting for her son to start school so that she could finally meet French women, go to French houses, take part in French lives, French lunches and dinners, but found nothing more than polite conversation in the schoolyard about children and homework, about swimming galas and birthday parties, but nothing about books, about theatre, about politics, forcing her sideways, me with her, to the Algerians in France, to Arabic newspapers and books, to headscarves and long skirts so that she could talk politics with the men in the shops, the old men and their sons at the tills, trading news on politics, on memories and stories of home, laughing and smiling with them as she never smiled with my father who was no longer a car mechanic but a post-office worker, a civil servant of the French state who shouted at her to shorten her skirt, to take off her scarf, shouted at her that she was married to a Frenchman, that that marriage made her French. But I'm not French, she said. I'm nothing. Nowhere. Woman in no-man's land. You're in my land, my house, no long skirts, no scarves. She shortened her skirts but still wore the scarves in the shops where the men talked to her about Arabic classes for her son, where the men talked to me in Arabic but I answered back in French.

Paul Reece, a nineteen-year-old signalman, and Richard James Furminger, a nineteen-year-old gunner, are part of the army convoy sent to South Armagh to examine the burnt-out vehicle used in the killing of Constable George Walsh.

It is Thursday, August 2nd. Paul Reece, from Crewe in England, and Richard James Furminger, from Colchester, England, have been in Northern Ireland for nine days.

The IRA has planted a 400 lb bomb in a culvert near the burnt-out car.

The investigation complete, the UDR leads the army convoy from the scene, travelling along the road between Armagh and Moy, close to the Irish border. The teenage soldiers are in a Land Rover in the middle of the convoy. The IRA bomb explodes. The Land Rover falls into the crater created by the bomb. IRA gunmen open fire on the soldiers in the Land Rover, killing the two teenagers.

They're not paying much attention to the Cardinal, said Mairéad.

They are not, said Bean Uí Néill. Maybe they'll listen to the Pope when he comes next month.

Maybe they will, Mam. Maybe they won't.

Mairéad scrubbed at the potatoes.

Will you go to see him, Mam?

Bean Uí Néill shook her head.

Too far away for me, Mairéad.

She tapped her chest, her head.

I have him inside me anyway, Mairéad. Morning, noon and night.

A woman in West Belfast calls the police on Thursday, August 2nd to say that her house has been burgled. She tells them that she is just back from holiday and is distressed by the discovery. The police check the woman's authenticity and send two officers to investigate.

The officers drive to her home in Clondara Street off the Falls Road. They are getting out of the Land Rover when the IRA opens fire from an upstairs window on the opposite side of the road, killing twenty-six-year-old Constable Derek Davidson, a Protestant married man with a four-year-old daughter, originally from Edinburgh.

Lloyd woke early, stirred by the light spilling into the hut. He dressed quickly and went outside to catch the sun rising out of the sea, the ball of red fire reaching across the surface of the still ocean, spreading crimson, scarlet, vermillion, stirring the birds on the rocky cliffs
feathered monks
in their cathedral choir
He sketched, in pencil
pagans at matins
heralding
the christ sun
He drew until the sun climbed out of the sea, the morning performance ending as the colours settled into blues, yellows and whites. He stayed a little longer, breathing deeply, the cool air cleaning his lungs, and returned to the hut empty of Mairéad, despite the strength of the light. He drew her anyway, imagining how the light would have fallen on her face, on the contours of her breasts, her hips.

He ate breakfast, tea and porridge, enough milk for both, gathered up his tools and went out to the cliffs. James was already there, on his belly reaching over the edge, sketchpad and pencil in his hands.

You're early, James.

I want the light, he said.

It's good today.

The way the sun sparkles on the rock, Mr Lloyd.

Lloyd set up his easel with a small canvas and painted the sun on the sea, the birds, the grass. He switched to pencil and drew James on his stomach with sketchpad and pencil.

island series: the artist's apprentice

They worked in silence, each cocooned in his attempt to draw, then paint, then draw again the fall of light on the water, on the rocks, the ripple of wind across the tufts of grass, through the wings of gulls and cormorants swirling in the sky.

At eleven, James produced a flask of tea, milk already added, two cups, and bread with jam and butter. They sat together and looked over the sea, at the birds banking and diving.

You don't mind, do you, James?

Mind what?

My painting your mother.

He shrugged.

It's not me you have to worry about.

Your grandmother?

No, she doesn't know about Mam. Not yet anyway.

So who do I have to worry about?

Francis.

Lloyd poured more tea.

Why would I worry about him? What's it got to do with him?

More than you think.

I don't care about Francis.

You should.

Why should I?

He's my father's brother.

Lloyd shook his head.

Francis doesn't bother me, James. But as her son, what do you think?

I'm irrelevant.

How can you be?

I have my life, she has hers.

That's very grown up of you.

Is it? She stays out of my head, I stay out of hers.

Lloyd shrugged.

I never managed that with my mother.

Maybe you had a big house. In a little house on a little island you have no choice.

There might be some truth in that.

Is she still alive?

Yes, both my parents are, though I see them seldom.

And your wife? When do you see her?

You ask a lot of questions, James.

You know everything about us. My turn to ask you.

That's fair.

So, when do you see your wife?

I'll see her when I get back to London.

Is she at your house now?

Maybe. Probably not.

Where is she then?

We live together sometimes.

And other times?

She's with another man.

Ah.

It gets worse.

How's that, Mr Lloyd?

She prefers his work to mine.

James shook his head.

That is bad.

They laughed.

I prefer your work to his.

You don't know his work.

I prefer yours anyway.

You're very kind, James.

And loyal, Mr Lloyd.

Yes, that too, James. Very loyal.

I thought that you were married.

So did I.

So you're not married?

I am and I'm not.

You've lost me, Mr Lloyd. My mother was married. Now she's not. You're either married, or you're not.

Maybe I'm half married. Sometimes married. Sometimes not.

So then your wife is half married too.

No, James. She is always married. Half married to me, half married to him. That makes her always married.

Which do you prefer? Being half married or half not married?

Good question, James.

Lloyd wiped crumbs from his chest.

I'm not sure, James. Sometimes I miss being married, some-times I don't.

James stood up and walked to the easel.

It's very good, Mr Lloyd.

I hope so.

You understand the light a lot better.

You're right, James. I do.

See, I'm useful.

You are, James.

You should include it in the exhibition, Mr Lloyd.

Maybe. We'll wait to the end of the summer. Decide then.

James laughed.

What's funny?

That's why she'll do the exhibition, Mr Lloyd.

I don't understand.

Your wife.

What do you mean?

A half-exhibition for a half-husband.

Lloyd smiled.

You're right, James. That's why she'll do it.

James packed away the flask and cups, the tea towel that had held the bread, and the two returned to their work, to their silence.

William Whitten, sixty-five, dies in hospital on Friday, August 3rd, from injuries sustained in June when the IRA bombed five hotels across Northern Ireland. The retired Protestant businessman, originally from Co. Clare in the Irish Republic, had been on holiday with his wife in the Marine Hotel in Ballycastle, Co. Antrim when the bomb exploded on June 19th.

Mairéad pushed open the door of the hut. Lloyd was still in bed.

Gabh mo leithscéal, she said.

He shook his head, to wake himself.

I'm sorry, she said.

It's raining, he said.

She nodded.

It is.

There's no light, Mairéad. You need to come when the sun is shining.

She shrugged, rain dripping from her hair.

Tá mé anseo anois.

Lloyd dressed.

What does that mean?

I'm here now.

Yes. Yes, you are.

He pulled on his boots but left them unlaced and drew instead, the rain dripping from her hair to her shoulders. He turned the page and set a chair in the middle of the kitchen, under the window, his laces flicking against the floor as he moved.

Sit there, he said.

She sat.

And take off your clothes. Only from your torso. Keep your skirt on.

She shook her head.

Ní thuigim. I don't understand.

He dropped his hands to his waist and lifted them over his head.

Á, tuigim.

He drew the droplets of rain falling onto her breasts, the grey light splintering on the beads of water. He drew her hair matted by the rain. And her face, moistened.

island series: woman after rain

He worked quickly but threw down the sketchpad. He laced his boots and went outside. He returned with three gull feathers. He gave them to her.

Hold them, he said. In your right hand.

She took them and he began to tug at her skirt, her mother's old garment of red wool. She stood up. He opened the hooks on the side and hitched the skirt until it sat under her breasts. He directed her back towards the right side of the chair. She sat down. He tilted her onto her left hip and placed her left hand flat on the chair.

Are you all right? he said.

Fine, she said.

He drew.

island series: woman with feathers, after gauguin

You can get dressed, he said.

She picked up her clothes and took a jar filled with milk from a pocket.

246

For our tea, she said.

Good idea, he said. Thank you.

They sat on chairs drinking tea and looked at his drawing of her with feathers.

It's beautiful, she said.

Thank you.

She pointed at Gauguin's name.

Céard é sin? Cé hé sin?

He's an artist. French. I'll show you his work. In the cottage. She nodded.

Nuair a bheas tú ar ais. When you're back.

She left and he continued drawing, indifferent to his hunger, glad of the rain that kept James away

not for him

son's eyes

as he drew the curves of her breasts, of her hips, the curls of her hair, eliciting from her, from himself, a beauty that he had not expected, had not felt running through his fingers for many years, ten at least, when he last drew Judith, when she was younger, as young as Mairéad, his fingers and body pulsing as he created her contours, laboured over each piece of her, her hair, eyes, nose and lips, her shoulders, breasts, stomach and buttocks, her pubic hair, her fingernails, her hips, thighs, calves, her ankles, feet and toes, picking his way along her body, digging his way into her, hour after hour of drawing then painting, matching paint to her skin, to her freckles, her blemishes, to her beauty, the work his only focus for weeks, his wife banned from seeing until it was finished, his artist wife renowned for her capacity with patterns and shapes, while he was renowned for drawing, for colours and tones, certain that this portrait of his artist wife would secure attention for them, fame, money, enough to lift them out of basement living where they would lie together, laughing, him in her, a single entity, she said, the perfect artist, he said, her skills and his blended into one, into an artist couple that would dominate the artistic world, his painting of her an introduction, a calling card that he finally, eventually finished, after weeks of work, and presented it to her, laid it at her feet, but she shook her head, flicked her wrist, adamant that it was too conventional, too traditional for the momentum they needed to create. Too predictable. Too boring. A likeness, yes, but nothing more. Nothing more than a photograph

damning it

me

us

He switched to landscapes

silent

in their opinions

and she drifted away, bored of his subtlety, the quiet nuance of his work, preferring instead the loud, the declaratory, the bold, the striking art that she began to sell to the wealthy, to those in penthouse apartments and refurbished, redesigned, remodelled Knightsbridge homes. She began too to hunt for a louder husband, for a man who wanted what she wanted, one after another until he was finally chosen, a modernist, committed, certain to succeed, the new half-husband the subject of the first solo exhibition in her new gallery, the old half-husband banished from the city of art to live alone, isolated, on an island, eating potatoes and fish, drawing a woman who was not his wife, not his half-wife, not his any wife, but an intimacy growing nonetheless with each twist and turn of his wrist, of his pencil, his charcoal, the half-husband creating works to confound his half-wife

beauty unearthed

hers

mine

Eamon Ryan is a civil servant in Dublin and has returned to his home town of Tramore, Co. Waterford, for a summer holiday with his wife and two children. His is thirty-two years of age.

He goes to the bank in the town with his two-and-a-half-year-old son on Tuesday, August 7th. Four IRA men, armed and masked, burst into the bank demanding money.

Eamon Ryan tries to leave the bank with his son and other customers. He is wrenched back into the bank by a gunman and is shot at point-blank range. His child stays beside him, sitting by his father's body as the raid continues.

James brought a cup of tea and a slice of bread with jam to
Masson.

Go raibh maith agat.

You're welcome, said James.

You should speak to me in Irish, James.

Why should I, JP?

It's the language of your ancestors.

So is English. Has been for centuries, JP.

Not on this island.

James shrugged.

I'm leaving anyway, he said. I'm going to London.

I heard that.

I'm doing an exhibition with Mr Lloyd.

You'll be world famous, Séamus.

I will. And my name will be James.

He left. Masson returned to his work, the drift from Irish on
the island accelerated by the arrival of the English-speaking
artist, the changes most obvious in Mairéad and James, as
Mairéad now speaks English intermittently and James regularly uses English in response to questions and comments
in Irish, as I did, in those shops, fathers and sons at the tills,
my mother irritated as I answered in French, annoyed by her

son's rudeness towards the gentle, civil men who wanted only to include me in their conversation when I wanted instead to look like the Frenchmen in that café that I passed every morning on my way to school, my father among them leaning sideways into the bar, looking onto the street, his morning coffee on the counter, a cigarette on the curl of his lower lip, greeting people as they passed, a nod, a wave, a hello, his gauge on the relationship, an acquaintance, a neighbour, a friend. He waved at me. His half-French son. He nodded at my mother. His non-French wife, against whom he would rail, in the evenings, after work. Her cooking, her clothes, her smell, her reading, shouting that she was too embarrassing to take to his friends, to his family, dressed like that, talking like that, smelling like that, and that she was thwarting his prospects at the post office, his chances of promotion, the jobs in management given instead to the yellow-bellied cowards who stayed home and married French women while he went to war, the yellow-bellied cowards who climbed into the upstairs offices, into bigger cars, bigger paycheques, who grew fat and smug, indifferent to his status as a decorated soldier, indifferent when those men should be on their knees in gratitude to him for his service to the country, for risking his life against the savages in Algeria, those dirty nomads who emerged from the desert sands to demand independence from France when it was France that paved their streets, educated their children, built their towns, their town halls, their schools, hospitals, houses, supplied their water, their sanitation. All of it built by France. Shouting now. At her. At me. Yelling. There was nothing there before France arrived, nothing, not even toilets, his anger pinning me to the floor, to a place midway between him at the kitchen table and my mother at the sink, washing dishes, her shuttered eyes telling me not to talk, to be silent about the fathers and sons at the tills, about the Arabic that I was learning, silent about the Algerian man who was teaching me grammar, history and politics, silent about the twice-weekly lessons that my father knew nothing of for my mother was careful that we were home before seven, home before him, the winter cold gone from us, from our coats, from our skin, the dinner already prepared, ready to eat at seven, when he walked in, simmering bile, her shuttered eyes telling me to stand still as he railed again against her, the town's whore who had thrown herself from one soldier to the next, hunting with her beauty for a Frenchman, a French fool who would fall for her and rescue her from that pit of a country. And I am that idiot, he shouted. That fool that crawled between your legs. I am that sucker. Sucked by you. Until now I am this, living like this, a man without prospects, a man married to a whore from that pit of a country.

I need to do homework, I said, and I went to my room, to do homework already done.

William Arthur McGraw is at the pub on Friday night, August 10th. He is a Protestant man from outside Garvagh, a village in South Derry. He is twenty-nine years of age and a bricklayer. Three of his brothers are members of the UDR. Another brother is a prison officer.

He accepts the offer of a lift home. The car stops outside his house. As he gets out, one of the men in the car shouts after him. He turns back towards the car and is shot six times in the face, chest and body.

His father finds him dead on the doorstep.

Mairéad carried cleaned clothes to Lloyd's cottage. She set them down on the kitchen table and looked through his books, for James was out on the cliffs and the Englishman was in his hut. She found Gauguin, opened the book and stumbled, almost winded by the vitality of the work, of the women, their bodies, their ease with themselves, with the artist looking at them, painting them. She steadied the book on the table and turned each page to look at the paintings, the drawings, thrilled by the yellows, oranges, blues, pinks, reds, by blue grass and yellow sky. She reached the end of the book and started again. She returned the book to the shelf but retrieved it early the next day and carried it to the hut, waking him though the light was again grey. She made tea while he dressed and restarted the fire. They sat side by side in front of the burning turf, looking at the paintings, soaking in their warmth, blending it with the warmth of the flames, of the tea.

He looked up at the windows.

The light is getting better, Mairéad.

Go maith. Good.

He lifted the mattress from his bed. She took off her clothes and lay down, partly covering herself with the sheet.

Actually, stand up, he said.

She pressed her hands into the floor and stood. He pointed at her knickers, white cotton greyed by washing, by years of wearing.

Those are wrong, he said.

He shook the pillow from its case. He brought it towards her.

My hands are cold, he said.

He wrapped the pillow case around her hips, tucking it into her knickers.

It's not perfect, he said. But it'll do.

She shook her head.

No. Not right.

She reached into her clothes and pulled out her green scarf. She wrapped it around her hips. He clapped.

Perfect, he said.

He put his hands on her hips and turned her slightly to the side, angling her so that her right hip was closer to him than her left. He lifted his hands into the air.

As though picking an apple from the tree, Mairéad.

She reached her arms upwards. He drew.

island series: woman picking apple, after gauguin

And lift your head, Mairéad. To look at the apple.

She tilted her head.

Eve in the Garden of Eden, he said.

She shook her head.

Ní thuigim.

Eve. Garden. Apple.

She smiled.

Tuigim. I understand.

She looked up at her hands, cracked and reddened from cleaning, her cuticles split, inflamed in spots, tender, sometimes sore, the hand cream in the yellow tub only a veneer at the end of each day, a coating when I need a lotion that repairs, that burrows into my skin, as he burrows now with his pencil, more deeply than before, his breath heavier than it was, his eyes more focused.

Reach your arms a little higher, Mairéad.

She reached up.

But still a bend in your elbows.

She bent her elbows.

That's it. Perfect. Thank you.

Penetrating. Digging. Deeper and deeper. And I want him to have it, Liam. To find it. This thing that is mine. Though I don't know what it is. Only that it is. Somewhere. Buried deep in the softness of my breasts, my belly, my groin. I want him to unearth it, this thing, this thing that is me, beyond the beauty that everybody sees, beyond that, beyond too what Mam sees, what James sees, what Francis sees, what JP sees, what JP thinks he sees, closer to what it is that you saw, Liam, all those years ago, the truth of me as I was then, I want that unearthed, captured, and taken away. Far from here.

He threw three pieces of turf on the fire to quell the goose bumps crawling across her skin.

Just ten minutes more, Mairéad.

She nodded, though her arms ached.

Far from here on the white walls of a London gallery, men

and women, with white wine, red wine, gin and tonic, a twist of lemon, pausing in front of me, the artist's latest subject, his object, a creature of beauty unearthed on a remote Irish island, a place so far from civilisation that he had to row across the ocean in a handmade boat, expecting at the end of that treacherous journey to find only old hags with their toothless men, but instead he found beauty, the young sleeping woman, Eve in the garden, woman sitting, woman lying, woman after rain, and they, the sophisticated men and women of London, will toast him, his bravery, his intrepidness, kiss his cheeks, shake his hand, this great painter, this great English painter, this great English painter of Irish women, his work encapsulating the exotic spiritualism of the Irish as I stretch for his imagined apple, my breasts, stomach and the silver traces of my boy's gestation rising and stretching with me.

He turned to a fresh sheet of paper.

island series: woman picking apple

Dig deeper, Mr Lloyd, though they will be furious, Francis and my mother, livid that I would stand like this for you, an Englishman. Standing in only your knickers, Mairéad, your arms in the air for an imagined apple. How could you? Lying down, a sheet over you, eyes closed, vulnerable in that sleep, but adored by the artist, watched over as you slept, protected, that we could tolerate, we could turn a blind eye to that, as we turn a blind eye to you and JP, but standing as you are standing, a bit of a scarf over your knickers, that is very different, Mairéad. Standing like that for an Englishman, for an English audience, that is beyond the pale, Mairéad.

He threw the sketchpad to the floor. Then the pencil. He stood up.

It's done, he said. Thank you.

She bent down and turned the pages, looking at herself as he saw her.

It's good, she said.

It will be great, Mairéad.

She turned more pages.

But not yet, she said. Not ready.

He shook his head.

I agree. Not ready yet. I don't have you yet.

She gathered her clothes and started to dress. He put water on to boil.

Will you have tea? he said.

I will.

She sat on a chair to pull on her tights. Lloyd began to whistle. She went outside and he followed, handing her a cup. They stood beside each other, again looking at the morning sea, the morning birds.

This could be my best work, Mairéad.

Tá áthas orm, she said.

What does that mean?

I'm happy, she said. But more to do.

He smiled at her.

Yes, Mairéad. More to do.

She returned the cup to him.

Thank you for coming this morning, Mairéad.

She turned towards the village.

Tomorrow, she said. Here.

He laughed.

Yes, Mairéad. Tomorrow. Here.

She walked from him. He shouted after her.

Tell James to let me know when Micheál arrives.

She waved at him.

I need to talk to him. To Micheál.

She walked back along the promontory, through grass saturated with dew, through strands of freshly woven web glistening in the morning sun. She released the hens and reached in to collect the eggs, some warm, but most already cold. She scooped up the base of her cardigan and gathered the eggs, twelve eggs in a woollen sling of blackberries and diamonds, the morning air cold against her belly.

You're late, Mairéad.

I went further than I realised, she said.

Bean Uí Néill snorted.

Any further than you realise and you're in the sea.

I lost track of time.

Set the table, Mairéad. Cut the bread.

Twelve eggs today, Mam.

At least the hens are doing as they are supposed to.

Mairéad picked the eggs from her cardigan and set them into a wooden bowl.

They're good hens, all right.

Bean Uí Néill poured the water into the teapot.

Did you see the Englishman?

No. I was over the other side.

How was your walk?

Lovely light today, Mam. The way it falls on the sea.

Bean Uí Néill set the teapot on the table.

You're beginning to sound like that Englishman.

Mairéad shrugged.

JP will be here in a minute, she said.

Starving as usual, said Bean Uí Néill.

He eats a lot, said Mairéad.

And not a pick on him.

No.

He's skin and bone. That's all there is to him.

That's all there is, Mam.

Mairéad spread the plates, bowls, cups and cutlery across the table. She unwrapped the bread and began to cut, white first, then brown. She fetched butter, jam and milk, and called on James. He came to the table dressed, but his hair tossed, traces of paint along the side of his neck. She wet her thumb with her saliva and rubbed at the paint.

He moved away.

Leave it, Mam. It's fine.

You should wash yourself properly.

What's the point? I'll only get more on me today.

Masson sat at his usual breakfast spot, beside James and opposite Mairéad. Bean Uí Néill placed four bowls of porridge on the table. They began to eat.

What's the plan for today, Séamus?

My name is James, and I don't have a plan.

What about you, JP? said Bean Uí Néill.

I'll work and then take a walk along the cliffs.

You should go to Mr Lloyd, said James.

I'm not in the mood for confrontation today, Séamus.

Mairéad poured tea and drank.

Are you all right, Mairéad? You look pale.

I'm fine, JP. Just tired.

Mairéad is always tired, said Bean Uí Néill. Into bed too late, out of bed too early.

It must be that, said Mairéad.

What's the forecast like, Bean Uí Néill?

Grand today, JP, but to be bad later this week. I imagine Mícheál and Francis will be here today or tomorrow.

Mairéad gathered the emptied bowls, the used spoons.

You'll need to get Mr Lloyd when Mícheál shows.

Why?

He wants him.

How do you know?

Mairéad lifted the crockery.

He said it.

When?

She went to the back kitchen, to the sink, the Frenchman returned to his cottage, to his desk, and James went to the studio, to work at the easel. His fifth piece for the exhibition. A portrait of three women, his mother on the right with her knitting, his grandmother in the centre holding the teapot, and his great-grandmother on the left with her pipe. *Mná na hÉireann*. Women of Ireland. After Rembrandt. The three of them looking out at me like the men of the Drapers' Guild, red on their skirts, black on their chests, dark shawls over their heads, though my mother's hair is bare. The three of them staring at me, the only man in the house and he about to leave, skedaddle away to live as he wants, a life that has nothing to do with their lives, nothing to do with catching food, preparing food, eating food, sleeping, waking to do the same again, one day the same as the next, marooned on a grey rock, repeating the cycle, over and over, again and again. Away I go. Away from the young widow island woman, the middle-aged widow island woman, the old widow island woman, three widow island women knitting, drinking tea, smoking her pipe. And waiting. Waiting for their men to crawl out of the sea. For their lives to restart.

Micheál and Francis walked by the studio window carrying boxes, the women behind them. Francis looked in and tapped on the window. He beckoned James. James shook his head. Francis tapped harder. James sighed, dropped his brush and followed them into the kitchen. Francis was holding up two books, one on drawing, the other on European art.

I suppose these are for you, James.

James nodded.

The one on drawing.

Francis paused, the two books still aloft.

Just one?

James took the book about drawing.

So, who is the other one for?

Mairéad stepped towards him.

It's for me, she said.

He laughed.

You?

Yes, Francis. For me.

Francis opened the book.

What do you want with a book like this?

Give it to me, Francis.

You know nothing about this stuff, Mairéad.

He turned the pages, slowly, one then another.

It's got naked women in here, Mairéad.

Give me the book, Francis.

Did you know it had naked women in here?

It's art, Francis.

He mocked her.

It's art, Francis.

He flicked the pages of the book.

Did you know, Bean Uí Néill, that your daughter is bringing pictures of naked women onto the island?

I didn't, Francis.

Francis shook his head.

That's not a good way to be going about things, Mairéad.

He closed the book. He handed it to her.

I hope you're not sucking up to that English artist.

She took the book. She put it on the dresser and unpacked the rest of the shopping. She sent James to fetch Lloyd.

He wants to talk to you about something, Micheál.

The two men sat at the kitchen table, waiting. Drinking tea. Smoking cigarettes. The women peeled potatoes and washed cabbage in the back kitchen. James returned with Lloyd. They sat down. Mairéad poured fresh tea.

I need a canvas, Micheál, said Lloyd.

For painting on?

Yes.

How do I get that, Mr Lloyd?

There's a shop in Dublin.

Micheál laughed.

I've never been to Dublin, Mr Lloyd.

I'm sure they can send it to you. I've written down the name of the shop.

Lloyd slid a piece of paper towards him.

I'll telephone when I get back across.

Thank you.

What type of canvas, Mr Lloyd?

Large, unframed, for oils. The best they have.

What's large? said Micheál.

Fifty-five inches by a hundred and forty-eight inches.

Micheál set down his cup.

I'll never get that, Mr Lloyd.

I'll pay you fifty per cent more than the cost in the shop.

Micheál smiled.

That's fair, Mr Lloyd. Right then. I'll do my best.

And I need wood, said Lloyd. One by two inches. Enough to frame the canvas and hold it in place with six or seven stanchions. And a box of short nails. Light ones.

That's not a problem, Mr Lloyd.

Thank you.

Lloyd stood up.

I need it by next week.

He left, and Micheál buried his head in his hands.

That damn man.

Bean Uí Néill laughed.

Good luck with that now, Micheál.

You understand English better than I thought, Bean Uí Néill.

It's good enough to laugh at you.

You're enjoying this too much, Áine Uí Néill. Where am I supposed to get a canvas that size? It's huge.

You may take a bus to Dublin, Micheál. Carry it home on your back.

I could tell him that I couldn't find it.

And lose all that profit? You're not going to do that, are you, Micheál?

He shook his head.

No, Áine. I'm not.

Francis opened the book on drawing still on the table. He turned the pages, slowly.

What's he going to do with the canvas, James?

I don't know, said James.

You're with him all the time.

I've no idea what he's doing, Francis.

What about you, Mairéad? What have you heard?

She shrugged.

What would I know, Francis?

You must see him sometimes. Out there. On your cliff walks.

She shook her head.

I walk the other side.

He pointed at framed drawings spread over two pages of the book.

The drawings in here are small, he said. The canvas he wants is huge.

He closed the book, his right hand resting on it.

I don't like his plan, said Francis.

Maybe he's doing the cliffs, said Micheál. Like he said he would.

He'd have to do that from a boat, said James. To get perspective.

Francis snorted.

Perspective, me arse.

James was silent.

Perspective doesn't catch you a fish, said Francis. Doesn't feed your mother and grandmother.

Bean Uí Néill poured tea for Francis. She placed a slice of bread on his plate. He smiled at her and ate.

What harm can he do? said Micheál.

A lot of harm, said Bean Uí Néill.

Some paint on a canvas, that's all it is.

She shook her head.

It's more than that, Micheál. We don't know what he's up to.

Ah, Áine. He's come here with a paintbrush, not a gun.

You can do a lot of damage with a paintbrush.

Micheál sighed.

You're being daft, Áine.

Am I? Look at the paintings in that book Mairéad brought into the house.

Ah Jaysus, Áine, he's not up in that hut painting naked women.

I know that, Micheál, but he'll leave with a huge canvas that will be his view of us. Of the island.

JP is writing a book about us, said Micheál. You don't mind that.

It's different, said Bean Uí Néill.

It is, Áine. But it's also the same.

She shook her head.

I won't understand what JP is writing, she said. But I will understand the picture.

Mairéad stood up and went into the back kitchen.

Maybe he'll make us famous, said Micheál. People will come from around the world to see us.

I don't like it, said Bean Uí Néill.

Micheál shrugged.

I probably won't find the canvas anyway, he said.

Oh, you will, Micheál. And you'll leave us with your mess.

Bean Uí Néill followed Mairéad. James fingered the shopping still on the table.

I'll take the orders to JP and Mr Lloyd, he said.

They both wanted shaving foam and razors, said Micheál. JP wanted soap. For Mr Lloyd there's a box of pencils and charcoal.

James delivered first to Masson, who was out walking, then to Lloyd who was in his studio, tidying his paint drawer.

You're causing a stir, said James.

Am I? And why is that?

Nobody understands why you want so big a canvas.

And they have sent you to find out.

No. I came anyway.

So you don't want to know why I want the big canvas.

James shrugged.

I never said that.

It's for a single work, James. The best piece of work I may ever do.

That's exciting, Mr Lloyd.

It's an Irish version of a Gauguin painting.

Can I see it?

No. Not yet.

I won't tell anyone.

I'm not ready to show you. To show anybody.

When will you be ready?

I don't know.

James turned to leave.

Stay. You need to tidy this mess. You've turned into a messy worker, James. Lids off tubes, paint drying out, brushes not properly washed.

I wasn't expecting you back, Mr Lloyd.

That may well be, but wash these brushes and sweep the floor.

Yes, Mr Lloyd.

James went to the sink in the back kitchen and rubbed white spirits into the brushes, weaving his fingers through the bristles, breaking down the paint, splashing flecks of white, grey, blue, black and red across the sink. He dried the bristles with a cloth and began sweeping.

Can I stay in your house in London, Mr Lloyd?

We'll see, James.

Is it far from your house to the art school?

No. Not far.

I can go to art school and be your assistant.

Only if you wash your brushes and sweep the floor.

Yes, Mr Lloyd.

And close paint tubes.

Yes, Mr Lloyd.

You used to be tidy, James.

My art is better when I'm messy, Mr Lloyd. When I forget about being tidy.

Lloyd nodded.

A true artist then.

That's right, Mr Lloyd.

He finished sweeping and retrieved his *Mná na hÉireann*. He perched it on a chair and knelt in front of the three women.

Not today, James.

I have to finish this, Mr Lloyd.

I need to work alone today.

So what should I do?

Lloyd shrugged.

Go to the cliffs, James. Practise drawing.

James stood up, slowly.

Get some rabbits as well.

James closed the door and Lloyd taped several sheets of paper together and stretched them across the kitchen table. He locked the doors not for him

apprentice eyes

He drew in pencil, Mairéad, standing, almost naked, to the right of the centre, reaching for an apple, the other islanders around her, James with two rabbits, Bean Uí Néill with her teapot, Bean Uí Fhloinn dressed in black, leaning on her stick, smoking her pipe, Micheál with his boat and bag of money, Francis with two fish, Masson in a beret holding his black recorder, all of them stretched across the horizontal plain filled with grasses, sea, cliffs, beaches and rock, filled with animals, tamed and wild, a gull, a hen, a dog, a sheep, a cormorant, a pig, a cat, a fish, a puffin, a cow, and he drew then the island's ghosts and spirits, the three drowned fishermen, half on land, half in the sea, their boat, nets and dead fish spilling from a bucket, and, in the distance, a darkened priest holding a cross, ethereal.

island series: where do we come from? what are we? where are we going? after gauguin

He rolled up the drawing and carried it upstairs to the room where he slept, setting it on the floor on the far side of his bed, away from James who was on the cliff, his eyes tracking the movement of light, left and right, up and down, scanning the surface for change and disparity, as though tracing rabbits, marking the fall of light into clefts and crevices as he marked a rabbit disappearing into the ground beneath him. He drew then, long vertical lines, his eyes and hands working together, a hum rising from his lips as he shaded and lightened, as he drew and redrew, page after page. And then he laughed. I am turning into you, Mr Lloyd. A madman out here on the cliffs, drawing and humming to myself, my hand out here on the edge dancing with my brain, swirling and twisting and turning and spinning, mind and fingers working as one, as they never do back there, back there killing rabbits, catching fish, pulling cabbage, planting potatoes, digging turnips, collecting eggs, cleaning sheds, back there listening to Francis, to my granny, to my mother, watching her, watching them, watching them watching me.

He drew waves pounding the rock, sea hammering the cliff, ocean crashing into the island. He drew water foaming and frothing, water splashing, water surging, page after page, none of it capturing the thunderous roar of the Atlantic Ocean on its passage east from America, south-east from the Arctic Circle. How do you draw noise, Mr Lloyd? How do I paint the clangour of battle between ocean and land, sea and rock? The sounds reverberating against the stone, cracking the air? The raucousness of gulls? Of terns? I draw them open-beaked, but still they are silent.

He hunched further into himself, and drew cormorants with open mouths, fulmars and terns in huddles of cacophonous chatter, but failed over and over to recreate the energy of their noise. The bursting crackle. As it is with JP's recordings of Bean Uí Fhloinn. I want that, Mr Lloyd. That energy in my painting. Those sounds of ocean and bird oozing from my painting hanging from the white wall of the London gallery. *Symphony of Bird and Wave* by James Gillan. Yes, I did it all by myself. Yes, at my age. An extraordinary piece of work, young man. Thank you. A prodigious talent. Thank you. The Mozart of the art world. Raw talent. An international discovery. Thank you. Thank you. Thank you. Mr Lloyd beaming proudly. His arm over my shoulder as we are photographed by the newspapers. *The Times*, the *Guardian*. Even the *Irish Times* sends a reporter to cover the opening, to depict this great Anglo-Irish relationship in art. News reports. Article after article. Despite all the troubles of Northern Ireland and the tensions between Dublin and London, a wonderful new exhibition showing the work of an English artist and his Irish protégé proves that art is greater than politics. Art as peacemaker, as bridge builder. A new religion that is neither Catholic nor Protestant. A spiritual experience without the priest.

He bowed and laughed.

And not a fish in sight, Francis Gillan.

He closed the sketchpad and walked to the hut, to tidy, to draw, sheet after sheet of birds, of rabbits, of sea and cliffs, but then grew hungry, too hungry to be away any longer. He tracked rabbits as they bounded through the grass, set three traps, crushed three skulls and walked back to the village, the rabbits over his shoulder, the sketchpad filled with drawings under his arm. *Triumphant Island Boy* by James Gillan.

He laid the rabbits and sketchpad on the kitchen table.

Good-looking rabbits, said Mairéad.

I'll gut them, he said.

Are you hungry?

Starving, Mam.

I'll get you something.

She scrambled eggs on a pan over the fire and cut two slices of soda bread.

Thank you, he said.

She sat opposite him and reached for the sketchpad.

May I look, James?

Only if you don't talk about it.

I won't, she said.

She turned the pages, slowly, stopping at each one to scrutinise her son's work.

It's very good, she said.

As good as his, Mam?

Different. Both good.

He laughed.

You have to say that. You're my mother.

I don't have to anything, James Gillan.

She turned the pages. He ate.

I feel like I'm out there, James. As though I can hear the sea, the birds.

He smiled at her.

I worked at that, Mam.

I can see that. It's very good.

Thank you.

Your birds are much better than his.

James nodded.

His birds are terrible, Mam. They must have none in London.

What does he say about it? About your work.

Hasn't seen much of it. Not recently. Too obsessed with his own.

That's how you artist types are, James. Obsessed.

She poured tea for them both, the rabbits' blood pooled and congealed beside them.

I'm going to go to London with him, Mam.

I know.

Do art there.

She patted his hand.

I didn't think you were going there to fish, James.

He laughed.

Will you be all right, Mam? All right if I go?

She shrugged.

There'll be no rabbits, Mam.

I know, James.

She closed her eyes, briefly. Opened them again.

Your granny will figure something out, James. She always does.

James used the last of the bread to mop up his eggs.

I'm doing an exhibition with him, Mam. Six of the paintings will be mine.

How many have you done?

Five are ready. Or nearly ready. A bit to do still.

I wish you luck, James.

You can come to visit me. See my work.

Maybe.

She gathered the crockery.

Will you miss me, Mam?

I will, James, but we're used to missing around here.

We are, Mam. Experts at it.

She stood up.

It's beds day today.

I'll be doing my own soon. In London.

You will.

Less work for you.

Indeed. I won't know myself. Lady of leisure.

She ruffled his hair.

I'll have your jumper finished before you go.

Thanks, Mam.

She lifted the crockery, spilling tea down her front.

That was stupid of me.

You'll be grand, Mam.

She nodded.

Will you clean the henhouse after the rabbits? she said.

I will.

He carried the rabbits to the back kitchen when his mother had finished the dishes, taking with him his grandmother's knife and cleaver. He cut into the belly, releasing a puff of heat, and nicked the innards, detaching the heart, stomach, intestines, kidneys, liver and lungs. He scooped them out with his hand and dumped them into a bowl but picked out the kidneys and liver to set on the draining board. He cut into the fur just below the head and, pressing his knife into the flesh, drew back the pelt with his left hand to expose the white pink body of the rabbit. He severed the head, shins and feet with the cleaver and rinsed the cavity where the stomach had been. He moved on to the next rabbit. And then the third. He threw the heads and feet in the bowl and rinsed the sink.

His mother stood beside him with the wicker basket of bed linen.

You're finished, James? she said.

I am.

She dumped the sheets on the floor.

The rabbits look good, James. Meaty.

They're well fed, all right.

He cleaved the three rabbits into twelve pieces.

Perfect, she said. I'll get them on now.

He picked up the bowl of innards.

I'll give this to the pig, he said. And do the henhouse.

Thank you, James.

She put the kidneys and livers on a plate and cleaned the sink, washing off the traces of blood and flesh left by her son. She carried a pot of boiling water from the fire, poured it into the sink and submerged the first of the sheets with a wooden spoon. She filled the pot again with cold water, added the rabbit pieces, the kidneys, the livers, then carrot, turnip, onion, salt and pepper. She carried it back to the main kitchen and hung it over the fire. It was midday. A six-hour simmer. Potatoes added at five. Parsley at the end. Job done. Men fed.

She returned to the sheets. JP's first. Before Mam turns up. Peering into the sink. Sniffing around. Bloodhound Bean Uí Néill. Fee-fi-fo-fum, the blood of an Englishman. She laughed and stirred the sheets, adding detergent that she frothed with the spoon. No, Mam. Wrong. She submerged the sheets. The Frenchman, Mam. That's what you smell. His smell. And my smell. You smell me, Mam. Your own daughter. The lust of her. The lust of her in the Frenchman's bed. That's what you smell, Mam. Though you know that. Bloodhound Bean Uí Néill. And pretend not to. Turn a blind eye. A blind eye that sees well enough. Sees what it wants to see. As it wants to see. It. Mairéad's bit of summer fun. A transience. That's all. Nothing more. And God forbid that a child might come of it. God forbid that. A child. A child like James, but speaking French. Rising from my loins to babble in a language nobody can understand. For JP will be gone. Long gone. The disappeared. But don't worry, Mam. There are condoms. French ones. She laughed. The writer with his French letters. Brought here especially, Mam. Imported. Illegally. Especially. Especially to fuck me, the young widow island woman. She scooped the sheets out of the water and dropped them in again, agitating the stains. Failing that, Mam, failing them, those French condoms, that writer with his French letters, there is always Francis. Francis at the ready. Waiting. In the long grass. Waiting for me to fall flat on my face so that he can pick me up and make me his. Francis the Saviour. Mould me then as he wants me. Has always wanted me. Even before Liam. Mould me, own me and turn any child that comes from me into an Irish-speaking fisherman. No English or French on his boat. The grand man that he is. The grand man prepared to take on the likes of me, the young widow island woman. The grand man ready and waiting for when the condom fails, for when the Frenchman leaves. When my son leaves. The grand man valiantly taking on that mad one still waiting on her drowned husband to rise out of the sea. She spooned the sheets out of the water, set them on the draining board. She added more washing powder, and, with the spoon, shook the tiny white and blue beads into a froth. She dropped the next set of sheets into the still hot water. Mr Lloyd's. She pushed them down, holding them still as water soaked into the fibres, drowning them as my father drowned kittens, pressing on the bubbles of fabric lifted by rising air, thwarting any escape, saturating each fragment that smells of him, the man who will take away my son, whip him from me, change him so that he returns only as a visitor, each year the visit shorter than before until it becomes annual, biennial, or not at all, as it is with my sister, my brothers, siblings in Boston who prefer now to go elsewhere, to see other parts of the world to this lump of rock, sand and shale, and James will in time become them, sending me letters and postcards, pictures of his paintings, of his children, his wife, of his holidays elsewhere, while I stay here, the young widow island woman, waiting for his father to return, waiting for him to return, waiting until I become the middle-aged widow island woman, then the old widow island woman. She pulled the plug and rinsed the sheets in cold water. She squeezed them, twisting and tightening the fabric, water flowing over her red, chafed hands into the draining sink. She carried the sheets outside and draped them across the line that stretched from the house to the wall of rock that marked the village boundary. She returned to the back kitchen. Her mother was at the sink.

I'll finish the rest, she said.

There's no hot water, Mam.

It's worse in winter, Mairéad.

She nodded.

I'll help James with the henhouse. Get me out for a bit.

She knocked her foot against the corrugated iron attached to the henhouse coarsely built of stone. Blue twine bound the door to the stone.

Do you need help, James?

Nearly done now.

Will you go painting after this?

Nah. I'll read for a while.

Why don't you go in to Mr Lloyd?

He doesn't want me around at the minute.

Why not?

Don't know. I'll wait till he goes back out to the hut.

What's he doing?

I don't know, Mam. He won't tell me.

What does he want the big canvas for?

Don't know.

Do you ever want to spy on him? See what he is doing?

He'd kick me out.

Do you see any of his work?

Sometimes. I've seen pencil and charcoal drawings of you.

Lying down?

He laughed.

You're sleeping, Mam. *A Young Woman Sleeping*. Remember? From the Rembrandt.

She glanced downwards.

Unless you sleep standing up, Mam.

She laughed.

I'm half horse, James.

Must be that.

Are they any good?

They are. Very.

He came out of the henhouse and handed her two eggs.

You missed these, he said.

Thank you.

They walked back towards the house. James pointed at the boat on the horizon.

They're back.

Good to have that rabbit stew, James.

I wonder if Micheál found the canvas.

I'll put the kettle on. You tell Mr Lloyd.

And JP?

Mairéad shrugged.

He'll come anyway.

Micheál and Francis dropped the rolled canvas on the table. It landed heavily, wrapped in brown paper.

You'll break the table with that thing, said Bean Uí Néill.

Francis propped the lengths of wood against the dresser.

Where is himself? said Micheál.

He's not in the cottage, said James.

I saw him leave, said Masson. About half an hour ago.

He must have gone for a walk, said James.

We may wait so.

I think we should open it, said Bean Uí Néill.

We can't do that, Mam.

We have a right to know what is coming onto the island, Mairéad.

Ah, Mam, it's his stuff.

It's our island. My house. I have a right to know what is happening.

You can't do that, Mam.

Masson patted Mairéad's arm.

Let your mother at it.

She's always at it, said Mairéad.

Francis began to undo the package.

Do you have Sellotape? he said.

We'll use string, said Bean Uí Néill.

Francis sliced the tape with a knife and folded back the brown paper.

Keep an eye out, James.

He'll be a while yet.

The canvas was creamy grey white, layer upon layer of rolled fabric.

It's huge, said Mairéad.

What's it for? said Bean Uí Néill.

Bean Uí Néill and Francis, simultaneously, without speaking, lifted the canvas and unrolled it, stretching it across the room, silenced by its reach from the fireplace to the door.

James, said Francis. What do you know?

Nothing.

I don't like it, said Francis.

Nor do I, said Bean Uí Néill.

It's only a bit of canvas, said Micheál.

You should never have got it for him, said Bean Uí Néill.
Micheál sighed and folded his arms.

Or brought him here, Micheál. With his English and his
art.

Ah, calm down, woman.

Don't tell me to calm down when it's your fault.

It's a bit of canvas, Áine, for a bit of paint.

A bit?
Micheál laughed.

All right, he said. A lot.

But for what, Micheál?

I know no more than you, Áine.

You must know something, Mairéad.

Why would I know something, Francis?

You got that book. The one with the naked women.

And?

Why are you interested in naked women all of a sudden?

It's art, Francis.

Well, we don't want it here.

Tell that to the Pope then too. His place is full of art.

The women aren't naked.

The angels are, Francis.
Francis dropped his end of the canvas onto the floor. He
pointed at James.

You must know something.
James shrugged.

I don't.

Mairéad, with Micheál's help, rolled the canvas closed again.

What does it matter, anyway? she said. He'll be gone soon and everything will be back to normal.

Whatever normal is, said Bean Uí Néill. I've forgotten at this stage.

They rewrapped the canvas in the brown paper, pressed the tape together and tied the package with white string.

Now, said Micheál. It looks perfect.

He'll know, said James. He notices small things.

Francis snorted.

You'll tell him, anyway, James. Little butler boy.

James left and sat on the wall outside, waiting for Lloyd's return.

Your package has arrived, he said.

Wonderful. Thank you, James.

It's very big.

Have you opened it?

Yes.

Thought so.

But Micheál has repackaged it. You'd never know.

Except that you told me.

True.

I wonder why you told me.

I don't know.

Fetch it for me, would you? I'll go to the studio.

He returned to the kitchen and took the package. Francis clapped, slowly.

Good little butler boy.

James walked to the studio with the canvas in his arms, blood pulsing at his temples, sweat building under his armpits. He dumped the canvas on the table, retrieved the lengths of wood, and stood beside the artist in the studio, the two scrutinising Lloyd's painting on the easel.

Your sea is getting better, said James.

Thank you.

The light is coming now from underneath.

It's your good teaching, James.

Must be that, Mr Lloyd.

As I said before, James, you have a good eye.

Better than yours?

Lloyd smiled at him.

Maybe. If you work hard enough.

James laughed.

And clean my brushes, Mr Lloyd.

Yes, James. And put the caps back on the paint tubes.

And sweep the floor. I know.

Lloyd tousled the boy's hair.

Open the package, James. Let's take a look at this canvas.

They stretched it across the floor.

It's perfect, said Lloyd.

He rubbed the canvas between his fingers.

It's already sized.

James shrugged.

More time for painting, Mr Lloyd.

We'll build the frame after dinner.

Tea, said James.

Lloyd smiled.

Tea, James.

Lloyd stored the brown paper, the string, and resumed his painting while James quietly, discreetly, knelt in front of his easel chair to work again on *Mná na hÉireann*, silence enveloping the studio, the cottage, and the cottage next door where Masson had returned to writing, in blue ink, a cup of hot coffee beside him, a relief from the endless tea, from the tension in the kitchen, hidden in the refuge of books and pens, as it was in childhood, in my bedroom with books and pens, away from my father, from my mother, comforted by the silence of my room, the solitariness of my school desk, my schoolbooks, French, English, Classics, Philosophy. Sometimes Latin. Even Greek. But never Arabic. There was no discussion of Arabic at school, of Algeria, of things Algerian, so that those texts from the Algerian teacher were pushed to one side, excerpts from newspapers, from the Koran, political and religious tracts that meant nothing to me for I knew nothing of my mother's country, cared nothing for it so that the translation work to be done for his Thursday classes eluded me, bewildered me. I tried to explain myself to my mother. Explain my indifference to the classes, the teacher, to the need for Arabic. She sighed, pulled on her scarf, and talked to the men and their sons at the tills who pressed even more books into my hands, pamphlets too, some in French, most in Arabic, read these, son, they will explain everything to you, and I read them, as best I could, children's books on the history of Algeria, on the relationship with France, but none of them explained anything at all, none of them explained what it was like to be the son of a Frenchman, of an Algerian mother, what it was like to be half French, half Algerian, half something, half nothing, a boy in no-man's land.

James stood up to look at his painting. He rubbed his knees.

I'll never make it as a priest, he said.

It's a sad day for the Church, James.

Lloyd looked at his work.

That's a good piece, James. Definitely one for the exhibition.

Thank you.

How many have you done?

That's the fifth piece ready.

One to go, James.

How many have you done, Mr Lloyd?

Not sure, James. I'll select mine when I'm in London. Not before.

Why not?

Makes me work harder if I think they'll all be included.

There's a logic to that, Mr Lloyd.

My wife doesn't agree.

Your half-wife.

He nodded. Smiled.

She thinks I should home in. Make choices sooner.

She has a lot of opinions about what you should be doing.

He laughed.

Oh, she does, James.

Will she have opinions about my work?

She'll like you. She'll love your work.

They worked together in silence until the evening meal. Bean Uí Néill served the rabbit stew. They ate. Francis cleared his throat and spoke, in English.

Why do you want the big canvas, Mr Lloyd?

Lloyd set down his fork, his knife.

To paint on.

Yes, but what?

Island scenes.

What type of scenes?

Why?

We should know what you are doing.

With all due respect, Francis, my art has nothing to do with you.

It does if it's about the islanders.

Lloyd shrugged.

You're not an islander.

I was born here, Mr Lloyd. I spend a lot of time here.

I see that.

So, I do have a say.

It remains my art, Francis. As I said, nothing to do with you.

Francis sat forward.

You're wrong there, Mr Lloyd.

Francis resumed eating. Lloyd ate too, in silence. He drank tea, ate tart and left. James followed.

That Francis is quite something, James.

He is, Mr Lloyd.

Who is he?

He's my father's brother.

Beyond that. Why does he have such a say about the place?

James shrugged.

He just does.

Lloyd stretched the wood along the floor of the studio.

We need a hammer and a saw, James.

James returned with the tools and they worked until they had eleven lengths of wood, two long pieces to run along the length of the canvas, top and bottom, and nine shorter pieces to frame and stanchion the canvas.

Has it always been like this? said Lloyd. With Francis in charge?

As long as I can remember.

They wrapped the canvas over the wood.

I thought it was Mícheál, said Lloyd. That he was in charge.

You'd think that. With the boat and all.

You would, said Lloyd.

James held the canvas in place. Lloyd hammered in the nails.

Mícheál pays Francis, doesn't he?

He does, Mr Lloyd.

But Mícheál isn't really the boss.

Not really. Not on the island.

Strange place you live, James.

That's why I'm going with you, Mr Lloyd.

Lloyd nodded.

I'd be going too, James.

They finished nailing wood onto one width of the canvas.

It's going to be huge, Mr Lloyd.

It will, James.

Have you ever done anything as big?

Lloyd shook his head.

It'll be my best work, James. I'm sure of it.

They moved to the other side of the canvas

newspaper ecstasy

half-wife delight

genius of british art

full wife delight

They again wrapped the canvas around the wood and nailed it in place.

I'd say he has a temper, said Lloyd.

Oh, he does, Mr Lloyd.

I wouldn't like to get into a fight with him.

You'd lose, Mr Lloyd.

They hammered the shorter cuts into place at each end of the canvas and spaced the seven stanchions evenly along the frame.

How will I get into art college, Mr Lloyd?

You'll be fine. They know me well.

Lloyd nailed short cuts of wood along the diagonal of each corner.

It holds the canvas upright, James. Stops it falling in on itself.

I thought that, all right, Mr Lloyd.

There's not much I can tell you, is there, James?

Not much, no.

They stretched the canvas across four kitchen chairs.

It's impressive, said James.

It'll be my defining work.

What's it of?

I'll show you when I'm finished.

If you ever finish.

Lloyd laughed.

I'll still be here next summer, James.

I won't be.

James walked the length of the canvas.

How do you paint on something this big, Mr Lloyd?

Top marks for spotting the problem, James.

Lloyd took his biggest brushes from his painting drawer.

It's about scale.

He went to the other room.

Come and help me, James.

They removed the mirrored door from the wardrobe and leaned it against the studio wall, opposite the canvas.

I look at the painting in the reflection in the mirror. Check the scale as I go along.

Can I watch you work?

Lloyd shook his head.

No, James. I'll be here on my own. You can work in the hut.

But I have to get ready for the exhibition.

We both do, James.

I like it here.

I like it there, but we have to acclimatise.

How long do I have to stay out there?

Lloyd shrugged.

Take what you need, James.

James gathered paper, pencils, paint and brushes and walked to the hut, towards the sun sinking into the sea.

The picnic baskets are packed and the sun is shining, the day perfect for the family outing to check the lobster pots. It is Monday morning, August 27th.

The Mountbatten family leaves Classiebawn Castle and drives the short distance to the pier at Mullaghmore in Sligo where they keep *Shadow V*, an old green wooden boat that is almost thirty feet long, large enough to accommodate seventy-nine-year-old Lord Mountbatten, his daughter, his son-in-law, his twin grandsons and their eighty-three-year-old paternal grandmother. The sea is calm.

Paul Maxwell, a fifteen-year-old schoolboy from Enniskillen, helps the family on board. He is a friend of Lord Mountbatten's fourteen-year-old grandsons, and has been hired to look after the boat for the summer, keeping it in order for Lord Mountbatten, a cousin of Queen Elizabeth II and a retired naval officer.

The passengers and picnic on board, they start the engine. Lord Mountbatten steers the boat away from the pier, towards the mouth of the harbour, unaware that the IRA has attached a 50 lb bomb to the underside of the boat, unaware too that an IRA man is standing on a cliff overlooking the cove, a remote-control unit in his hand.

Lord Mountbatten motors beyond the harbour wall.

The IRA man flicks the switch. The bomb explodes, shredding the boat, killing Paul Maxwell and Nicholas Knatchbull, one of Lord Mountbatten's twin grandsons. Lord Mountbatten dies at the scene, from injuries to his legs.

Did you hear, Mam?

I did, Mairéad.

Two boys. James's age.

Where is he?

Out on the cliffs, Mam.

Let him stay there.

Out there. Away from this.

Mairéad bowed her head, closed her eyes.

Stay away from this, James.

A British Army convoy is driving through isolated lake country close to the Irish border at 4.40 p.m. on the same day, Monday, August 27th. The sun is still shining.

The convoy, a Land Rover and two trucks, is moving soldiers between army bases. It is passing through Narrow Water, near Warrenpoint in Co. Down.

The IRA is waiting on the convoy and has hidden an 800 lb bomb in a trailer of hay bales parked on the side of the road. The convoy passes the trailer. The bomb explodes, killing six members of the Parachute Regiment travelling in the second army truck.

The surviving soldiers run for safety. IRA gunmen open fire from the other side of the lake, in the Irish Republic. The British soldiers return fire, killing Michael Hudson, an Englishman on a birdwatching holiday. The British soldiers radio for help.

British Army reinforcements arrive in Land Rovers and helicopters, seeking shelter behind a stone wall. The IRA explodes a second 800 lb bomb, planted behind that stone wall, killing twelve more soldiers, their body parts scattered by the force of the explosion. No trace is found of Lieutenant-Colonel David Blair who had arrived by helicopter, and the only remains of nineteen-year-old driver Anthony Wood is his pelvis, welded by the heat of the first bomb blast to his seat in the army truck.

Eighteen soldiers are killed by the two bombs, sixteen of them members of the Parachute Regiment:

Donald Ferguson Blair, twenty-three, single, from Kilsyth, Scotland

Nicholas John Andrews, twenty-four, married, from Bromyard, England

Gary Ivan Barnes, eighteen, single, from Ipswich, England

Raymond Dunn, twenty, single, from Swindon, England

Anthony George Wood, nineteen, single, from London, England

Michael Woods, eighteen, single, from Blackburn, England

John Christian Giles, twenty-two, married, from Stockton-on-Tees, England

Ian Albert Rogers, thirty-one, married, from Bishopstoke, England

Walter Beard, thirty-three, married, two children, from Borehamwood, England

Thomas Robert Vance, twenty-three, engaged to be married, from Belfast, Northern Ireland

Robert Nevis England, twenty-three, married with one child, from Aldershot, England

Jeffrey Alan Jones, eighteen, single, from Gwent, Wales

Leonard Jones, twenty-six, married, one child, from Manchester, England

Robert Dylan Vaughan-Jones, eighteen, single, from Corwen, Wales

Christopher George Ireland, twenty-five, married, one child, from Bedford, England

Peter James Fursman, thirty-four, married, from Crick, England

Two soldiers from the Queen's Own Highlanders:

David Blair, forty, married, two children, from Edinburgh, Scotland

Victor MacLeod, twenty-four, single, from Inverness, Scotland

James turned the dial on the radio until the man reading the news was speaking in English. Lloyd listened, staring down, into his cup, at the skim of milk growing over his cooling tea, watching as it thickened, as the fat congealed.

My tea has gone cold, he said.

James turned off the radio.

Lloyd lifted his spoon and stirred, blending the fat back into the milk, into the tea. He drank, his swallow the only sound at the table for the others were silent, eyes dropped to the table or lifted to the ceiling.

He returned the cup to its saucer.

It's a lot of death, he said. For one day.

It is, said Masson.

Lloyd turned the cup on the saucer, clockwise.

A lot of death, he said.

Anticlockwise.

It's hard to understand, said Lloyd.

What is? said Masson.

That amount of hatred.

Masson sighed.

Is it?

After all we have done for this country? said Lloyd.

After all you have done to this country.

That was a long time ago.

Was it?

Yes.

It's unfinished business, Lloyd. A border that should not be there.

Mairéad stood and gathered the cups.

Is there any whiskey? said Lloyd.

Mairéad shook her head.

You drank it, Mr Lloyd, said James.

Lloyd nodded.

I did, didn't I? That was a mistake.

It was, said Masson.

You drank it too.

Our mistake then.

Unusually conciliatory of you, JP.

It's an unusual day.

Lady Brabourne, eighty-three, dies in hospital in Sligo on Tuesday, August 28th from injuries sustained when the IRA bomb exploded on *Shadow V*.

James knocked and opened Lloyd's door.

Granny sent me over with this.

He set tea, milk and buttered bread on the table. Lloyd closed the studio door behind him.

Thank you, James.

Lloyd picked up the pot.

Would you like some tea?

I would.

Good. Get the cups.

Lloyd poured, still standing.

You'd miss the chairs, wouldn't you, Mr Lloyd?

We could sit on the floor. Outside is a bit damp.

Inside is too, Mr Lloyd.

That's true.

They stayed standing, hips leaning against the table as they ate and drank.

How is the work going, Mr Lloyd?

It's going well, James.

May I see it?

Not yet.

When?

Maybe soon.

That woman died.

Which woman?

The woman on the boat. The old woman.

I'm sorry about that.

James drank more tea, ate more bread.

It must be weird, Mr Lloyd.

What is, James?

To be English here. Now. At this time.

I suppose it is.

Are you scared?

Lloyd shrugged.

Of what?

The bombs going off and you out here on your own.

I don't suppose they're after English artists.

I don't suppose they are, Mr Lloyd.

Not much of a headline, is it, James? 'IRA bombs English landscape artist.'

James laughed.

No, not much.

Lloyd leaned into James, whispering to him.

Unless you think Francis is after me.

James whispered back.

Francis is after everybody.

They laughed.

Maybe he'll come after you, James. For painting with an Englishman.

He has me in his sights, all right.

Lloyd gathered the cups and plates and handed them to James.

Can I paint today, Mr Lloyd?
Not today, James.
Can I see what you're doing?
Not today, James.

John Patrick Hardy is having dinner with six of his ten children at his home in North Belfast on Tuesday, August 28th. It is just before five in the evening, and someone knocks at the front door. He walks from the kitchen through the hall and opens the door. A man shoots him in the chest. He falls backwards. The UVF gunman fires a second time, killing John Patrick Hardy, a forty-three-year-old Catholic man, an unemployed mechanic.

He took the drawing from the side of his bed and stretched it across the table. He drew over his depiction of Francis holding two fish, darkening him, a balaclava over his face, a gun in his left hand, a detonator in his right, a trailer stacked with hay bales behind him, a British Army truck driving towards the trailer. He painted his redrawn Francis onto the canvas, using greys and dark greys among the red, yellow, blue, pink and green, twisting the gunman's shoulder and head until his eyes stared from beneath the balaclava at the artist, at the woman, the man, wandering around the London gallery, glass in hand.

Gerry Lennon is packing fruit into the window display at Levy's grocery store on the Antrim Road in North Belfast. It's 9.30 on Saturday morning, September 1st. A young man from the UVF comes into the shop and shoots the twenty-three-year-old Catholic man in the head and back. Gerry Lennon dies in the shop.

James carried the teapot, the milk jug and the bowl of porridge through the morning sunshine to Lloyd's cottage. The door was open. He stepped in to put them on the table, to knock then with his hand, rather than kick with his foot. But the table was covered. With a huge drawing. In pencil. One he had not seen before. He stared, open-mouthed, still holding the teapot, milk jug and bowl, struggling to absorb the scale of the drawing, the depiction of Bean Uí Néill with her teapot, Bean Uí Fhloinn with her pipe, Micheál with his boat, Masson with his black recorder. As I had them. In my work.

The teapot suddenly heavy, he set it down on the hearth, scraping the metal against the stone. He looked again at the drawing, at himself holding a rabbit and paintbrushes. He looked closer, at the shadow beneath the pencil, at the rubbed-out drawing of him holding two rabbits.

Lloyd emerged from the studio.

I told you to knock, James.

Lloyd began to roll the drawing.

I've seen it, Mr Lloyd. You're too late.

Lloyd slowly turned around, holding the drawing to his chest.

Thank you for bringing the tea, James.

You copied my idea, Mr Lloyd.

What idea is that, James?

My idea about representation. Giving each islander a symbolic object.

Lloyd smiled at the boy.

I've taught you well, James.

I've been reading too, Mr Lloyd.

That's good, James. That's important.

So I know all about symbolism, Mr Lloyd. About representation.

Lloyd returned the folded drawing to the table and moved towards the teapot.

Would you like some tea, James?

You stole from me, Mr Lloyd. Stole my idea.

Lloyd laughed.

Did I, James?

Yes, you did.

Lloyd poured tea into two cups. He added milk and handed a cup to James.

It may be, James, that you built on what I did first.

What do you mean?

James with Two Rabbits. You saw that, took it and expanded it.

You still stole from me. Took the bit I expanded.

Lloyd ate the porridge.

That's what artists do, James. Take from each other, learn from each other. That's what we're doing here, in our little artist's colony.

James fingered his cup.

It doesn't seem right, Mr Lloyd. That you can just take my idea like that.

Lloyd shrugged.

We're feeding off each other, James. Getting ideas from each other.

James drank the tea. It was tepid, almost cold.

Will you at least credit me, Mr Lloyd? Tell them that it was my idea?

It'll be obvious in the exhibition that I learnt from you, that you learnt from me.

James nodded, slowly.

I suppose it will be.

Lloyd emptied his cup.

So, do you want to see it, James?

I think so.

It's not finished yet.

Lloyd pointed at the studio.

In you go, James.

He took James's cup.

No food. No drink.

James walked through the door, into a room filled with colour, vibrant blues, greens, reds, yellows, his mother at their centre, the green scarf on her hips, reaching for an apple above her head, her skin glowing, shimmering in the island light, her nakedness a startling contrast to the other islanders stretched across the canvas in dark clothing lightened by dashes of blue, red, yellow and pink.

It's beautiful, Mr Lloyd.

James moved closer to the painting and walked slowly up and down its length, absorbing its vitality – the lush blue sea and sky, the gulls and terns banking and swooping, the island animals casually wandering among the humans, untethered, living alongside each other, the island's ghosts and spirits too in their midst.

It's wonderful, Mr Lloyd.

Lloyd smiled.

You like it, James?

I do, Mr Lloyd. Very much.

It's a blend of Gauguin and Manet. His *Déjeuner sur l'herbe*.

And my work, said James.

Lloyd laughed.

Yes, yours too, James.

James pointed at the painting.

Is that Francis? With the balaclava?

It is.

James shook his head.

He won't like it.

He won't, James.

James pointed again. At the dead men by the boat, with their nets and fish.

Is that my father?

Lloyd nodded.

Do you mind, James?

Do I have any choice, Mr Lloyd?

James walked again, but stopped in front of his own figure

with a dead rabbit in one hand and three paintbrushes in the other.

When do I get rid of the rabbit, Mr Lloyd?

When you've graduated as my apprentice.

How long will that take?

We'll see.

James turned to look at the painting in the mirror.

It's truly wonderful, Mr Lloyd.

Thank you, James. Now I must get back to it.

Lloyd picked up his brushes and his palette.

Close the door after you, James. Both doors.

James strode out across the island, muttering, mumbling, cursing, swearing, kicking at the grass, it was mine, Mr Lloyd, my idea and you stole it, stole from me to use as your own.

He reached the cliffs and flopped onto his stomach to peer over the edge, to watch again as sun and shadow danced across the rock, picking out pinks, reds, oranges, blues and yellows, colours that once seen cannot be unseen. He pummelled the ground. You showed them to me, Mr Lloyd. The colours, the light. Taught me how to see, how to see the unseen. Why? So you could steal from me? Take my ideas. Gave me too the feeling of pencil and charcoal on paper, of paint on canvas. And the smell of paint. Of linseed oil. Of white spirits. The sensation of paint drying on my skin. Speckles of grey, green, blue and white across my hands at the end of the working day that feel better than the silver and black scales of fish. Better than their stinking smell. The smell of me if I stay. The smell of me if I do not leave with an Englishman who steals from me.

He buried his head in his hands and stayed on the edge of the cliff as the clouds came, then the rain. He drifted back towards the village, indifferent to the water seeping into him, stopping at Bean Uí Fhloinn's house. She smiled at him and pointed him towards the chair beside the fire. She poured tea for him.

You're wet, she said.

I am.

Drink the tea.

She stood up and wrapped her shawl around his shoulders.

That'll warm you up, she said.

Thank you.

She sat down again and lifted her knitting, looking at it rather than at him as she spoke.

Not long now until you leave, James.

It's not.

Are you looking forward to it? It's a great place by all accounts.

He shrugged.

I was, Bean Uí Fhloinn.

But now you're not?

I'm not sure of Mr Lloyd.

She nodded.

It's hard to be sure of an Englishman, James.

He's been very good to me, Bean Uí Fhloinn.

He has, James.

But he has stolen from me.

She laughed.

What can he steal from you? You have nothing.

He sighed, his body sinking into itself.

He stole my idea, Bean Uí Fhloinn. He put it in his art.

That's a hard theft, James.

It is.

He sipped his tea.

He says it happens all the time in art.

She set down her knitting and took up her pipe. She packed it with tobacco and settled the smoking pipe in the corner of her mouth.

He's a magpie, James.

And?

That's what magpies do.

You mean it's in his nature?

She nodded.

He's an Englishman and an artist.

James laughed.

So he's only being himself.

That's it, James. That's who he is. What he is.

He lifted the cup to his mouth and drank.

Henry Corbett is twenty-seven years of age and is at home with his wife in their small terraced house in North Belfast. It is midnight on Monday, September 3rd. Four gunmen from the Ulster Defence Association burst into the house. He runs from them but they open fire, shooting the Catholic man nineteen times. He dies in his house.

Bean Uí Néill lifted a bottle of whiskey from the shopping.
Jameson.

It's the one I promised you, said Micheál.

That'll do, she said.

She took four cups from the dresser.

The Englishman was looking for some the other night, she
said. After that Monday.

Francis scoffed.

I suppose he wanted to celebrate.

Must have been that all right, Francis, said Mairéad.

Bean Uí Néill opened the bottle.

No time like the present, she said.

They toasted and drank.

It's been awful up there since, said Bean Uí Néill. That poor
man stacking vegetables.

Collateral damage, said Francis. That's all.

What about the children, Francis?

What about them, Mairéad?

The two children killed on the boat.

As I said, collateral damage.

One of them was Irish, Francis. The same age as James.

A true Irish boy wouldn't work on the boat of a British lord.

He was a child, Francis. With a summer job.

Francis shrugged.

He should have thought more carefully about the source of his employment.

Jesus, Francis. That's sick.

He shrugged again.

That's the way of it, Mairéad.

Of what, Francis? What is it?

War, Mairéad. The way of war.

Against old women and children on a day trip on a boat?

Francis emptied his cup.

The boat of a colonial warlord, he said.

The boat belonging to the children's grandfather, Francis.

He sat back into the chair.

He's a legitimate target, Mairéad.

You've lost me, Francis Gillan. How is an old man with his family a legitimate target?

He's a member of the British royal family. A cousin of the Queen.

And the young Enniskillen boy?

Francis refilled his cup.

As I said, that's the way.

So James could be next because he paints with an English artist?

He could be.

Then they'll be after you because you took money from the English artist. Rowed him with your bare hands to an Irish-speaking island.

317

You're being stupid, Mairéad.

Am I? Where does this end, Francis?

In a united Ireland, Mairéad. One free of British rule.

And you'll blow up innocent children to get it.

Mairéad swallowed the last of her whiskey.

You're pathetic, Francis Gillan.

She gathered the deodorant, coffee and pens ordered by Masson, the paper, pencils and newspapers requested by Lloyd.

I'll deliver these, she said.

She went into Masson's cottage. He was writing.

You're here, Mairéad.

I am.

She set the shopping on the edge of the table, away from his papers.

Coffee? he said.

She sat down, jerking her head backwards, towards her own house.

Francis is in there driving me mad.

Masson laughed.

Francis is always driving you mad, Mairéad.

She laughed too.

You're right, JP. He is.

What's he doing to you this time?

Defending the killing of those children. Of the old woman.

A stain on his otherwise perfect day.

I don't think he cares, JP. Collateral damage, he calls it.

Nice and neutral.

He tidied away his deodorant, coffee and pens but left the paper, pencils, paints and newspapers on the table.

Are those for Lloyd?

They are.

She laughed.

Actually, I think it's James. But Mr Lloyd is paying.

What colours this time?

Mairéad pushed the papers to one side.

More blue, she said. And green.

He's very quiet these days, Mairéad.

Mr Lloyd?

Masson nodded.

Maybe he's afraid to come out.

Masson laughed.

That Francis might get him.

He might, said Mairéad.

Masson placed a cup of coffee in front of her, a spoon, some sugar and some milk.

It's the last of my coffee.

I am honoured, she said.

They drank.

It's good, she said. Thank you.

He lifted her hand and kissed it.

So what does he do in there all day, Mairéad?

We could ask the same of you, JP.

You could. Though you know me well enough by now.

Yes, you're in here hunkered over that recorder like some madman.

He smiled.

That's me.

Muttering to yourself. Muttering the mutterings of Bean Uí Fhloinn.

He laughed and kissed her hand, her cheek, ran his fingers through her hair.

How is your work, anyway? she said.

Good. Almost finished the comparative work.

What does that mean?

Examining whether the language loss has shifted much over the past five years. Whether the islanders are speaking a lot more English.

And?

Some are. Some are not.

Whose language has changed?

Bean Uí Fhloinn hasn't shifted at all.

That's hardly a surprise.

My star student.

Stubborn goat.

He sipped his coffee.

Yours though has changed.

In what way?

Your inflections have altered, as though you are listening to English.

That's strange, she said.

As though you're listening to Lloyd a lot. Absorbing his English.

She drank her coffee.

As though you're learning it. Somehow.

He added more milk to his coffee and stirred.

What are you doing with Lloyd, Mairéad?

She shook her head.

Nothing.

He stared at her, then stood up.

I need to get back to work, Mairéad.

He gathered the cups.

How much longer will you stay, JP? You're here longer than usual.

I can't leave before Lloyd. I need to see his impact on the language.

Make sure I don't start blathering English.

Or worse, he said. Bean Uí Fhloinn.

That'll never happen, JP.

She lifted the paper, pencils, paints and newspapers.

Will you come tonight? he said.

I don't know, she said. We'll see.

I don't see so much of you any more, Mairéad.

There's a lot going on. James isn't going back to school.

I heard.

Art college in London. Living with Lloyd.

Quite a change for him. For you.

She picked at the edges of the newspaper.

What do you think, JP? Do you think James should go?

He shrugged.

I know nothing about it, Mairéad.

She shredded a corner, dropping newsprint to the floor.

I hope it's the right thing, she said. With everything going on. That he'll be safe, JP.

It'll be a hard time to be Irish in London, Mairéad.

She nodded.

It's always a hard time to be Irish in London.

She opened the door.

Try and see what he's doing on that canvas, Mairéad.

She laughed.

You want me to spy on him?

I do, Mairéad. Come back with top information.

I won't see anything. He has his curtains closed.

What is James saying?

Nothing. He's out in the hut.

Banished?

Mairéad smiled.

He spends all day out there drawing.

The pair of them will end up mad.

That's us all, JP.

She tapped on the door and pushed it, but it was locked. She knocked. Lloyd pulled back the curtain, peered at her and opened the door. She handed him the bundle of paper, paints and pencils.

Thank you, he said.

She turned to leave.

Do you want to see it, Mairéad?

I do, Mr Lloyd.

She slipped though the half-opened door. She followed him into the studio, the dusky daylight augmented by four lanterns

on the floor. He stood to one side so that she could see herself, naked but for her scarf, reaching up for an imagined apple,
her son and mother either side of her, beyond them her grandmother with Francis and Micheál, and in the background a
priest, a cross and an upturned boat, three men scattered around
it. She inhaled sharply, briefly, then closed her eyes. Father, Son
and Holy Ghost. Incantation. She opened her eyes.

The island, she said.

She looked again at the painting, at Mountbatten and the
children on *Shadow V*, the soldiers dead on the beach, beside
the seals.

What do you think?

It's wonderful, she said. Beautiful.

And Liam?

She bowed her head.

He's always with me, Mr Lloyd.

She walked from one end of the painting to the other, absorbing the blues, greys, greens, browns and blacks, but the splashes
too of vibrant colour, yellow, orange, pink, red and gold, soaking in his inclusion of hens, dogs, cats, fish, birds and seals, of
the island pig and her litter, and the island milking cow. The
heifer too. Swimming in the sea by herself. A sea tinged intermittently with red. Blood red.

It's very, very good, she said.

He bowed, slightly.

Thank you, Mairéad.

She reached out to touch the painting, her hand attracted
by the glow of her skin, the young widow island woman as

323

they have never seen me, my skin, my body, shimmering with energy, with vibrancy, a vitality that will be whisked away from here, carried off to live in London, in Paris, in New York, to live as Liam and I were going to live, vibrant, vital, flitting from one gallery to the next, from theatre to bookshop, wine glasses in hand, red for me, white for him, though we had tasted neither, drinking whiskey and tea on our wedding day, laughing that it would soon be wine and champagne in Boston, where his brother lived, where his brother had earned enough to buy tickets for Liam, for me, for our child, so that all that remained was the visa, the one that arrived after the drowning, the visa that Francis wanted to take as his, me with it, though I was not having it, not having him, so that talk of Boston faded, and talk of wine, of champagne, of theatre, of galleries was washed away by winter rains. But I can go now, Liam. Leave. Get off this rock. Escape. But stay too, setting the kettle on the fire, the day in motion, waiting on you to come out of the sea, into our bed, into me.

Lloyd put his hand on hers, gently.

It's still wet, he said.

She dropped her hand and again walked the length of the canvas, up and down, several times, smiling, then laughing, the young widow island woman as they have never seen me, those mainland women, over there.

She shook Lloyd's hand.

Thank you, she said. It's perfect.

He smiled at her. He kissed her then on her right cheek.

It's my best work, Mairéad.

She left, walking a distance from Masson's window in the hope that he would not see her. He came out after her. He called to her.

So what did you find out, Mairéad?

About what?

About what he's doing in there?

Oh, nothing.

What were you doing in there?

He asked me to tidy up. To clean cups.

Did you?

I did, she said. And I swept the floor. He's a messy man. Masson remained as he was, leaning against the door frame to watch her walk away, leaving him quickly, hurriedly, but then slowing as she approached her own house, her own door, the changes in her gait the same as my mother's each time she left the old men and their sons at the tills, rushing from their shops, from their streets, fretting that my father would pass in a post van, on a post bicycle, that he would find her where he did not want her, dressed as he did not want her dressed, walking quickly, trotting, jogging until she was back again in our area, near our apartment block, and then she slowed, her body heavy, lugubrious, her shoulders slumped as we approached the building, as we climbed the concrete stairs, as she turned the key in the door, relieved each time to find the shared home empty of him with enough time for her to change out of long skirts into shorter ones, out of darker colours into the brighter clothes that he preferred though she was increasingly comfortable with covered legs and a scarf hanging loosely over the back of her head. Just as she was wearing that evening, the evening we got home to find him already there. Steeped in beer and French television, demanding to know where we had been and why she, my mother, was wearing those dark clothes and scarf when he had told her not to. And she told him. Straight out. Your son is learning Arabic. Classical Arabic. Literary Arabic. The language of my people, my culture, my history. He sprung out of the armchair and shoved her, my mother, against the wall, shouting that his son was French and would be raised as French. Speak French. Read French. Play with French children. That his son would never learn Arabic. And that he was anyway sick of all this Arabic crap, this Algerian crap, that fucking couscous that she cooked for hours, steaming the apartment until condensation dribbled down the windows. And all I want is a decent rabbit stew and apple flan. To eat as my friends eat. As the bosses in my office eat. And he lunged then at her books. At her newspapers. Tearing them. Ripping them. Then at her. At my mother. Slapping her. Across the face. Punching her. In the stomach. In the chest. Knocking her to the floor. Kicking her. My son is French and will eat French food. He unbuckled his belt, yanked it from the hooks of his jeans. He lifted the black leather into the air above her, my mother, my beloved mother cowered into the corner of the kitchen beside the bin, emptied before she left, a fresh liner inserted. The belt came down, through the air and onto her back. She yelped. He lifted the belt again. It came down a second time, on her legs. And he shouted. You Arab slut. The belt rose again. I should never have married you,

you Arab whore. The belt landed, on her hip bone. I should have left you there with that child inside you, left you in that godforsaken country. The belt rose, the belt fell, my mother a tightened ball, hands and arms over her face, over her head. I should have married a Frenchwoman. None of this Arabic crap. The belt on her back. My son will speak French. On her legs. Read French. On her back again. Lashing her. Legs. Hip. Back. Buttocks. Shoulder. My. Son. Will. Be. French.

He stopped then, and, panting, gathered the belt into his hand. My mother sobbed, quietly, as quietly as she could and reached her hand towards my foot. I stared down at her, my mouth open, my body still, silent, speaking neither the tongue of my mother nor the tongue of my father, watching as my father rethreaded his belt, aware as he returned to his beer and his television, as my mother let go of my foot, that my father tongue had become my mother tongue and my mother tongue a silence for she spoke little after that. She stopped reading too, sitting instead at the window looking over the distant sea, leaving the apartment only to fetch food, return-ing every Thursday with rabbit and apples. My father praised her cooking. And her shorter skirts. And the bright colours of her clothes. He said that I was free to be as French as he was. A proper French boy, he said. Eating proper French food.

He saw James then coming back from the cliffs, a rabbit in each hand, the sketchpad under his arm.

You've been busy, James, he said.

Masson stepped away from the doorframe.

I'll follow you, he said. See if there's a cup of tea.

James stretched the rabbits across the table. He set down his sketchpad.

A handsome pair, said Micheál.

Francis picked up the sketchpad and flicked through the pages. James stood still, his hands by his side.

I hear you're off to London to be an artist, he said.

I am.

Let's hope you're a better artist than you are a fisherman.

James laughed.

That's the hope, Uncle Francis.

When are you leaving? said Micheál.

Soon enough, said James. As soon as Mr Lloyd's work dries.

What's he working on, James? said Masson.

James shrugged.

He's being very mysterious, said Masson.

No big mystery, said James. He's just working on his own. Artists do that.

Francis dropped the sketchpad onto the table.

You'll be doing a lot of that in London.

What? said James.

Being on your own. Lonesome Irish lad stuff.

What do you know about it? said James.

I know enough, said Francis.

You've barely left this place.

James drank tea, ate two scones, and carried a serving to Lloyd, his sketchpad tucked again under his arm. He kicked at the door with his foot. Lloyd opened the door and let him in.

Thank you, James.

You're welcome, Mr Lloyd.

Lloyd took the food and nudged his head towards the studio.

Go in. Take a look. Tell me what you think.

James again walked its length.

I like it more every time I see it, he said.

That's good.

Lloyd stayed at the studio door, eating and drinking.

I can't wait to see it in daylight, said James.

That will be a good moment.

Can I open the curtains?

No, James. Too many disapproving eyes.

It's a long list, all right.

Lloyd smiled.

Your grandmother will throw me off the cliff if she sees this.

She will, Mr Lloyd.

And Francis will shoot me.

He will. You'll be well dead from the pair of them.

Lloyd stood beside him.

Maybe Francis will like it, James. All that soldier blood running into the sea.

He'll see only my mother. Then himself.

You're right, James.

James laughed.

There'll be steam coming out his ears, Mr Lloyd.

You sound like you might enjoy that.

Oh, I will.

What about your great-grandmother?

Hard to know. Not as locked into the priests' way of thinking as my grandmother.

But she prays?

Oh, she does that. Night and day. But to God. Little time for the priests and their rules.

A direct line, then.

No middlemen for her, Mr Lloyd.

James resumed painting. Lloyd remained in front of his canvas scrutinising Mairéad, the glow of her skin and its reflected shimmer on the islanders around her, on the animals, the rock, on the wind-burnt grass. He walked alongside the canvas, checking it, analysing it, and looking at it through the mirror for scale and evenness, muttering as he examined his work, to himself, to James, it'll be my best work, James, my masterpiece, this mammoth work a comeback and calling card that will turn the head of a half-wife, turn a forgotten, dismissed, overlooked artist into a celebrity, an equal to Freud, to Auerbach, to Bacon. No, he laughed. No. Better. Better than all of them. Better than those dealers' darlings, this seminal work of mine pushing theirs aside, rendering their work, rendering them, so insignificant that my half-wife becomes my full wife and my full wife promotes me, hangs this groundbreaking work from the walls of her esteemed gallery, that coveted space, and extols me on opening night as the Gauguin of the northern hemisphere, as the existentialist of British art who lived on a remote Irish island for almost four months, alone, isolated, a hermit in a hut, without electricity, without running water, on a diet of fish and potatoes, lauding me as the great British artist who stripped everything back to ask the same questions as Gauguin, *D'où venons-nous? Que sommes-nous? Où allons-nous?* Where Do We Come From? What Are We? Where Are We Going? And here you have it, ladies and gentlemen in your silk scarves and Rolex watches, ladies and gentlemen of the press, of *The Times*, the *Telegraph*, the *Guardian*, the BBC, the questions are presented once more by this great British artist. But not in the French colony of Tahiti where Gauguin painted. Closer to home. Closer to all of us here this evening. The questions he poses are about Ireland. About us. About the British relationship with Ireland. The former British colony of Ireland. Lloyd, like Gauguin, is prodding at the questions still unanswered of how we exist together on this earth, on these islands, human, animal, spirit, all of us passing through the same stages of birth, life and death, side by side, cheek by jowl, intertwined in this coexistence, this co-dependency that he understood properly, thoroughly, as he lived on the island, on a rock surrounded by ocean where existence is stripped back to essential living, relationships too laid bare on the remote rock, and he asks us through this magnificent work, no, challenges us, to reflect on our relationship with the earth, with each other, and on the relationship between Britain and Ireland, the sea between us tinged still with the blood of ordinary people, of men doing the dishes at home, of women out shopping with their mothers, of children on a boat with their grandfather, the blood too of teenage English soldiers and young Irish men who call themselves 'Freedom Fighters', the violence and chaos of those deaths, of that bloodshed, living alongside the beauty of the people, of the landscape, a disrupted, upended Garden of Eden, a suspended state, a state of unfinished business where the ghosts of the past shimmer still in the present. A spontaneous round of applause from the men and women in their silk scarves and Rolex watches, from the men and women of the press. Lloyd has created this magnificent work, ladies and gentlemen, by drawing not only on Gauguin – with a nod en passant to Picasso's *Guernica* – but by drawing too on primitive art and naive art, his long-time interest in these art forms stirred by his relationship with James Gillan, an island boy whose astonishing naive art is also shown here this evening. Lloyd befriended James, known too by his Irish name of Séamus, and was struck by the boy's natural ability as an artist. By his natural capacity to see as an artist, to interpret as an artist. From the beginning, the boy's work reminded Lloyd of the work of ancient Chinese artists who painted in a linear style that gave equal representation to all, to people, to animals, to spirits, a perspective abandoned in European art in the Renaissance, when the linear narrative that we see too in ancient cave paintings was abandoned to allow the artist to focus instead on a single point, a single person, creating a dominant position in the painting. A dominant position in society. Lloyd, this great British artist, is unpicking all of those assumptions and habits in our ways of seeing and returning us to the more egalitarian roots of the naive period. Ladies and gentlemen, I ask you to join me this evening in raising a glass to toast Lloyd, this great British artist whose work is as radical today in London as Manet was in Paris when he presented *Le Déjeuner sur l'herbe* to the Salon. As Manet mixed the classical with the modern, Lloyd has radically blended primitive, naive, impressionist and post-impressionist art to create something utterly original and new.

Lloyd smiled. Then laughed.

What's funny, Mr Lloyd.

My wife loves telling people what to think.

Your half-wife.

My wife.

Lloyd stepped across the room to stand by the easel. He looked at James's painting of the cliffs, at the pinks and blues sparkling in the sunlight.

It's good, James. I think we should include it.

That will be my sixth work, so.

James carried the painting to the corner of the room to dry. He returned *Mná na hÉireann* to the easel.

Bit more work to do on this one, he said.

I like it very much, James.

I won't be selling it.

Lloyd nodded.

Then that's the one that everybody will want to buy.

James resumed work on his mother, on her eyes, on the lines shimmering under the surface of her skin, soon to rise, to break through.

How big is the gallery, Mr Lloyd?

The perfect size for what we are doing. And very central. People love going to it.

Will I be there?

Of course you will. It's your work.

Do I need a suit? A jacket?

Just as you are, James, is perfect.

James nodded.

I could wear the jumper my mother is knitting.

Ideal.

It'll be brand new.

Perfect.

I'll walk around the gallery as the island boy in his island jumper.

You'll be good at this, James.

I will, Mr Lloyd.

Would your mother come to London, James? For the exhibition.

James shook his head.

She won't leave here.

Ever?

She's waiting on my father.

Lloyd startled.

But he's dead, James. Drowned.

She's still waiting.

James pointed at his painting.

They're all waiting, he said. All waiting for those men to come out of the sea.

Maybe you should rename it. *The Waiting Room*.

James looked again at his work.

Maybe I should, Mr Lloyd.

Lloyd returned to his own canvas.

I think I will consider this done now, James. Let it fully dry.

How long will that take?

A few days.

And then we'll go, Mr Lloyd?

Yes, James. Then we'll go.

Lloyd looked again at his work.

You have inspired me, James. With your linear narratives.

That's not linear, Mr Lloyd.

It is, James.

My mother is still at the centre. Everybody else in a supporting role.

You're wrong, James.

It looks like an album cover, Mr Lloyd.

James laughed.

The Boomtown Rats, Mr Lloyd. Bob and the Rats. Mairéad and Islanders.

Lloyd shook his head.

No, no, James. It's much more than that.

Maybe, Mr Lloyd. But it's nothing like my work.

I think it is, James.

In my paintings everybody is equal, everybody has a story. It's not like that in yours. Mam is top dog.

She is very beautiful.

James shrugged.

That doesn't give her greater value, Mr Lloyd.

To me it does.

Then you're not painting like me, said James. You're painting as yourself. An Englishman on an Irish island.

What does that mean?

You're turning the island into something it isn't.

You've lost me, James.

Mam isn't the centre of things. She isn't top dog.

So who is?

James shrugged.

It changes. All the time. Winter. Summer. The job to be done.

Lloyd shook his head.

You're deluding yourself, James. Francis is top dog.

Only when he's here, Mr Lloyd.

But he's always coming back.

That's true.

Anyway, James, it's my interpretation of the island.

That's grand, Mr Lloyd. It's just nothing to do with my work. My work is different. Yours is like everybody else's work.

That's not very kind, James.

A beautiful woman at the centre. Everything dotted around that. Painting done. Job done. You're all doing that. Have been for centuries.

You know very little about art, James.

James shrugged.

I've been reading, Mr Lloyd. Looking. I know enough.

I really find your tone objectionable, James. This art is utterly original.

336

Is it, Mr Lloyd?

Yes, James, it is.

James shrugged again.

To me, it's a version of what has gone before. An amalgamation.

James laughed.

Magpie art, Mr Lloyd.

And yours will be better, James?

I suppose we'll find that out when I get to London.

I suppose we will, James.

Hugh O'Halloran, a twenty-eight-year-old Catholic father of five, dies in hospital on Monday, September 10th from injuries received two days earlier when he was beaten by a gang of republican men with a hurling stick and a pickaxe handle.

It's going mad up there, Mam.

It is, Mairéad. Attacking and killing their own.

Mairéad mopped where her mother had swept.

Francis would say our own.

He would, Mairéad.

But you're not.

I'm not.

Mairéad reached the mop under the chairs.

You used to.

I did.

Not any more, Mam?

I don't know what to think any more, Mairéad.

They heard a tapping against the dresser. It was Lloyd. Bean Uí Néill turned off the radio.

I have a question, he said.

Bean Uí Néill began to shout for James. Mairéad stopped her.

Fág é mar a bhfuil sé, she said. Yes, Mr Lloyd?

When will Micheál be back?

Amárach. Tomorrow. B'fhéidir. Maybe.

Thank you. I will leave then. Go back with him.

Mairéad nodded.

What about James? she said.

He wants to come with me, Mairéad.

She reached the mop under the dresser.

Tuigim. I understand.

Will I take him, Mairéad?

She worked from left to right, a single sweep, and then back to the open floor, towards the door, where Lloyd was still standing.

Do you want him to come with me, Mairéad?

She pushed the mop towards him.

Idir, she said.

What does that mean?

Between, she said.

She mopped around his feet.

Between you and James, Mr Lloyd.

She forced the mop between his feet.

Your decision, Mr Lloyd. Not mine.

Lloyd stepped away from her and left, for the cliffs, walking the route of that first evening, through the vegetable patch, by the lake and up the hill, no longer noticing the steepness in the back of his legs, the wind through his hair, his body acclimatised and bent slightly forward at the hips to walk as the islanders walked. He reached the top and fell to his knees, to his belly, leaning over the edge to look once more, one final time, at the rock shimmering in the evening light, at the birds preparing for night

as it was

in the beginning

is now

He laughed.

self-portrait: finding god

He stayed until the sun left, soaking in the clefts, the hollows, remembering them and the last of the light flitting across the rock, the tumult of sea, of wave after wave crashing against the rock, gnawing at the earth, its force and power reverberating through the cliff into his bones

and ever shall be

He shivered and stood up. He walked to the hut, arriving in darkness. He lit the lamps and moved about in light and shadow, the hut tidier than he had left it, his drawings stacked into four neat piles, the pillow, blanket and mattress returned to the bed, the table cleaned. He lit the fire, shook the tea caddy, rattling the teaspoon and dried leaves. He looked inside. Enough for a final cup of tea. He tasted the water in the bucket

fresh enough

my thanks, james

He put water on to boil and took the drawings to sit in front of the still stumbling fire. He lifted a bundle. Birds. Terns with heads that were too big, gulls with heads that were too small. He fed them to the fire, a surge of light and heat eradicating his early ignorance, his need for tuition by the island boy, rude now, cocky in his assertions of amalgamation and magpie art. He laughed

cheeky pup

He picked up more drawings, of the light on the sea, on the cliffs, and threw sheet after sheet to the flames.

self-portrait: playing god

The water boiled, he made tea and returned to the fire, sipping at the hot blackness as he sifted through the drawings of Mairéad, keeping most of them to take with him, to include in any future exhibition on the evolution of his work. He turned his attention to the fourth pile, of James, of James with the rabbits. He moved through the sheets, pleased with them, with the freshness of life and death, delighted by the vibrancy, the vitality, but then paused. It was not his work. He scrutinised a sheet. It's James's drawing. His hand. Not mine. His drawings slipped among mine, his drawings of rabbits freshly killed exuding a vividness missing from mine. He scrunched up the sheet. Then another. Six sheets. Seven sheets. He threw them on the fire, staring as the flames smothered and devoured the boy's art, art that is better than my art.

He gathered the sketches of Mairéad, extinguished the lamps and pulled the door of the hut tightly behind him, his last time on the promontory. He glanced around, but only briefly, cursorily, and hurried back towards the village, muttering, mumbling, swearing as he walked, pummelling his fist against his thigh, against James, the apprentice better than his master.

He barged into his cottage, into his studio, and lit the lamps along the floor. He squeezed fresh paint onto his cleaned palette and painted over James, the boy no longer holding the rabbit and paintbrushes but four fish, two in each hand.

self-portrait: being god

He quenched the lanterns and went to bed, though Mairéad was still up, by the fire, sewing the back of the jumper to the front, grey wool in the darning needle, stitching one side tightly to the other, closing off gaps, shutting out the wind, the rain that comes sideways at the island men. She added the sleeves then, first the right, then the left, and stretched the completed jumper across her lap, stroking the blackberries that will keep him warm as he crosses the Irish Sea, the diamonds that will shield the centre of the chest as he waits in the wind for the train to take him to London. Away. From here. From me. Though I will travel with you, James. Alongside you on the boat, on the train, alongside you on the white walls as we hang together in London, mother and son, an exhibition, a celebration, my beauty captured before it fades, yours as it grows, blossoms, an Irish child artist into a great Irish artist, for your rabbits are better than his rabbits, James. Your birds, too. Their movements through the air more vibrant in your drawings. As though you understand them more. Have studied them more. She tucked the sleeves behind the back, and folded the jumper. You're not better than him yet, James. But you will be. In time. She smiled. And he knows that, James. That you will be better than him. In time. And you have time. Lots of time. Time that your father never had. She laughed. He never wanted to be a fisherman either, James. Hated the sea. Hated boats. But that was all he knew. Had the chance to know.

She returned the wool, the knitting needles and the darning needle to the basket by the chair and stood up. She laid the jumper on the kitchen table for James to see in the morning and went out into the night air, the stars abundant, the moon on the cusp of fullness. It was cold, the summer gone, though still she dawdled, taking her time to reach Masson's cottage, her eyes resting on the stars and moon, relishing the quiet of others sleeping on the island while she was awake, the place entirely hers, as it had been ours, Liam, out on the cliffs, down by the sea, across in the hut, on the floor in front of the fire where I lay for the artist, where I lay with you, where James was made. She smiled. Our own little artwork, Liam. Our collaboration. She pushed at the door of Masson's house. She went inside, the mildew thwarted by the smell of coffee fragments burning still on the stone hearth. One last time, JP, for you will not be back, and I will not see you again, for there will be no camera crews, no newspaper writers, nobody rushing up here to meet Bean Uí Fhloinn, the last Irish speaker on the island, for nobody will care now about your study, JP, about the language, its history, its demise, the shift towards bilingualism in this most remote corner of Europe. The camera crews, the newspaper writers will come to this land only to talk of soldiers and guns and bombs, the story now, to write stories of death, of hatred, of fear, of tit-for-tat, retaliation on top of retaliation, a downward bilious spiral until the killers stalking the streets in the dead of night no longer remember what it is they are retaliating.

She climbed the stairs and slipped into his bed.

In the morning, James saw the jumper.

Thanks, Mam.

It'll keep you warm, James.

I'll wear it on opening night, he said.

She wrapped her arms around herself.

You'll look very smart, James.

James Gillan, The Island Painter.

He carried breakfast to Lloyd and knocked on the door. Lloyd didn't respond. The door unlocked, he went inside, the cottage stilled by sleep. He quietly set the breakfast on the table and went to the studio, to check the dryness of *Mná na hÉireann*, to absorb the smells of oil and paint that will soon be my smells, the Irish island boy in London, no longer smelling of salted water, dead fish and rotting rabbit blood, but of lemon ochre, of carmine, of Prussian blue, Persian blue, of grenadine, Payne's grey, olive green, scarlet vermillion, of linseed oil and white spirits. He laughed. My new smells. My new way. No more school. No more priests. No more Francis. And no more fish. He touched *Mná na hÉireann*. Dry. Ready to go. One of six. Five more to select. To take with me. The rest I will leave behind, here, in this room, for Mam to find when she comes to clean, to scrape the paint off the walls, off the floor, to return the room, the cottage, to how it had been at the beginning of the summer, before Lloyd arrived, before I knew about painting instead of fishing.

He walked behind Lloyd's canvas to reach his paintings in the corner. He carried them back across the room and set them out on the floor, under the window. Twenty-two paintings. Time to choose, James Gillan. To select your darlings. He walked from one side of the room to the other looking down, choosing but tracking too the development of his art, the rapid shift over one summer from childish, primitive art to representative art, distillations of island life. He examined his paintings of Bean Uí Néill, of Bean Uí Fhloinn, and stepped across the room to look at Lloyd's canvas, to scrutinise how much the English artist had copied him. He laughed. Utterly. Completely. Their clothes, their gestures, their postures identical, as though Lloyd had come down in the middle of the night to copy from me. And then he halted. In front of himself. His altered self. Why had I not seen it sooner? As soon as I came into the room? A boy with fish. An island boy with fish. No longer an artist, an apprentice. No longer holding brushes but fish. I am a boy with fish. An island boy. Hunter. Gatherer. Provider. But not artist. He doesn't see me as an artist. Does not want me to be seen as an artist. For there is only one artist. And it is not you, James Gillan.

He heard Lloyd then, coming down the stairs. He stilled his breath, his anger, and slipped back into the kitchen to stand by the table, his hands behind his back, his face static. James Gillan, little butler boy.

Morning, James.

Morning.

Lloyd poured tea.

Would you like some?

James shook his head and turned to look through the window, at the sea.

It's a good day, said Lloyd.

It is.

Lloyd lifted his bowl of porridge.

I do miss the chairs, James.

I'd say that, Mr Lloyd.

Lloyd ate. James was silent.

So what do you think? said Lloyd.

Of what? said James.

I heard you, James. In the studio.

James looked at his feet.

Why did you do that, Mr Lloyd?

Lloyd spooned more porridge into his mouth.

Do what?

You painted over me. Turned me into a fisherman.

It's my painting, James.

James turned to him.

It's my identity, Mr Lloyd. And I'm not a fisherman.

It's a representation of the island, James. Nothing more.

It's much more.

It's not.

It's how you want me to be. How you want me to be seen.

You're being ridiculous, James.

You're the artist, Mr Lloyd. I'm the island boy who fishes.

James, you're over-interpreting this.

James lifted his face, holding onto tears welling in his eyes.

An artist can't over-interpret, Mr Lloyd.

You're not an artist, James. Not yet.

And I won't be if you present me like this.

You need to calm down, James.

I'm supposed to be part of the exhibition. An artist in the exhibition.

And you will be.

James ran his hands through his hair, using the heel of his palms to whip the water from his eyes.

No, Mr Lloyd. I'm an exhibit. A fisherman.

Lloyd shrugged.

It's a representation of the island. Nothing more.

Lloyd poured more tea.

It's me as you want me to be seen, Mr Lloyd. As you want me to be interpreted.

Lloyd added milk and drank.

As I said, you're not an artist yet, James.

And I won't be if you present me as a fisherman.

Lloyd gathered the crockery and pushed it towards James.

I'll be packing today, he said.

James shook his head.

But the canvas is still wet, Mr Lloyd.

Only in parts, James. It'll be fine. I'll put dry canvas over the wet parts.

The boy inhaled, deeply.

Does that work, Mr Lloyd?

Well enough. Stops it sticking.

James lifted the dishes from the table.

I'll fold the canvas tomorrow, James. Will you help me?

James shrugged.

Maybe.

He returned to the house, to the back kitchen. His mother and grandmother were baking.

Can you get some rabbits today, James?

James splashed water across his face.

I can, Granny.

The men are coming across, she said.

So I hear.

And you'll be going across with them.

That's the plan.

You, Mr Lloyd and JP.

He nodded.

It'll be a busy boat, Granny.

And a quiet island, James.

James walked towards the door.

Do you want two or three rabbits?

Three.

He hunkered down in the grass and waited, the sun warming his back, the corncrakes calling still to each other, though the puffins were already gone, out at sea on their way south, their path already mapped. As mine had been. Micheál's boat tomorrow, my drawings and paintings with me, waving goodbye to my mother, my grandmother, my great-grandmother, three women on the slipway, in darkened clothes, huddled, weeping, *Mná na hÉireann, At the Pier*, and then onwards, across the country to the other sea, the sea smaller, the boat bigger. A rabbit stepped into the net. He yanked it tight, grabbed the thrashing rabbit by its hind legs and hammered it to the ground, smashing its head. He picked the rabbit out of the net, set the trap again and sat back down to wait. And then the train to London, to Lloyd's house to live with the smell of paint and the half-wife who is becoming again the full wife. Another rabbit came out of the hole. It bounced into the net. He snared it. A third rabbit emerged, despite the commotion. Stupid fucking rabbits. Stupid thick rabbits. He grabbed the third rabbit with his hands, lifted it into the air and slammed it against the earth. I'm sick of rabbit stew, anyway. Sick of eating the same fucking thing. He kicked the third rabbit, although it was already dead. Sick of being the hunter. The gatherer. He swung the second rabbit over his head and smashed it on the ground, blood splattering across the grass. Sick of being the provider. The rabbit killer.

He walked back to the village.

A good slew, James, said Mairéad.

It is, Mam.

You'll lose the knack of it in London.

I won't miss it, Mam.

You will. More than you know.

Then I'll kill them in Hyde Park.

Mairéad laughed.

They'll have you arrested.

She laughed again, burying her head in her hands.

Can you imagine the faces of the children? Of their mothers?

I'll be in jail forever, Mam. The Irish Rabbit Killer.

They leaned into each other.

I'll miss you, James.

I know, Mam.

Micheál and Francis arrived. They dropped the shopping on the table, beside the rabbits.

Another feast, said Micheál.

My last supper, said James.

It'll be a good one, James.

Bean Uí Néill set the teapot, scones and crockery on the table. They sat down.

Are you nervous, James?

No, Micheál.

It will be exciting, said Mairéad. A new life.

There's nothing wrong with this one, said Francis.

There is if you don't like fishing, said James.

Mairéad ruffled his hair.

So what's the name of the school you're going to? said Micheál.

I don't know. He hasn't said.

And when will you start?

I don't know that either.

You don't know much, do you? said Francis.

I'll know soon enough, said James.

You're taking an awful risk, James.

Why's that, Francis?

Going off with an Englishman you barely know.

James shrugged.

I know him well enough.

And being Irish in London, said Francis.

He'll be grand, said Mairéad.

The police are picking up Irish lads all the time. For doing nothing.

I'll be quiet, said James. They'll barely notice me.

Francis shook his head.

They'll notice you, James. They'll know everything about you.

There's nothing to know, Francis.

They'll make it up, James. Even when there's nothing to know.

James finished his tea, his scones and stood up.

I'll take some to JP and Mr Lloyd, he said.

He carried two cups of tea and a plate of four scones, stopping first by Masson who was clearing his desk.

Perfect, James. Just what I need.

When will you be back, JP?

Next spring. When my book is published. I'll bring television and newspaper people to meet Bean Uí Fhloinn.

I won't be here, JP. I'm going to London.

So I hear. It's exciting for you.

Thanks, JP. Though Francis is giving out.

Francis is always giving out.

He went then to Lloyd, in the studio. He was throwing used paint tubes and pencils from the drawer onto the floor. James handed him the food, the tea visibly cold.

I stopped by JP.

Not to worry, James.

Lloyd ate, drank. James stepped towards his work, still on the floor.

I'll pick my six, he said.

Lloyd nodded.

James selected *Mná na hÉireann* and five others, mostly on

paper, of rabbits, of the village, of the cliffs, of boats on the sea, and *What the Ant Saw*. He laid the six paintings between sheets of cardboard and, with white string, tied them into a bundle that he set on the floor by the studio door, beside Lloyd's easel, already collapsed and ready for the journey.

That's done, Mr Lloyd.

It's good work, James.

James nodded.

A good start, Mr Lloyd.

James gathered his remaining paintings into a pile that he returned to the far corner of the room.

Do you want me to sweep, Mr Lloyd?

Lloyd shook his head.

It's a bit soon, James. But get the brush, and I'll do it when I'm ready.

James returned with the yard brush.

It'll be a good exhibition, Mr Lloyd.

A great one. My best.

James pointed at his paintings, still by the door.

Will I put them in your suitcase?

Not yet, James. I'll include them when I am doing my own.

James left, with the cup and plate, and Lloyd resumed his work emptying the drawer, repacking the mahogany chest, though most of its original contents had been used or worn down, the paints, turpentine and linseed oil emptied and drained, the cloths dirtied and hardened, the tape, primers, pencils, pens, inks and charcoal depleted. The jars and bottles were too grubby to bother carrying back, though the small easel, palette, palette knives and brushes were in good order, well used but still functioning. His black apron was pristine, unworn.

He slipped his drawings between the pages of his books and packed the books into the chest. He covered them with a layer of clothing, then added his canvases and paintings, layers of paper and cardboard between them, rolls of shirts and socks tucked around them to hold the artworks in place. He closed the lid of the chest, locked it.

He swept the floor, cursorily, pushing the detritus of his stay into a pile under the window, screwed up sheets of paper, used tubes of paints, jars, containers, cloths. He went into the back yard to return the brush. Masson was sitting on a chair, his eyes closed, fragments of turf scattered about his feet.

I gather that you too are leaving tomorrow, said Masson.

I am, said Lloyd. My work is done.

As is mine, said Masson. Except the conclusion, which I will write in Paris.

And what is that? said Lloyd. Your conclusion.

That the English are deeply intolerant of the Irish language.

Lloyd laughed.

We hardly need a book to tell us that.

That the English have done their best to portray Irish as the language of the poor, of the stupid.

Lloyd shrugged.

It's not very original thinking, is it?

It needs to be said.

It has been said.

It needs to be said again.

Lloyd returned the brush to the lean-to, setting it down beside the shovel encrusted with cement. He stopped as he passed Masson on the way back to his cottage.

I finished that work, he said. Do you want to see it?

The big canvas?

Yes.

Very much.

Masson followed Lloyd into the studio. He stood in front of the canvas. He nodded, slowly.

It's very, very good, Lloyd. Better than I had expected.

A compliment.

Masson laughed.

They do happen. Sometimes.

I'll take it, said Lloyd.

But it's derivative, said Masson.

Lloyd shook his head.

It's a reinterpretation, yes, but not derivative.

Maybe, said Masson. That's for others to decide.

Lloyd nodded.

I agree.

It will garner a lot of attention for you, Lloyd.

That's the hope. For the island too. Turn it into a tourist spot for them.

What? said Masson. The Tahiti of the northern hemisphere?

Lloyd shrugged.

Why not?

It would destroy this place, said Masson. Annihilate the language.

It'll bring money, said Lloyd. An income other than fishing.

The language won't survive that.

That's not my concern, said Lloyd.

It is mine.

Masson walked the length of the canvas, stopping in front of Mairéad.

Have the islanders seen it?

Lloyd shook his head.

Only Mairéad and James.

That's probably for the best.

Probably.

Francis won't like it, said Masson.

I gather that.

The women won't either. Bean Uí Néill. Bean Uí Fhloinn.

It'll be gone in the morning, said Lloyd.

And that's it? You just whip the painting off the island, the islanders as you want them.

You do the same thing, Masson.

Masson shrugged.

Peut-être, he said. Maybe not.

The Frenchman left and Lloyd levered the nails from the frame with his penknife. He stretched the canvas along the floor and rolled it, a square of clean dry canvas over James. He wrapped it again in the brown paper, tied it again with string.

self-portrait: departure time

Masson walked up the hill, through the village, to Bean Uí Fhloinn's house. He tapped on the door, poured tea and sat opposite her. He lifted both her hands, kissed them.

My last visit, he said. I'm off tomorrow.

She smiled at him.

You are.

Will you come down to the house for tea?

She shook her head.

Not with all you buckos.

Masson laughed.

It's too much for me, JP. All that squabbling.

It's too much for me too, Bean Uí Fhloinn.

You never stopped, JP. All summer.

It's a small island for a Frenchman to share with an Englishman.

It seems that the world itself isn't big enough for the pair of you.

He lifted her hands again and kissed them, right then left.

It gives me a pain in the head listening to you both, JP. Áine can bring me my meal here, as she usually does.

You're a wise woman, Bean Uí Fhloinn.

I've been around long enough, JP. I've seen most things by now.

Masson nodded, slowly.

But not his painting.

The big canvas?

The very one.

Have you seen it, JP?

I have, Bean Uí Fhloinn. It's huge. And we're all in it.

Me as well?

You are. With your pipe.

She shook her head.

He said he was doing the cliffs.

It's not the cliffs, Bean Uí Fhloinn.

No?

It's the island. The islanders.

He said he wouldn't do that.

Mairéad is in the middle of it. Posing for him.

That's what she was up to.

That's it.

Bean Uí Fhloinn drew heavily on her pipe.

She's not wearing much, Bean Uí Fhloinn.

She's not?

He shook his head.

Only that green scarf she has. Around her hips.

And that's it, JP?

That's it, Bean Uí Fhloinn.

She nodded, slowly.

She kept that very quiet.

She did, said Masson. They both did.

I knew there was something going on. Out there in that hut. I said that to you.

You did, Bean Uí Fhloinn. That very thing.

She drew again on her pipe.

Does Francis know?

Masson shook his head.

It's a big secret down there. Curtains and doors closed.

He'd go mad if he knew, JP.

He would.

He'd put a stop to it.

He would, Bean Uí Fhloinn.

His own sister-in-law. Liam's wife. You better not breathe a word of it, JP. Not a word.

I won't, Bean Uí Fhloinn. Not a word.

He kissed her on the cheek.

I'll be on the slipway in the morning, she said. To wave you off.

He kissed her on the other cheek. He smiled at her. He kissed each hand.

I know I can rely on you, Bean Uí Fhloinn.

He closed the door and walked down the hill, whistling. He met James coming up.

Are you off to say goodbye to your great-grandmother, Séamus?

My name is James. And yes I am.

They'll love Séamus in London. It's a great Irish name.

They'll be happy enough with James, JP.

Masson packed until it was time for the evening meal. Bean Uí Néill set plates in front of them, fuller than usual. The largest portion went to James. She ruffled his hair.

A fine last meal, James, said Micheál.

The last time I'll eat rabbit, said James.

They ate, silence along the table until Micheál spoke.

It'll be winter soon enough, he said.

Another month, said Mairéad.

That's early, said Lloyd.

Earlier here than other places, said Micheál.

What's it like here in winter? said Lloyd.

Micheál shook his head.

Hard, he said. Nothing happens but the wind.

Beidh sé go hálainn, said Bean Uí Néill.

They laughed.

What did she say? said Lloyd.

That it'll be wonderful, said Mairéad.

Lloyd laughed, Masson shook his head.

That's very good English, Mairéad.

She smiled at him, the green scarf through her hair.

Thank you, JP.

You learnt a lot of English this summer, Mairéad.

She hesitated, but continued in English.

I have, JP.

I'm sad about that, he said.

She shrugged.

James is going, JP.

And?

Caithfidh mé Béarla a labhairt. I have to speak in English.

Caillfidhear do theangaidh, said Masson.

She closed her eyes.

Your language will be lost, Mairéad.

She shook her head.

It's me that will be lost, JP.

Bean Uí Néill cleared the dishes. She placed an apple tart on the table. And a bowl of cream. Mairéad poured tea.

We'll leave at eight tomorrow, said Micheál. Get you over in time for the bus.

Breakfast at seven, said Mairéad.

Masson stared at her. She laughed.

Ar an seacht a chlog, JP.

Micheál and Francis left to smoke, to stand at the village wall. Masson resumed his packing and Lloyd walked down towards the cove. James followed him.

I want to see it one last time, James.

You'll see it in the morning, Mr Lloyd.

It'll be busy then.

It will.

Lloyd walked ahead of him, down the narrow path.

What about the canvas, Mr Lloyd?

What about it?

We need to take it off the frame.

I've done that. It's ready to go.

Lloyd turned right into the ruins of the first village. James followed. Lloyd sat on a pile of rubble.

You're on the Protestant school, said James.

What? On this island?

James nodded.

There was a Protestant school and a Catholic school.

That's unbelievable, James. A place this size.

During the famine. You got soup if you went to the Protestant school.

If you were in the Catholic school?

361

Nothing.

Lloyd shook his head.

We weren't very nice, were we?

You were not.

But that's the past, James. It's different now.

James picked paint off his hands.

I hope so, Mr Lloyd.

Lloyd looked at the sea, at the sky, at the birds swirling over the water, one last feed before night.

It's a beautiful place, he said. It'll be hard to leave.

No, it won't, said James.

James peeled a strip of red paint from his left thumb and dropped it to the ground.

It'll be very easy, Mr Lloyd.

Lloyd rubbed his hands along his thighs, flattening the corduroy of his trousers.

About that, James.

About what, Mr Lloyd?

I'm not sure it's such a good time for you to be coming to London.

James closed his eyes.

I knew this was coming.

What?

Has Francis been talking to you?

Lloyd shook his head.

No. I've been thinking about this.

James peeled paint from his left hand. Sky blue.

Thinking about what, Mr Lloyd?

It's not a good idea for you to come with me. Not now.

James dug his nails into his skin.

And why's that, Mr Lloyd?

Given everything that has been going on. Mountbatten, the soldiers, it's not a good time.

Is that right, Mr Lloyd?

It's not a safe time for you, James.

Nobody will notice me, Mr Lloyd.

Lloyd shrugged.

It's not a safe time to be a young Irish man in London.

James closed his eyes.

You have to take me, Mr Lloyd. Let me do this.

Lloyd shook his head.

I'm sorry, James. I can't.

He opened his eyes.

You can't just leave me here, Mr Lloyd. Start me off as an artist and then abandon me.

I have no choice.

James laughed. Scoffed.

You do, Mr Lloyd. You have so many choices.

You should go to Dublin, James. Go to art school there.

James shook his head, slowly.

Why didn't I think of that, Mr Lloyd?

Lloyd nodded.

It's not a bad idea, James.

James spoke very slowly, enunciating each word.

I don't know anybody in Dublin, Mr Lloyd.

You'll get to know people.

363

I don't have any money to go to Dublin, Mr Lloyd.

Lloyd stood up.

I'm sorry it's not working out for you at the moment, James, but it's beyond my control.

Lloyd started back up the path.

What about the exhibition, Mr Lloyd?

What about it?

Will I still be in the exhibition?

Lloyd stopped and turned around.

Yes, of course, James.

So people will come and see my work.

They will, James.

Maybe teachers from the art school?

Definitely.

They might see my work and still take me in their school.

That could happen, James.

Lloyd resumed walking. James shouted after him.

You don't mean a word of it, do you, Mr Lloyd?

Lloyd waved, but did not turn around.

I will do my best, James.

James turned from him and stared at the sea, my father's grave, the fisherman's grave. He stood up and clambered along the cliff and out across the island, away from Lloyd, away from the village, from his mother who was in the back kitchen, cleaning after the evening meal, drying dishes, wiping down the sink.

Francis stood in the doorway.

How's it going there, Mairéad?

Grand, Francis.

He nodded.

What do you want? she said.

He stepped towards her. Close to her.

Jesus, Francis, back off.

You didn't say that to Mr Lloyd.

What are you on about?

When he was painting you. When you were taking your clothes off for him.

She walked around him and returned to the sink.

How do you know about that, Francis?

There are no secrets here, Mairéad. You know that.

She shrugged.

So now you know, she said.

We don't approve of what you're doing, he said.

She laughed.

Who's this 'we', Francis?

We've had a meeting. And I've been sent in to talk to you.

She resumed wiping the sink.

So, she said. Talk.

As I said, we don't approve of what you've been doing.

I need a list of names, she said. Of this 'we'.

You're out of line, Mairéad.

She walked around him and picked up the sweeping brush.

Are you done now, Francis?

She began to sweep the floor. He snatched the brush from her.

As I said, you're out of line, Mairéad.

She shrugged.

What line is that?

My line.

She laughed.

What I do has nothing to do with you, Francis.

It's everything to do with me.

She sighed and moved towards the door. He blocked her path with the sweeping brush.

You're my sister-in-law. Liam's wife.

As I said, Francis, what I do has nothing to do with you.

He flicked his fingers at her face.

Stop it, Francis.

We tolerated your bit of summer fun with the Frenchman, Mairéad.

Again, none of your business, Francis.

Your bit of widow fun.

He flicked at her face again.

But this is too much, Mairéad. Posing naked for an Englishman.

Nothing to do with you, Francis. None of your business.

She lifted the sweeping brush. He blocked her with his arm.

It is my business, Mairéad.

Have you even seen it, Francis?

What?

The painting, Francis. Have you even seen the painting?

I don't need to, Mairéad.

It's a work of art, Francis.

And?

I'm in a work of art.

He shook his head.

You're Liam's wife.

And?

I'm Liam's brother.

And?

Liam's wife is not taking her clothes off for an Englishman.
She laughed.

She can fuck a Frenchman but not take her clothes off for
an Englishman. Is that it, Francis?

You're a slut, Mairéad. An English-speaking slut.
She laughed again.

Which is worse in your mind, Francis? Fucking a Frenchman or speaking English with an Englishman?

Liam was too good for you, Mairéad. We all said that.
She shook her head.

Don't you dare, Francis. You know nothing about Liam.

He was my brother.
She snorted.

He thought you were a fucking idiot, Francis.
He yanked at the scarf in her hair.

Slut, he said.
She put her hand on the scarf, stopping its fall.

You'd be happy enough if I was your slut, Francis Gillan.
Her mother arrived then, into the kitchen. Mairéad sighed
and moved towards her.

You can back away now, Francis. Leave me alone.
He laughed.
Bean Uí Néill stepped into the doorway of the back kitchen,
blocking the evening light.

We won't have it, Mairéad.

Have what, Mam?

You. Like this. It's too much, Mairéad.

In the morning, at seven, James brought breakfast to Lloyd. He set it on the table. Lloyd sat down.

Do you want some tea, James?

James shook his head.

No, thank you, Mr Lloyd.

That's a shame, James. I'd like us to have a last cup of tea together.

Not to be, Mr Lloyd.

James rolled back his shoulders and put his two hands in his pockets. He stared at the Englishman.

We had a deal, Mr Lloyd. An arrangement.

Circumstances change, James.

Only if you let them, Mr Lloyd. If you want them to.

James returned to the kitchen to eat breakfast, at the table on his own with Masson, his grandmother at the fire, his mother still in bed.

Are you ready for the big trip, James?

I'm not going.

Why not? You're packed, aren't you?

I'll go across later. When the teachers call me to the art school.

Masson nodded.

I'm sorry, James.

James closed his eyes.

I'll see you then in the spring, James, when I come back with the camera crews.

James shook his head, his eyes still closed.

No, he said. I'll be gone by the spring.

Not too long to wait then, James.

Not long, JP.

He finished his porridge, drank his tea and walked away from the village, out along the island's edge, watching from the cliff as Lloyd moved down the path to the cove, carrying the rolled-up canvas with Micheál, one in front of the other. Masson followed with his recorder, Francis and the old men in their wake with the suitcases, mahogany chest and easel. James stuffed his hands deeper into his pockets.

They rowed out in three currachs to Micheál's boat. Lloyd climbed on board and sat alone with his canvas perched on the seat, away from the watery traces of heifer manure swirling still around the floor of the boat. Masson sat near Francis who was pulling ropes into the stern.

The old men in the currachs waved them on. Micheál started the engine and turned the boat away from the island, towards the mainland, the noise of their leaving drowning out the gulls and terns squawking in the cove.

The islanders rowed back to the slipway, lifted the currachs from the water and carried them over their heads, out of the cove. They set them down at the top of the slipway and walked up the hill towards the village, backs stooped, legs buckled.

James remained on the edge, watching until Micheál's boat disappeared from view. He walked back along the clifftop to the cottage and into the studio, into the lingering smell of paint, linseed oil, charcoal and white spirits. He looked around the emptied room, at the canvas frame scattered in fragments across the floor, at the six paintings for the exhibition in London, bound in cardboard and white string, waiting still by the door, as he had left them, as Lloyd had left them.

Gabriel Wiggins is washing dishes in the kitchen of his West Belfast home shortly before midnight on Wednesday, September 12th. He is fifty-six years old, Catholic, and a father to fourteen children.

Someone knocks on the front door. He turns on the hall light, but quickly turns it off again. He doesn't open the door. The UVF gunman shoots through the glass, killing Gabriel Wiggins, an unemployed gardener.

Acknowledgement

These four works were essential to my writing:

*Lost Lives: The Stories of the Men, Women and Children
    Who Died as a Result of the Northern Ireland Troubles*
    by David McKittrick, Seamus Kelters, Brian Feeney,
    Chris Thornton and David McVea (Mainstream
    Publishing, 1999)
An Index of Deaths from the Conflict in Ireland 1969–1993
    by Malcolm Sutton (Beyond the Pale Publications,
    1994)
A History of the Irish Language by Aidan Doyle (Oxford
    University Press, 2015)
Language Conflict in Algeria by Mohamed Benrabah
    (Multilingual Matters, 2013)

I am deeply indebted to Helen Nic Aodha, a master's student at University College Dublin specialising in the Irish language of Dú Chaocháin, Co. Mayo, the dialect used in this book. My gratitude too to Professor Regina Uí Chollatáin, Head of Studies at the UCD School of Irish, Celtic Studies and Folklore, and to Caoimhe Ní Bhraonáin of the Irish and Celtic Studies department at Trinity College Dublin.

My thanks also to Peter Straus and the team at RCW literary agency, to Louisa Joyner, Anne Owen and all at Faber, to Claire Gatzen, to Jenna Johnson and everybody at Farrar, Straus and Giroux, to Sarah Bannan, Head of Literature at the Arts Council of Ireland, and to Sinéad Mac Aodha, Executive Director of Literature Ireland. Thank you all for your faith in me and this work.

I am profoundly grateful to Maeve Magee for her support of my writing. Heartfelt thanks too to Shibéal Megan, Duncan Fort, and to Sophie and Patrick Trane.

And, as ever, to Laurie, Anna and Sally, and to Johnny – thank you.